Swallowed Whole

E.M. Eden

COPYRIGHT

— · —

Dedications

For the ones of us that started by writing smut on the internet at 3 a.m. instead of sleeping.

This one's for you.

Stay nasty and dim your AO3 screen. It's better for your eyes.

Trust me.

◆

« and also »

◆

For Bethie –

for always trying to push me into getting my work out there professionally.

Hands down, the best mom a girl could ask for.

---·---

CONTENT WARNINGS

This story is dark, twisted, and a little too intimate.
It's not here to comfort you—it's here to crawl under your skin and stay awhile.

Enjoy the start of the Saturate Me Trilogy.

This book contains mature and potentially distressing material, including:

A slow burn that might make you want to yell at the author

Obsession and psychological manipulation

Voyeurism and stalking (non-consensual surveillance)

Gaslighting and emotional control

Explicit sexual content

Power imbalance between characters

Substance use (alcohol, cocaine)

Violence and threat of harm

Toxic, manipulative relationships

Death and implied murder

Reader discretion is advised.

CONTENTS

1

I can't believe this is what my life is turning into. This mockery of my autonomy being stripped away so publicly. There are hundreds of guests waiting for me. Hundreds of guests that were invited by my father.

None of them matter. None of them care.

This is yet another thing that's being taken from me for the sake of my family.

For the sake of "our" legacy.

He told me it wouldn't take long.

Just a few months, Sage. Make it just a few months.

A few months of my life I'd never get back.

I know the plan. I know it will work. I know things will be over quickly, but that doesn't make it any easier. If my mother were still here, she would never stand for this. She would never let my father pawn me off like this, even if it were just for a few months.

His name is Adrian Hart.

From what I've been told, he's the epitome of self-obsessed, ill-advised, childish bad decisions. He has no self-respect. No self-control. Nothing he owns that he ever had to work for. Everything in his existence was handed to him on a silver platter by his father, Andrew

Hart. He's been hand-fed by a golden spoon clasped in silk covered digits, and now, it's come back around to drag the Hart family to the pits of hell where they belong.

My hair has been pinned up into a half-up, half-down style, with expensive jeweled pins and smooth silver threaded all throughout. Nothing on my body was picked by me. Everything was carefully crafted and hand-selected by my father, orchestrated to make me look like the perfect bride.

The dress was form-fitted at the waist, the corseted bodice spilling down into a ballroom gown with a long wedding train. It was stark white; lace embroidery draped in beautiful layers. I hate it more than anything else.

My hair is so dark that it clashes with the porcelain-colored garb, and the pink they've plastered on my cheeks makes my ice-blue eyes look atrocious.

Everything about today is the opposite of what I would have chosen for myself. From my makeup to my hair to my dress to my husband.

The golden ring on my finger feels like a noose. All of this, everything, is the opposite of what I want. And I have no choice but to let it happen.

The ceremony hall is packed full of reporters and people who do my father's bidding. Each one is here because he demanded they be here. He wouldn't dare let the Hart family have more acquaintances in this building on a day that's so important. Every detail has been tailored to make my family look superior, to keep the Harts in their rightful place underneath my father's boots.

He hates them.

I hate them.

And now, I'll be forever tied to one of them.

The overhead lights are blinding. The smell of flowers is nauseating.

Everything is wrong.

Yet everyone in the room stares at nothing but me when I step through the double doors. The piano rises in volume, but I can barely hear it over the rushing of my own blood in my ears.

My father's arm is crushed under the force of my grip, but I won't dare release it. If I must be uncomfortable, then so does he.

He walks me all the way to the altar and kisses me on the cheek like he has so many times before. I used to think it was sweet.

Now, it feels like he's sealing my death sentence with a pretty lace bow to match this awful dress that I'm drowning in.

I know he sees the disappointment in my eyes. I know he does. I want him to. I want him to cringe every single time he looks at me. I want him to know that what he has done to me is hurting me, and I hope it hurts him too.

Adrian Hart has sweaty hands. They're nauseatingly warm, damp and clammy feeling, just like the sheen clinging to his hairline.

He has blue eyes, too. Not blue like mine, not even close. Adrian's eyes are more like a muddy blue, not quite pretty enough to be gray, but not vibrant enough to swim in.

His hair is dark, a rich dark brown instead of my pitch black. It's styled so perfectly that there isn't a hair out of place.

He looks like a boy, one that still trips over his shoelaces and has a nanny to tie them back up. His nose is sharp and straight, all smooth skin and lacking any markings. Not even a pore can be seen. He's tall and lanky, all limbs and no muscle. The kind of body that looks good in a tailored suit but holds no weight to it.

There's nothing to him. Nothing special.

He's just another rich boy born into privilege and lacking will. I know he's never had to fight for a single thing in his life, and perhaps that's what makes me most angry.

Even in this very moment, he can't look me in the eyes while we're wed in front of hundreds of people.

I don't hear a single word that the officiant says. Instead, I stay laser-focused studying my almost husband.

He's too pretty. Too polished. Too young, even though we're the same age.

I could kill him. I want to kill him. Sooner, rather than later.

Honestly, I could take these pretty diamond-encrusted hairpins and gouge his eyes out. Maybe then he'd stop looking at me like I've turned into Cerberus and am getting ready to chew his fucking head off.

I get so lost in glaring daggers at him that the officiant clears his throat and I cut my eyes over to look at him. He graciously repeats the vows, and I recite the meaningless words, knowing they're dead before they even leave my lips. How callous of me.

The kiss is underwhelming, just a childish peck on the lips. Like teenagers trying it out for the first time. There's no love here. No passion. Just two bodies who know nothing of each other, except that they're meant to produce an heir. They're meant to bring peace.

But there can be no peace here.

I won't let there be.

I plan to fight tooth and nail. I plan to be difficult. I won't let them use me. I won't let this boy use me. This spoiled man-child. This fucking snake.

A Hart, my husband? No, I will die before I willingly allow this man to love me.

"Tonight, we stand together as one family, now united despite our tragic and harrowing pasts. For years, the north and south side have run parallel, neither stepping foot over the territory lines.

Our family names have been spoken with respect for decades; our legacies carried on the shoulders of those that have bled for them. But a divided family cannot prosper. A house that is split cannot stand.

This marriage is not just between my daughter and Adrian Hart. It is between the Ledgers and the Harts. It is a promise that we will come together with this unity.

That old scars can give way to new beginnings.

I look at my daughter tonight, beautiful and strong, and I know she will bring honor to both of our families.

I look at her husband, dear Adrian, and see the future they will forge together.

May this marriage bring peace where there has been blood, prosperity where we have struggled, and may it bring forth not only profit and power, but also love, family, and a future life itself.

To the Harts, and to the Ledgers, and the bond that will reign strong forevermore!"

Ian Ledger's voice booms over the room, and the toasts and cheers come soon after.

I can't remember much of the rest of the reception, brooding among people who passed me around like hors d'oeuvres. So many people touch and admire me, so many tell me how lucky and beautiful and blessed I am.

But I don't feel blessed. I don't feel beautiful. I don't feel like myself. I feel like this is all a charade, and later the curtain will drop, and I'll be laid bare for all to see.

For now, I'll play my part.

For now, I'll bat my eyelashes and laugh and smile with perfectly crafted teeth and soft pink lipstick.

"Remember what your purpose is," my father whispers in my ear as he hugs me, long and stifling.

What my purpose is?

To my father, my purpose is to breed and to ravage. To murder. To claim what he feels belongs to us. To the Ledgers.

My purpose... I will show them what my purpose is. They will see in the future just how much this hurts me. I'll make sure they do.

And none of them will see it coming when I burn it all to the ground.

2

The woman who leads me to the bridal suite is infuriating. Everything about her grates on my nerves. She talks in this nasal sickly-sweet tone, gushing about all of the beautiful details that the room has. The Hart family has spared no expense, so it seems.

Rose petals.

Wine.

Limited clothing.

Lingerie that's somehow just my size.

I hate it all.

If it were up to me, I'd douse this fucking gown in gasoline and set this entire hotel on fire.

It feels childish as the woman helps me undress out of the heavy garments. Each piece of lace that's removed makes me feel like it'll never end.

The dread is finally starting to settle in, and I can't stand it.

I know what must happen. Hell, I've even imagined and dreamt about it. This exact scenario has run through my mind probably a hundred times over in the past few weeks, and every single time, it's had a different outcome.

One of two things will come next.

One, the sex ends up decent enough and I at least get some sort of satisfaction out of it. It would be just my fucking luck if my terrible choice in marriage partner ended up being blessed in the bedroom. At least that would make it bearable.

Two, he's awful, and it all sucks, and I end tonight hating him even more.

I'm betting on option two.

The silk robe that's left for me is humiliating.

It feels nice on the skin, but it's spritzed with some perfume that smells flowery and awful, like some bitter old realtor that doesn't know how not to suffocate the room.

Another thing I hate about this night.

It's meant to show off my bare legs. To entice. To make my new husband size me up and want me even more. Not that it's needed. I know I'm nice to look at. A little plumper with my fuller breasts and thighs, but there's never been a man that hasn't begged to put his hands on me.

I'm sure this one will be much the same. Men are such simple creatures after all.

When my betrothed finally does arrive, the urge to slam an ashtray upside his empty fucking head strikes so fiercely that I nearly reach for it on the bedside table.

Not only is he tipsy, stumbling around a bit as he tries to get through the door, but he's still sweaty.

Still sweaty, damp, and disgusting.

He smells like alcohol and cheap cigarettes and some kind of spiced cinnamon cologne that reminds me of someone's great uncle, or a teenager that hasn't yet realized you can wear something other than Axe body spray.

The only decent thing about him is his pretty face.

His pretty face that I currently want to connect with the curb out back by the dumpsters.

He giggles like a schoolboy when he stumbles into the door, and the sound is even more grating on my nerves than the woman from before.

They've been married less than two hours, and he's drunk already.

This is what he's been doing while I've been getting deconstructed and prodded and fondled by some woman as she fit me into lingerie. Drinking.

"Oh, there you are," his voice is agitating, a little high-pitched, but that's probably made worse by the alcohol. He stumbles my way with a beer tight in his grasp, sloshing around so much that it spills onto the tile floor. And then he giggles at that, too. Like making childish messes is somehow amusing.

"Here I am," I try to keep my voice level and nonchalant. Like this isn't ruining my life. "Did you have difficulty finding me? Or, what, the hotel you booked was just hard to find on a map when one is impaired?"

"Impaired?" Adrian scoffs, pointing his bottle at me with a clumsy step forward. "I'm not impaired. I'm p-perfectly fine and capable. Besides, I have a job to do still."

"The job being me?" I give him an unimpressed glare, just barely managing not to cross my arms. "Let me guess, you needed the liquid courage? What, never been with a woman before?" That certainly gets a rise out of him. Just not the one I was hoping for.

"Of course I've been with a fucking woman," he practically spits, spilling more beer onto the floor, his voice rising in anger. Mouthy and hot-headed, just like his bastard father. "You're fucking lucky my Daddy picked you or you'd never be in such a good spot."

"Me? Lucky?" I scoff and then school my face back into a mask of indifference. "I meant no offense, dear husband. I only meant you may need the alcohol to relax after the long, stressful day we had," I soothe him with falsities, and Adrian's eyes drift, his lips pinching as he scrutinizes me to see if I'm telling the truth. "I assumed you had been with many women. At least that's what the rumors all say."

"The rumors?" Adrian echoes distantly before his lips form into a smug little smirk. The alcohol is certainly affecting his decision-making skills, because there can't possibly be any way that he is *this* easy to manipulate. "What rumors might that be?"

"Oh," I tilt my head in a bashful show of shyness. "You know... about.. well," I bite my lip and Adrian licks his and staggers a few steps closer. I can tell he's been with another woman some time recently. His collar is all messed up, makeup on his breast pocket where some tramp has rubbed against him. That explains the messy hair and the faint floral perfume lingering on his clothing. The way it mixes with the cigarette stench makes my stomach roll.

"Oh, I know," Adrian says, voice dripping in conceited pride. "Anyway," he takes another swig of his beer before he drops it on the edge of the table, knocking it over in his drunkenness. It rolls to the side and clatters loudly when it drops to the floor.

I try not to cringe when he starts stepping closer, tugging at his buttons. "We gonna do this shit or what?"

"What shit?" I feign curiosity despite my stomach rolling. If I could wipe that smug look off of his face, I'd do it in a heartbeat. I can't wait to watch it fall from his lips when I finally pull the rug from under his feet.

"We have to fuck," he shrugs as he drags his sweaty shirt from his body. "They did tell you that, didn't they?" Adrian is skinny just like I assumed, body full of spite, spoiled rotten pride, and liquor. He's not attractive from the neck down and I know this is going to be the hardest part of this marriage, having sex with someone that doesn't physically appeal to me.

He could at least take some pride in his figure. If I have to be perfectly polished to make him look good, the least he could do is pick up a weight or invest in a gym membership with all of this fucking money he's got laying around.

He's built like a twenty-year-old cosplaying as a grown man.

But I have a job to do.

"They did," I grit my teeth. I can't believe this man is my husband. I can already tell that he thinks he's God's gift to women, and I wish I could return him straight back to the sender. I'm betting that this will be terribly dull and excruciatingly quick. "You want to do that at this very moment?" *Please say no, please say no, please say no.*

"No time like the present, huh, doll?"

Fuck, I can't catch a break.

My father is going to pay for this.

The pet name makes me want to gouge his eyeballs out again.

Where the fuck did I put those hair pins? Maybe I'll strangle him with a pillow once he falls asleep.

"Besides, I'm tired. And you know our parents will check, those fucking bastards." It takes everything in me not to agree that his father is a fucking bastard, and mine... well, he's not favoring too much better at this point in time.

"Right," I mutter as he stalks up to me. I hold myself perfectly still, resisting the urge to smack his hand out of the way when he reaches out.

He trails a slow finger up my pastel pink baby doll lingerie. Not picked out by me, of course. But I can tell his hands are shaking. Even drunk, this pathetic little man doesn't have the courage to just do what needs to be done. He hesitates even now, despite knowing there's no way out of this. He's stuck in the same place that I am... right under our fathers' thumbs.

"Right," he repeats, and the tremble in his voice is so obvious it's insulting. "Well, we have a duty to our families to see this through and c-consummate the marriage," he stumbles through it, again like a child that's never felt the touch of a woman.

"Of course," I agree at once, nodding my head with what I hope seems like eagerness. "Let's do it now."

I try to stay relaxed as I watch this idiot fumble around. His clothes are dropped in a haphazard manner, littering the floor in spots that make no sense. He nearly trips when he leans forward, impaired by the liquor running through his veins.

Those hands... those God-awful clammy hands aren't all that rough with me. In fact, it's embarrassing how soft they are. Not a day of labor has met his palms. They're smoother than mine are, lotion softened and manicured. Everything about him is polished, even his nails, it seems.

Those unfamiliar hands map a trail up my sides, fumbling and shaking where he tries to fake through his nerves. A poor attempt at proving he's the man here.

Still, I let him place these alcohol-bitter lips on my skin, across my neck and up a path across my jaw. I let his hands cup my breasts through the flimsy lingerie, and I let him place shallow, meaningless kisses on my lips, making soft noises to encourage him to get a move on.

He tastes like cheap whiskey, bad decisions, and the regret that I know is going to sink into my bones any second now.

It seems he can't even hold my gaze. Each time our eyes meet, he looks away, until finally, he spins me around and all but shoves me into the comforter.

I wonder if he has to do it this way because he can't perform if he has to look me in the eyes.

There's no work up to it.

Nothing special.

Just a few flimsy fingers that lack finesse or excitement before he's working his hips in a way that holds no skill.

I need him alive. I need him alive. I need him alive.

I keep telling myself over and over again, ignoring all the other sensations.

There's nothing here for me anyway, and I've had better sex with myself than what he has to offer me.

Just a few more minutes, Sage. Just a few more minutes and then it's done. Just a few more...

I try to think of anything else. I agreed to this. I agreed to this, right? You knew this would happen, Sage. It doesn't have to be pleasurable, but it has to happen.

Anything other than the dry friction that's making me embarrassingly raw while he chases after his release.

Literally anything is better than thinking of what's going on right now.

It would all be easier to stomach if this idiot was at least decent in bed.

But *this* bad? How can anyone be *this* fucking bad at sex? And a man? It's literally one of two things on their mind twenty-four-seven, and he can't even get this right?

How on earth did I end up with a pathetic, Axe-body-spray-giving, limp-dick two-minute man?

This *cannot* be what my life amounts to.

I might toss my father's entire plan and just kill everyone.

At this point, that might be what happens. Just a full cleansing of all of the immediate men in my life.

Maybe I'll research bomb-making videos and just light this entire place sky high. Or maybe that entire gaudy cream-colored mansion that I've heard Andrew Hart speak so much about.

Would that put me on a government watch list? Probably so. I'll have to hire someone to do it with my new husband's money. Is that too callous? To kill him with a hitman paid by his own bank account?

The clock on the bedside table glares red, like the devil himself placed the numbers there. I watch it tick to the next one and wonder how many more seconds I have to endure.

Maybe tonight, he'll drown in the balcony hot tub.

Or I'll place a pillow over his mouth and suffocate him before I shove another bottle between his lips and claim he choked on the beer.

Maybe tonight, I'll just fucking *kill* him.

There's a long dramatic groan before I feel a little warmth between my legs, hot breath forcing down on my shoulder blades, and a body that weighs barely anything collapsing beside me.

The feeling is disgusting.

He acts like *he* did all the hard work when I'm the one that had to endure all his sloppy, uneven thrusting.

He's gasping for breath while I'm cringing at the cum that I can feel dripping out of me. Two minutes. A whole limp two-minute performance. That's what we're working with?

That's how fucking easy my new husband is. God help me. How am I supposed to put up with this man for an entire year?

At least his poor stamina brings a little comfort. Even if I do have to endure this chore often, it'll be quick. Little men need little time it seems.

Well, okay, that's not exactly fair to him.

He isn't, like, actually little, from what I felt. Below the belt at least.

But he's skinny as fuck, and his brain is probably the smallest thing about him.

I don't even glance down to see what lies between his legs, too scared that I somehow miscalculated what it felt like, and I'll end up with more disappointment added to the laundry list for today.

Instead, I swallow back the bile in the back of my throat and turn my head to face him. Only, his exhaustion is seemingly gone. Because now he's asleep with his mouth open next to me, breath stained with beer, cigarettes, and pink lipstick.

An embarrassment.

That's what this is.

A bad omen.

I need him alive. I need him alive. I need him alive.

I try to remind myself as I stumble from the bed sheets and into the bathroom so I can wash off the evidence of this awful day.

The water is furiously hot as I harshly scrub at my skin until it's rubbed raw. Even the soap here is floral. Even the shampoo here is floral. Like it was done on purpose.

I wonder if the other woman he fucked on our wedding day likes this scent.

Maybe he had to have it here so he could stomach being married to me.

Maybe we're both trapped in this.

I hate it.

I hate him.

I hate *all* of this.

He thinks he's got me right where he wants me.

His fucking father thinks he's worked everything out in his favor.

They think this marriage has saved them all.

That the violence is over and things will quiet down, and the death toll will plummet.

But the death toll is only going to rise.

For both the Hart family and the Ledger family.

With what they've forced me into, with this trap they've set, not only for me, but for my dear loving husband as well, I will make sure there is hell to pay.

One way or another, I'll be free.

I'll claw my way out of this cage on my left hand if I have to.

I'll make sure of it.

3

I almost feel bad that I want to kill Adrian so badly.

The rage that he incites is almost enough to make me want to off myself just to escape him.

It's not even that he's cruel or heartless or rules with an iron grip like his father.

It's that he's spineless.

It's that he's a child.

I have to do everything. The cooking. The cleaning. The laundry.

I left my father's empire to become a fucking maid. Except that's not right either because Adrian already has a fucking maid. Only they don't do their job.

Because Adrian doesn't like to be disturbed before ten in the morning.

Because Adrian likes his laundry done only on Sundays.

Every single thing is handed to him on a silver platter.

He can't even so much as get himself a glass of water.

I mean, be so serious with me. Are his hands so limp and dainty that he can't even pick up a glass and move two feet to the fridge to fill it with ice?

So, if not for my insistent grumbling as I snatch his dirty underwear from the middle of the living room floor, it would sit there for an entire week or until he ran out of clothing.

Not to mention that Adrian is asleep more than he is awake.

He drinks from sun-up to sun-down, and he eats like a toddler. His father even sends him an allowance, and of course I don't get a penny of that money.

Infuriating.

That's what it is.

"Dad, I'm telling you that there aren't any fucking secrets to give," I hiss into the phone. "He's a goddamn child! He doesn't leave the house except to party and go to the bar. His own father had to come here to wake him up from a two-day bender. They're enabling him, Dad! You have to do something, or I'll be stuck here forever dealing with this shit!"

"Watch your fucking mouth, Blue!" My father snaps back. The nickname plunges like an ice pick straight into my heart.

Blue.

It used to be a shared thing between us. Our matching ice blue gazes used to light up every room. Now I can't stand the fact we share even that.

"Dad, you told me this would be easy! That it would be over quick. It's been two weeks and all he's done is drink and sleep! You have to get me-"

"I don't have to do jack shit, Sage," he cuts me off, impatient and fed up already. "Or did you forget that I'm in charge here?"

"You promised me," I whisper, and the hurt is clear in my voice. Even I can hear it. There's no way he doesn't.

This is a betrayal that I'm not sure I'm going to be able to recover from. One that I think will settle into my bones, and no amount of reassurances or apologies will be able to rid me of it.

"We don't always get what we want, Sage," he sighs, twisting the knife even further. "You know what sacrifices have to be made, Blue. We talked about this."

"I know, but you never let me have a say in anything! You never listen when I talk, you just-"

"This conversation is over, Sage," he cuts me off again and I feel it. That hatred. It's building even now. "Drop it and do what's expected of you."

The line goes dead, and I stare down at the phone in my hand.

This must have been what my mother felt like before her death. Like she'd been abandoned by the one person left that was supposed to love her.

That's how I feel right now.

My father. My own flesh and blood. He's abandoned me to the Hart family.

To suffer alone. To listen for secrets.

To take back what belongs to "us."

This is nothing less than a betrayal.

The lines are being drawn, and I'm stuck in the middle, in between the Harts and the Ledgers that both want what the other has.

It's me who suffers. Me who has to endure. Me that has to see the plan through to fruition.

I'm the one harmed by both sides, no matter how I navigate this marriage. My father has offered me up as a prize, all while knowing I'm collateral damage.

I am all that I have left, and I don't have to put up with all of this childish behavior.

Maybe it's my father to blame for what happens next.

Or maybe it's all just me and I get satisfaction when I see Adrian floundering like an idiot.

I storm into the kitchen and rip open the cabinets, searching for the largest pot I can find. I make sure the water is cold and dump some extra ice in there for good measure.

And then I lug it all the way upstairs and into the bedroom.

I kick the door so hard that it flings open and collides with the wall, and still, he doesn't stir.

With all of my huffing and puffing and this loud door, he doesn't so much as groan.

"You've got to be fucking kidding me," I grit my teeth as I cross the room.

I stare down at him for a moment, taking in the way his normally ethereal features are now scrunched and unattractive. The way his mouth is parted like he's getting the best sleep of his life while I'm cleaning up after him. The way he's curled up in a ball, like he needs protection even from his five-thousand thread count Egyptian cotton sheets that he's currently drooling on.

I stare down at him, and all I feel is hatred.

I lift my arms, even though they shake from the effort.

And then I dump the entire pot of water on the bed.

Adrian startles so hard that he nearly falls off the bed. He flails, kicking the comforter all over and knocking pillows onto the floor as he gasps in shock at the cold.

"W-what the ever-loving fuck are you d-doing?!" He stammers through the chill of the ice water drenching his body. He scrambles to orient himself, spitting out water and pushing his slick hair back from his eyes.

"I am sick and fucking tired of you sleeping all goddamn day!" I scream at him, and the sincerity in my voice must finally register with him, because he settles a little to stare at me, eyes studying my flushed face and the angry furrow of my brow.

"Are you not fucking tired of this?" I continue yelling, dropping the empty pot on the ground. He flinches when it clatters to the expensive marble flooring. "Seriously, are you not fucking tired of this? All you do is sleep and party, Adrian! That's *all* you do! Your fucking father treats you like a pathetic child that doesn't know his ass from his mouth! Your own family's underlings are laughing at you! Did you know that? They literally talk about you in the halls like you're a spoiled brat that can't lift his own goddamn fingers to even type on his cellphone!"

I'm breathless and panting by the time I'm finished screaming, and Adrian looks so thoroughly chastised that I almost feel bad. Almost.

"This ends today," I firmly declare. "I am serious. Do you fucking hear me? We're making some changes starting today. Get up, get dressed, and meet me downstairs in ten minutes or so help me God, I will shoot you between the eyes. Am I fucking clear?"

"Yes," Adrian clenches his jaw as he responds, but he *does* respond. I can only stand to look at him for a few more seconds before I sigh in exasperation and trudge out of our room and down the hallway to the staircase.

I'm so aggravated that my voice easily carries across the house.

"If you're part of the maid service, please come downstairs right now!"

I yank open a drawer in the kitchen that I saw someone using the other day, and then I snatch a pen up and start hastily scribbling "Maid Services" at the top before slamming it on the counter

They stagger in one after another, and it infuriates me to no end that there's over a dozen maids here, and yet they don't do anything but enable my husband.

Adrian filters into the room behind them and hesitantly crosses to stand beside me, but he immediately averts his gaze and looks away.

"How many cleaners do we have here? Raise your hand!" Four hands instantly go up, and I point at the first two that lifted theirs. "You two can stay. The other two, you're fired. Please get out," I point to the door, and there's whispers and gasps that follow. A spoon clatters onto the countertop as one of the maids' mouths falls open.

"You can't fire my staff, I-"

"I don't want to hear it, Adrian!" I snap, turning to glare at him. He pulls himself to his full height, suddenly finding some sort of backbone to continue facing me. "You are a laughingstock. You don't even know how to run your own household, and these people are enabling you. You're going to learn some fucking responsibility starting today, and if you push back, I'll make sure your father knows exactly what you've been doing with Daddy's money!" I challenge him.

But I can tell the threat works.

Just as I knew, Adrian has no guts. No shame. All he has is fear. All he has is his father to hand him whatever he wants. It's pathetic.

If poor Daddy Hart knew that Adrian was using all his money and skimming coke off the top of his desk, he'd kill him.

"Who cooks?"

Four more hands hesitantly go up, and I point again at the ones on each end.

"You two, you're fired. Get out."

The process continues until I cut the staff in half, and then I pick the pen up and start scrawling on the paper.

"I will make sure that each of you gets a five dollar an hour raise starting today, and I don't care how you do it, but you'll need to divide up all your tasks and make sure they're done. Starting today, this house will be cleaned every day. I don't mean like scrubbed from top to bottom. I mean dishes done, laundry done, counters cleaned. That kind of thing. Starting today, I don't care what Adrian told you to do. Every fucking day, no matter how many times you must do it, if you find his clothes on the floor, you go find him and tell him to pick them up immediately and put them in the laundry. And I don't care how many loads of laundry it takes, but you will wash clothes as soon as there are enough clothes for one load. No more piling it all up until Sundays. Am I understood?"

The chorus of yeses sounds like the sweetest song.

"And you," I turn on Adrian and level him with an ice-cold look of hatred. "You will stop leaving your clothes and dishes all over the damn house. Starting today, I will be waking you up every single day, no later than eight in the morning-"

"Sage, you're being fuc-"

"Do you remember what I said about shooting you between your fucking eyes?" I yell in exasperation. "What about that didn't you get? I'm not playing around, Adrian, I'm fucking sick of this!" I slap my hand on the countertop, and he goes silent, glaring at me, but complacent at least.

"Your father is letting these people talk shit about you as they please! They think you're ridiculous and childish and you don't care? Does it not piss you off every time they undermine you? You are the only fucking child of Andrew Hart. The one meant to inherit and run all of this, and these people act like you're some fucking schoolboy on the street!" I stress, urging him to understand.

"I'm not doing this for no reason, Adrian. I'm doing this because this is my life, too, now. I'm stuck with you just like you're stuck with me. Everything that you do reflects on me, and I won't let you run us into the ground and make us a laughingstock. You have to make some changes here or they're going to push you out of this family, and all this money and freedom, and bullshit that you partake in, it will *all* disappear, and you'll be left with nothing!"

Adrian's jaw tightens just enough for me to see it, but after a moment, he finally slowly nods his head, like he gets where my anger is coming from. I hope he does, because for everyone's sake, I need him to.

If he doesn't start making these changes, I'm going to burn everything he loves in the backyard and make a show out of it.

"I'm not doing this to make your life difficult," I try to soften my voice, willing him to understand where I'm coming from. "I just need you to work with me here, Adrian. You have so much potential, and you waste it by sleeping away. You can do and be so much more than you are, and I know that you can. No one else knows or believes it, but I do. And I'm asking you, please, just to work with me here," I plead, feeling a little emotional with the weight of the words.

I don't want to have to rely on or ask this man for a single thing, but I have no choice. I have to make him think I care. I have to make him agree.

"Can you at least try? At least try to make some changes, and I promise you that things will get better. All I'm asking you to do is try."

"Alright," Adrian mutters, and I take a deep breath as I hear it.

"Alright?" I ask again, and he slowly nods his head.

"Yeah, alright," he agrees, holding my gaze.

"Alright then," I breathe out and try to release some of the tension in my shoulders. "Then we will do it together."

Together.

I fucking hate it.

But we will do it together.

I will build my husband into something palatable.

Even if it kills me to do it.

Even if I have to burn this empire to the ground to do it.

4

My husband is like a dog.

A cute, innocent little dog that you picked up from the animal shelter and think they'll be your forever partner-in-crime.

Except he's actually a Doberman that weighs over one hundred pounds and doesn't realize they're knocking everything over and draining you dry because they eat so much.

Not to mention that he's actually not so innocent.

Instead, he's like a dog stealing licks off of your plate.

Messy, ill-mannered, and doesn't understand the word "no."

The thing is, you have to condition a man just like you would a dog.

When they don't listen, you pop them on the nose and firmly let them know they're doing something wrong.

When they make messes, you rub their nose in it so they'll understand that they have no choice but to stop.

That's how I have to treat Adrian.

I think I've been training him well enough.

At least the brat knows how to do laundry and wash a plate now.

Only now, an even bigger problem is forming.

Andrew Hart has been foaming at the mouth over the changes Adrian's making.

From asking more questions in the family meetings to inquiring about small possibilities to learn about the business, to becoming interested in what's going on around him... he's trying.

Adrian is *trying*.

I can see that, at least.

But unfortunately, that means everyone else can see it as well.

It's difficult to put a name to whatever Adrian's efforts are.

It seems like no matter how hard he tries, he still seems to fall short of everyone else's expectations. Even mine.

Just yesterday, Adrian made me coffee as a token of good faith, trying to show me that he's at least attempting to pay attention to me. But even then, the coffee was black, whereas I take mine with hazelnut creamer and a shit ton of too much sugar.

I waited until he left the house to pour it down the drain.

Dogs have to think they're doing a good job, or they'll revert back to bad habits.

Today, Adrian told me he's going to pick up payments for some drug shipments.

Our family doesn't deal in drugs. We deal in guns.

And Adrian? Well... he's already got an alcohol problem, so I don't need him jumping off the deep end.

I already gave him the full breakdown of this needing to go well, even begged and pleaded for him not to fuck this up.

His father's been chomping at the bit to find a way to blame him for something, and this is his first real opportunity to prove himself.

I almost wonder if his father chose this task because he expects for Adrian to fuck it all up.

I pray to God that he doesn't.

Over the past two weeks, Adrian's been putting more effort into making this as civil as possible.

The small talk is excruciating, but I'll admit, he's become a little more palatable. When he's not being a total snob or drunk off his ass, he's pretty decent to be around.

On Fridays, we've been kicking the maids out for the day so we can have "alone" time. If alone time means attempting to "hang out." We eat dinner together. We continue the small talk. We drink some wine to make each other more tolerable.

And at the end of every Friday night, we end up back in bed.

Where Adrian lacks in most areas, he, *shocker,* also lacks in bed.

The one good thing about him is that he knows how to use his tongue. Not during kissing, apparently, but in all other areas. It's his one saving grace and my one break.

Still, I've been taking every measure not to let this man impregnate me.

My father doesn't know.

His father certainly doesn't know.

But I just can't do it.

I'm biding my time and counting the days down until I can get out of here.

Anything to speed this process up.

I go through the motions of my day, cleaning up around the house, planning dinner, looking over paperwork and reports about our sales and shipments.

The hours all blur together, and still, I can't stop glancing at the clock in the foyer.

I've paced a hole in the marble flooring, like cattle tracing the same path again and again and again.

Three.

Four.

Five.

Six.

Adrian should have been back by now.

I pace the entire length of the house from one side to another, frantically dialing his number, trying to get through.

It rings to voicemail every single time.

And I know.

Deep down, I have this sinking feeling that Adrian's gone and fucked it all up.

Like he always does.

He forwards my calls to voicemail. Over and over again.

"Adrian, so help me, if you've fucked-"

The front door clamors open and my husband appears.

As his father throws him into our foyer, my heart starts beating so fast I can feel it in my throat.

I stumble backward as he lands at my feet, groaning and tear-stained as he rolls across the ground. The sound of his knees slamming into the marble flooring seems to echo in my ears.

Andrew Hart stands over him, undoubtedly regretting the very day that he was born.

I'm starting to share that sentiment.

The only problem is... I actually have a tiny shred of sympathy.

Don't get me wrong. It's buried. Somewhere deep, deep down under mountains of resentment and an amount of hatred that would take years to get a full grasp on. But it is there.

At the end of the day, Adrian and I aren't so different.

We're both being forced to live a life that has been chosen for us, and Adrian has been crumbling under the weight since his birthright placed a claim on him.

There's no navigating around it.

There's no hope to take a different path.

Andrew Hart controls his past, present, and future.

And now, I'm getting a firsthand glimpse at how his hatred burns just like mine does.

No one is safe from him.

Not even his son.

Not even his heir.

"What is this?" My voice trembles, but I try to will it back steady. Andrew Hart is a very dangerous, very powerful man. Even I know that. I don't even mean to question him, but the way he's careless with Adrian as he slams him into the floor is baffling.

"Your-" he grits out and spits at his feet towards Adrian. "Pathetic, idiotic, cowardly excuse of a husband has failed me yet again."

"Failed?" I whisper, brows knitting together in confusion. I can feel the panic rising in my blood. This isn't part of the plan.

This isn't part of the plan.

It can't be.

I was meant to stay far away from this man.

Far away from the rest of their family.

"Failed," he snarls, knocking over a vase in the entryway. I startle backwards and bump into the archway as Andrew crouches down and pushes Adrian's head into the floor.

His nose makes a sickening crack, and I take another step back to put some distance between me and his father. Still, a metallic scent fills the space around us, and I know blood has been spilled.

"And now he's going to pay for it," he spits the words out like they burn his tongue.

"Daddy, I didn't-"

"You did!" Andrew pushes his head harder against the floor like an ant being squished beneath a boot, and Adrian pathetically whimpers and begs him to stop.

"You'll be out of here tomorrow," Andrew says, flat and final. His voice is nothing short of deadly and it makes even me shiver instinctively.

"Out?" I whisper in confusion, dread pooling like ice in my veins. I don't even realize when I take a few steps forward, nearly stepping on the broken glass littering the floor.

"My son needs to learn how to be a fucking man, and not this pathetic little cunt that can't do anything but drink himself into oblivion and snort my fucking product," Andrew's voice drops so low that I know he means every word of it. He hates Adrian more than I do.

"Tomorrow. He'll be shipped off to a specialized unit-"

"Father-"

"Shut the fuck up, Adrian!" His father roars, and Adrian whimpers under his hand.

"You're sending him away?" I practically whisper the question.

This wasn't part of the plan at all.

"For how long?"

"For as long as it fucking takes," Andrew shoves Adrian's head down one more time before he stands up from his crouched position and levels me with an unimpressed stare. "He's lucky I could call in enough favors to even get him there. Say goodbye to your darling wife, Adrian. Tonight may be the last night you ever get to see her," he spits on Adrian's trembling form one more time, and Adrian makes a wounded sound.

Andrew Hart pulls a case from his suit and tugs a cigar free.

All I hear is the flick of a lighter as he walks out of our home.

Once I hear Andrew's car door slam shut, my eyes lower to the man trembling underneath me.

My husband, cowering on the ground like a child, crushed under the weight of his father's legacy.

Sympathy.

Maybe that's my fatal flaw.

Because I still feel it when I look down upon the man I swear to hate.

"What the fuck did you do, Adrian?" I whisper, struggling to grasp how I'm going to work this out.

Adrian either just opened a door or slammed one in my face.

This isn't what my father promised me.

This isn't even close.

This is worse.

And I will have to pick up the pieces, but I'll make sure someone bleeds for every single shard.

5

Adrian shudders and pulls away from me every time I dab the cotton ball across his face.

I yank him back every single time. He's lucky I even feel a shred of sympathy for his busted-up face.

Honestly, he's lucky that his father didn't just shoot him and save himself the public humiliation of having to ship his coke and alcohol addicted son off to God knows where.

At least, that's what Andrew Hart did to my mother years ago.

He took my mother from me.

I wonder if he'll take my husband.

If anything, *this* is the one thing that we have in common. The only shred of similarity that bonds us together. We both have shitty fathers, it seems. Unless you count the fact that his father probably wants us both dead.

"You couldn't have just done what you were told?" I quietly speak into the little space between us. Adrian clenches his jaw at my question and tries to pull away again, but I grip his chin tighter to keep him there. Still, he lowers his gaze and looks away from me like he can't stand to see the disappointment etched on my face.

I can't quite hide it from my voice though.

"They set me up, Sage. I didn't-"

"They set you up and yet you still *fell* for it, Adrian," I cut him off in frustration. For a moment, nothing else is said as I carefully spread some antibiotic cream across his nose. At least now I won't feel so bitter about how polished and pretty he is.

"I get it, okay?" I continue in a quiet voice. "Your father is a piece of shit and so is mine. But Adrian, now you've put yourself in an even worse situation. What are we going to do now?"

"I don't need you to remind me how much I fucked up, Sage," Adrian grumbles as he hops off of the counter and trudges into our bedroom. "There's nothing to do. Daddy is going to send me off just like he said." I trail after him with antibiotic cream still stuck to my fingers, too worked up to worry about it.

"You really think he's going to send you away? And to the military? What the fuck is he hoping to accomplish with this? Can he even do this?" I rapid-fire questions at him and Adrian drops his head to rest it in his hands before he lets out a long sigh.

"He can do anything he wants, Sage; he's Andrew Hart. He's probably hoping they'll kill me off so I won't come back. At least then he can pretend I died with some kind of honor," he rolls his eyes and sits down heavily on the edge of the bed. I move to stand in front of him and Adrian looks up at me with clear exhaustion in his eyes. "This is my life, Sage. It's yours now, too. You can question it all you want, but my father just wants me out of the picture."

"You don't really believe that, do you?" I ask, and the disappointment is clear in my voice. "You're his only son."

"He never wanted a son," Adrian sighs. "Everyone knows it, Sage. I'm a fuck up. I know it. You know it. Everyone else sure as hell knows it. Nobody wants me here. Least of all my father. He only kept me because he needed someone here in the event of his death. But we both know he'd never let the family go. He's planning to die of old age before he shares it with me. It was always his plan to get rid of me eventually."

"Adrian," I sigh and move to sit down beside him, and we both know this isn't going to end well no matter how we look at it.

"There's no point in talking about it, Sage. He won't go back on what he said. I've got no choice but to go," Adrian says in a soft, defeated murmur. It's perhaps the most emotion I've heard from him since our wedding.

"You'll be able to contact me at least, won't you?" I ask, and Adrian cracks a smile on the corner of his mouth. I want to smack it clean from his face.

"What? Are you pretending that you'll miss me?"

"Shut up," I grumble, but Adrian actually lets out a small laugh.

"Really, Sage," he says after a moment, and his voice is still soft when he turns to look at me. "Will you miss me? Even a little bit?" He asks.

I don't know why the question bothers me.

I hate Adrian.

I do.

I hate everything.

But we have been cohabitating for nearly a month now, stuck together more than we are apart. He's the only solid that I've had since this catastrophe started.

I don't love him.

And I don't need or want him.

I can't stand his attitude or the condescending, self-loving head on his shoulders.

But now with him being sent away, I might be all on my own.

This time, I might truly have to come to terms with what this marriage means.

This time, I might be stuck dealing with something far worse in Adrian's absence.

His father.

"All you do is annoy me to fucking death," I breathe out, and Adrian chuckles again, but it sounds a little defeated, like he expected the answer. "But you're alright for a spoiled rich kid," I grumble and push myself to stand back up. "You probably need to pack some things up just in case he makes good on his promise. And maybe shower," I suggest and gesture towards him. "You smell disgusting."

"Gee, thanks. My wonderful wife. How sweet of you," Adrian quips sarcastically, but he does get up to head back toward the bathroom, and all I can do is think of how uncertain my future will be.

I wonder if Andrew really will make an example out of Adrian and the choices he's made.

It only takes eight hours for me to find out.

Andrew Hart makes good on his promises, apparently.

He shows up bright and early the next morning, practically dragging Adrian out of our house.

I have no choice but to hug him to keep up appearances, but then his father rips him away and shoves him into a car while I sit back and watch.

I don't want it to, but my heart seizes up a little in my chest.

Adrian is my only comfort here. My only solace.

He was supposed to be the one I share my life with. Well, at least until I decided to kill him, but we're not counting that right now.

It stings a little to watch Andrew drag him out by the collar.

We knew it was coming. But still, it's difficult to come to terms with.

Adrian and I stayed up nearly half the night, both too anxious to get any rest.

Somehow, we managed to find some common ground this time.

Adrian wants to be better.

So he says.

He wants to *be* better, and he wants to *do* better.

He wants to step into the family business, for real this time, and show his father that he can do more than just drink and party and skim a little coke off the books in hopes that no one will notice.

And I'm going to make it happen.

We're going to make it happen together.

While Adrian fulfills his duties wherever his father is shipping him out to, I'm going to do what I can to make things better here.

No matter what it costs.

I hope for the sake of both of our lives that Adrian was being honest when he said he was going to try.

That's all I can think when I watch their car disappear through the iron gates.

6

The house is silent.

Too silent.

With no staff there on my first Friday alone, it's almost frighteningly quiet without hearing Adrian's footfalls down the barren hallways.

For starters, the clang of liquor bottles slamming into the tables as he noisily finishes one off is missing.

Plus, there's the absence of dishes banging against the stainless-steel sink while I forced Adrian to wash his glasses out.

Even I've grown quieter.

There's no more huffing and puffing while I clean up his lingering messes. No clack of my shoes as I rush from here to there making sure he isn't spilling alcohol on the floor.

The house itself seems to mourn him.

It's like he's already dead.

Except that can't be right, can it?

I certainly haven't killed him yet.

But I start to worry because what if his father did? What if he took Adrian away to get rid of him under the guise that he died serving his country?

That would sure be a way to gain sympathy.

I don't want to worry about him, but it's hard not to think that Adrian could be dead in a ditch somewhere right now while I'm studying chips in the cream-colored paint.

I have to force the thoughts not to stir in my head while I survey everything about my new fortress.

For now, I set my mind on a new task.

Making this place *mine.*

Everything about this house is not a home.

It's a palace.

One meant for control.

For societal falsities that bring no comfort.

I'm not sure if it's meant to keep people in, or to keep people out.

Perhaps that's why Adrian hated being here.

I wish I could pinpoint exactly what the discomfort is about this place, but perhaps it's simply because it isn't mine yet.

It's too cold. Too impersonal. Too impractical.

There's no warmth or touch of personality.

I have a vision.

At least, a vision about what I'd like my home to look like. I don't give a damn if Adrian agrees or not.

But this place needs some color. It needs some life. It needs to lose some of its stark white walls and dull edges.

It needs me.

Right now, it's a soulless, barren hellscape.

Just a pre-designed empty shell meant to contain Adrian's drunken rages.

It starts with the alcohol.

I don't even mean to do it.

But I walked past that same bar top one too many times, and the rage fills me all over again.

This place needs to be cleansed.

It needs to be polished.

It needs *Sage's magic eye for decking shit out in an early-2000s vampire* aesthetic.

It needs some dark crimsons and charcoals to pair with this black marble and gold flooring.

I drag the large trash can from the kitchen into the dining room. Or Adrian's version of a dining room. Alcohol lines all of the countertops. Each one filled with booze, cheap and expensive alike.

I pop the top from every single bottle and pour it down the drain, watching the liquid swirl away into oblivion.

The sharp, biting scent of cinnamon fills the kitchen, burning my throat as it flees from my grasp.

My poor husband doesn't even have good taste if this shitty ten-dollar bottle of whiskey is anything to go by.

Every single bottle empties until I hear them clink when they fall to the bottom of the trash can.

Adrian isn't even around to mourn it.

And I won't have it here as evidence of how my husband gave in and fell for one of his many vices.

Every single room seems similar.

I find liquor bottles all over the place, some hidden, some half-drunk.

Adrian couldn't just let it go.

He couldn't just give it up.

Maybe that's what is most infuriating about him.

He has so much potential and yet he wastes it on trivial things like liquor.

Once I'm finished with the downstairs, I trudge up the staircase and start all over again.

Only I get hung up on Adrian's study.

The only room in the entire house he didn't want me entering.

But Adrian isn't here.

And I'm claiming this house as my home.

The door creaks on the hinges when I push it open, and it thuds off the wall like a bad omen.

I shouldn't pry.

Really, I shouldn't.

I know better.

Curiosity killed the cat and all that.

But the room feels like a beacon pulling me in, and what secrets might lie here are too tempting to overlook.

There's dust lining the bookshelves. A thin sheen of it covering the desk.

Adrian's only been gone a few days, and yet this place looks like it hasn't been touched in weeks.

At least, that's what I first thought.

It goes to show that I am my father's daughter.

Because I know that I'm missing something here.

Something that I refuse to let go unseen.

There's no way Adrian isn't housing secrets in this room. Why else would he tell me not to go in here?

What doesn't he want me to see?

It's not like there's anything that can be worse than all the other shit I've been subjected to since the start of this marriage.

When I take a step back and glance around the room again, I see the same film of dust. It coats nearly every surface.

Nearly.

I almost hesitate to approach the one shelf that seems out of place.

At first glance, it seems almost comical.

The shelf is full of boring non-fiction titles. The history of whiskey production. A historical recollection of technological inventions. Other nonsense titles no one would reach for.

But I reach for them anyway.

It starts with the book on the far-left corner.

The spine is a little worn, evidence of grimy hands that have repeatedly reached for it.

But the spine isn't what interests me.

It's what's hidden within the pages.

Like the first photograph that I find.

It almost looks like me.

Almost.

The dress is eerily similar. So is the corsage wrapped around a thin, dainty wrist.

Only the nail polish is different.

I pull out the Polaroid and hold it towards the light, and my heart stutters in my chest.

The strands of blonde hair barely entering the frame encourages my pulse to hammer in my bloodstream.

When I flip it over, I barely realize that my own hands have started to shake.

There's a date on the back of the photograph.

Two weeks after my wedding.

No.

Absolutely not.

This isn't me.

I know it isn't me.

I drop the photograph on the ground and flip the book over, shaking it violently until two more photographs fall out.

I crouch down and snatch them from the floor.

These Polaroids are similar to the first.

But that face isn't mine.

That blonde hair isn't mine.

My hair is nearly blue with how pitch black it is.

My eyes are pale blue and striking, not muddled down like these green hazels staring up at the camera with my husband's thumb on thin lips. My lips are plump and full.

This woman isn't me.

And yet the date on the back shows just two days before Adrian left for whatever hell his father sent him to.

I drop the book and reach for the next one.

The bile that rises in the back of my throat is suffocating.

Picture after picture falls out, each one seemingly worse than the first.

This woman is wearing my wedding dress.

My dress that I didn't even get to pick out.

My high heels.

My corsage.

My husband's suit jacket as he fucks her in my dress.

The photographs are proof that even the day before he was sent away, he was cataloging his life with this woman.

While he was supposed to be trying with me, while he was supposed to be home with me, he was seeing this woman.

The woman he actually wanted.

I can't get over the bitterness building in my chest. It rises and rises, and it feels like my heart's been torn in two.

I know Adrian doesn't love me.

I don't love him either.

But at least I was fucking trying to tolerate him. At least I was trying to be what he wanted. What he was promised. At least I endured his touch and his kiss and his roaming hands. At least I tried to salvage his image and mold him into something great.

At least I tried to make the best of this nightmare.

All while my husband has been playing house with another woman.

How fucking *dare* he!

This right here is why I should have fucking killed him myself.

I take back all of the sympathy I might have felt for him.

He's just like his father. A fucking spineless leech who sucks the life out of everything that he touches.

A pathetic excuse of a man who I should have let drown in the hundreds of liquor bottles!

He's stolen my youth from me.

My prime years, and I'm sold off like cattle to a man that doesn't want me! To a man who can barely stand on his own two fucking feet.

A man who fucks other women in my wedding dress. The very same dress he had someone else peel me out of.

No.

No, I won't let Adrian get away with this.

He is going to pay.

My husband is going to pay.

Andrew Hart is going to pay.

My father is going to pay.

All of these men that think I'm under their thumb will pay.

I wanted to burn their empire to the ground, but I think I can do something better.

I'm going to build my own empire.

And I'm going to watch everything they love crumble.

I'm going to steal it from them.

7

ELLISON

There are only a few things that I know are solid truths about life.

First and foremost, sugar goes on Frosted Flakes.

Seriously.

They aren't shit without at least a tablespoon sprinkled on top.

Secondly, and just as important, the band Dance Gavin Dance has had more lead singer scandals than I've had Subway sandwich footlongs.

Thirdly, the FitnessGram Pacer Test is cruel and unusual punishment.

Last and not least, the final truth I've come to learn is the newest one.

It only recently came to light, but I think it will rise to the most absolute law before long.

The fact is: I want to kill Adrian Hart.

No, wait, scratch that.

I want to drag him out into the middle of the desert and siphon sand down his windpipe while he chokes on every word he's ever said.

Actually, scratch that, too.

I want to tie his fingers to thick bands of rope and drag him from behind a truck at one hundred miles per hour so there's no chance he'd ever recover.

Whatever terrible tortures there are in the world, I want him to experience them firsthand.

Preferably by my hand, but I'll take what I can get.

Anything to make him learn when to shut the fuck up and keep his goddamn hands to himself.

His slender fingers reach out to caress a strand of blonde hair from a young girl in the village. The high-pitched giggle is sickening considering this girl is probably no older than seventeen.

The runt never cares.

He's used to being handed everything on a silver platter without consequence or fear of retaliation.

Even here, where the entire hierarchy is based on command and respect, he doesn't fucking care.

The men here, me, the guys, the ones who work alongside us... they've all spent more than half of their lives preparing for this unit. They've poured their blood, sweat, and tears into it.

Just for some fucking prep kid with soft hands to saunter in here like he's on a two-week vacation down in Mexico.

I guess Daddy's money stretches all the way to the Middle East.

We aren't supposed to touch.

We aren't supposed to interact.

We aren't supposed to draw attention.

We aren't supposed to be noticed.

Our rules are there for a reason. Both our protection and theirs.

The kid doesn't give a fuck.

He breaks every rule that's set, and then he whines when he's disciplined.

Adrian Hart is vermin.

He's pathetic.

Inferior.

The guys have started calling him my twin. Maybe, but I'm the superior sibling that probably tried to absorb him in the womb.

I wish I could have finished the job.

That could be true. Maybe we are blood-related. That might explain the otherworldly phenomenon of how eerily similar we look. Like twins. Only, I know that I would have been successful in eliminating such a weak individual in the womb.

Men like Adrian Hart are a plague to humanity. Weak-minded, ill-tempered dogs. He lacks control and finesse. He cannot even sign his own name without the pen holding a tremor.

Perhaps I'm biased. Perhaps I'm jaded from all the action I've seen up close and personal. Maybe one too many bullets have penetrated my skin. Or maybe I'm just a sick fuck who wants to see a weaker man suffer.

Whatever the reason, the truth still stands that I want Adrian Hart to meet his death, slow and torturous.

For two weeks, he has failed to learn. He has failed to succeed in *any* task given to him.

While they encourage me to take him under my wing, I cannot help but notice the differences between us.

His voice shakes when addressing a man bigger than him.

And I might only be two inches taller, but I've got at least thirty pounds of muscle on the runt, and he fucking trembles every time he looks me in the eyes.

His posture is lazy, and he lacks control of his limbs.

Every single time I hand him a gun, he nearly pops himself in the face with the recoil, and he complains the bullet casings burn when they fly back.

His thought processing is slow and delayed, almost like a teenager that never finished fully developing.

Half the time he speaks, he stutters, and the other half of the time, he slurs his words so badly that I feel the rage simmering all the way to my hair follicles.

But that probably has to do with the fact that he's a fucking drunk.

There's no authority in his voice. No intelligence in his offered suggestions.

He hesitates in everything that he does.

We could never be a perfect mirror image of each other.

But I won't lie. Even I see the similarities in our appearance.

Adrian Hart has eyes that are a little more blue. Height that is nearly two inches shorter. A nose that is perhaps a little straighter than mine. His body is lean where mine is crafted from years of dedication and hard work.

But if someone cut us open, I've no doubt that even my blood would be better suited for survival than his.

I'd almost be willing to bet my life on it.

Perhaps I will save that for later.

For now, I pick him apart and watch as he crumbles under the weight of my expectations.

I keep my voice level and instruct him as expected of me.

I push and I push and I push, and he still doesn't get better.

His arrogance will be his downfall, and I will be the one to send him packing back to his Daddy.

War has no place for cowards like Adrian Hart.

Why I was chosen to mentor and keep him alive, I'll never know.

I want to rid myself of his presence, and I will, one way or another.

He simply doesn't belong here. His father bought his way into hell, and now he's met me.

There's nothing of importance about this pathetic excuse of a man.

Nothing memorable.

Nothing worth knowing.

Or so I thought.

I hear it in passing.

It calls to me like a siren trying to lure me out to sea.

I don't mean to look.

In another world, my knowledge of Adrian Hart's existence would be obsolete.

He wouldn't exist to me.

And yet the compulsion to glance over his shoulder takes hold of me like hands ripping the oxygen from my windpipe, and I cave.

It takes one look, and I plunge into the depths of fascination with the creature on the other side of the dim-lit screen.

Eyes that pool like crystal blue rivers glare daggers at Adrian Hart.

A voice that captivates me to my very core, so full of hatred and disdain for the man staring back at her, tugs at my blood vessels to bleed just for another chance to hear it caress the shell of my ear.

"Have you learned nothing, Adrian?" That melodic voice rasps and swirls around me, and I could drown in it. So easily, I could drown in it.

It's not even directed at me, and yet I'd be willing to give in to whatever this woman so desired of me.

I'd do *unspeakable* things to have even her enraged disdain directed at me.

I've killed men with my bare hands. It's common in this line of work. And yet... and yet, I'd kill a million more to have this woman direct even her barest amount of frustration on me.

Even in her anger, the control that she wields is enlightening. The clarity in her eyes as she looks at Adrian is so obviously tempered for the sake of civility.

"It's not your concern, Sage," Adrian spits the words back at her.

Sage.

The object of all my desires is named Sage.

The knowledge nearly chokes me.

Much like I wish it would choke Adrian.

Whoever this woman is to him, he does not deserve her.

He does not deserve to even be in her presence. A man so inferior, so pathetic, so ill-equipped and oblivious.

The way he spat the words at her... no, he does not deserve her. So much wasted potential in the span of a single breath. He's nauseatingly naïve.

Every little thing about him is sickening, from his spoiled rotten core to his glaringly obvious misfiring brain cells.

I'd give anything to have the life that Adrian Hart has had.

If it were mine, I would wrap an iron-tight fist around it and milk it dry of all of its potential.

The money, the world, the conviction at claiming even his very name.

I would make it all mine.

Flip it upside down and manipulate it into an added limb that only I could wield.

I'd take control of every aspect of his life.

His money. His cars. His home. His lifestyle.

I'd take it all and then I'd drain it dry until every fabric of Adrian Hart was ripped apart at the seams, and all that was left was what I created from the ashes.

I'd make it mine.

And I'd make *Sage* mine.

Adrian Hart doesn't deserve it.

He doesn't deserve her.

He has the world in his palms, and he spits on it at every turn.

I could make it mine.

Whatever she required of me, I'd give it to her.

I could do it right.

Whatever it is.

And if I don't know how, then I'll learn it.

I'll mold myself into exactly what she needs.

Whatever amount of time it takes. Whatever amount of blood it takes.

"You have wasted every fucking opportunity your father has given you, Adrian! Why can't you just listen to me for once?"

Yes.

He *has* wasted every opportunity.

Finally, an intelligent, beautiful creature that sees what I see.

A waste.

It wouldn't be wasted if it were mine.

She wouldn't be wasted if she were mine.

"Why can't you just listen to me? I'm trying to help us."

I would listen to you.

I would listen to anything you have to say.

I would do whatever you asked of me.

I wouldn't waste what you give.

I wouldn't let you feel this anger.

I'd put you on a pedestal.

I'd worship the very ground you walk on.

You'd want for nothing.

You'd ask for nothing.

I would give it all to you without question. Without reason. Without restraint.

Whatever your heart desired, I'd give it to you, Sage.

I'd relinquish all control to please you.

"Adrian, I can't do this without you," Sage says in a defeated tremor.

No.

You won't do it alone, Sage.

I'll make sure of it.

8

— . —

SAGE

I had half a mind to burn Adrian's house to the ground.

But that would probably make me seem a little unhinged.

So instead, I chipped it all away one idea at a time.

First, I trashed every single shred of floral-scented shit from the house. Every single fucking thing that reminded me of that blonde adulterer, I torched it in a barrel in the backyard.

The matchbox seems to haunt me from the kitchen drawer, and my mind keeps flicking back to the handle like it's itching to burn this place to the ground, too.

Perhaps it was still a tad dramatic, but it felt cathartic enough that I didn't let the house get torched with it.

I ripped the guts out of Adrian's office.

Now it belongs to *me*.

The fancy tan polished wood has been replaced by black marble, glinting gold and cold like I feel on the inside. All of Adrian's off-white bookshelves have been painted black and stained to perfection. Those dreary books have been replaced with my own collection, and that white Office Depot cheap desk has been thrown out and replaced with expensive dark stained oak.

And the scent... ah, the scent. I can finally breathe again without feeling like there's pollen clogging my nose.

Now, it smells like vanilla.

My absolute favorite scent. Timeless. Classic. Sophisticated.

The frat house and cheerleader scents are finally expunged, and now it just smells like me.

Everything that man put in this office is gone, and now all that remains is me.

Then, it came time to do a clean sweep of the money exchange in this house.

The staff never stood a chance.

I call them in one at a time, and while I feel a tinge of guilt at cutting them loose, I know that our money, now *my* money, can be better allocated elsewhere.

I ask all of them the same questions.

The one that cuts the deepest doesn't seem to shock a single one of them.

Did you know my husband was having an affair?

They all knew. I can tell immediately that they had planned to take Adrian's secret to the grave.

They knew all along that he was hellbent on humiliating me, on betraying me at every turn even when he looked me in the eyes and told me he was trying.

These fucking vultures knew all along. I can tell by the way they lower their eyes as I stare them down. They shake in their boots like it was *them* that was betrayed and not me.

They were going to sit back and collect a paycheck from my dear husband with no regard for how I might feel at their expense.

Well, they can take my husband's secrets and their final paychecks straight to hell.

My planner is full by the time I've cut all interior staff.

No more maids gossiping in the halls and picking up Adrian's dirty laundry from the floors.

No more chefs handcrafting the menu every single week.

No more of any of it.

Now it's just me and my own fucking conscience living here.

I can't tell if that's better or worse, so I push the thoughts down altogether.

I met with the interior designer on Sunday, and she was beyond intrigued by my declaration to grind down every inch of Adrian's betrayal and cover it in my own style.

She'll start with my bedroom, and then move to the foyer, tackling room by room until it finally feels like home, and until then, I've got some work to do.

Adrian's bodyguards trail behind me with every step I take outside of this house, which isn't very often.

But I know I need them on my side to bring my plans to fruition.

I'm not naive enough to trust that their hands are clean.

Growing up under my father's devious instruction, I know that secrets make friends in this line of work.

I've no choice but to assess which men might still be salvageable.

And to do that, I'll have to somehow separate the good from the bad.

It starts with my two shadows.

With names like Dallas Ward and Aaron Johnson, I'm not expecting the pair to share many brain cells between the two of them.

But I know I'll have to put it to the test.

Only, I was hoping to have more time to figure out just how to do that.

Andrew Hart barrels into my home like he owns the place.

Which, he might, but that's not the fucking point.

The fucking point is that he barrels into my home, the *one* place I'm supposed to feel safe, and thinks he can dictate what I can and cannot do within the confines of my own home.

"You've been busy, dear," his voice is dripping with condescension. So fucking fake, just like his snake of a son. "I don't think my son would take too kindly to you playing house while he's away bettering himself for the sake of your future family, would you?"

"Is it playing house if this is our shared home?" I play it off as a joke, but Andrew's eyes tighten just a fraction, and I see his anger boiling just under the surface. He hates me. It's so glaringly obvious that I could laugh. But I know better than that. He would cut my tongue out of my mouth if I laughed in his face.

"Be that as it may, you are causing a bit of a stir, yes? Best leave the redecorating for when Adrian returns. Or are you turning over every stone in this place in search of something?"

Andrew smells like bitter castor oil and cigar smoke. A deadly combination that I can't help but think may provide the perfect accelerant for when I torch everything he's ever loved.

"What do you mean?" I feign stupidity, and Andrew's lips twitch slightly in amusement. He thinks I'm an idiot like his darling son. "I just didn't like how bright it is in here and it feels so cold and-"

"And where are the staff? Why are *you* cleaning this kitchen? Where are the maids?"

He doesn't know, my mind whispers, thrilled at gaining the upper hand. He doesn't know I got rid of the staff.

"It's Friday night, and Adrian and I agreed to let the staff have Friday nights off. I was just cleaning up my-"

"As I said, you will drop it and leave it for when Adrian returns. Whenever that may be," he sneers as he turns away from me and cuts his eyes across the kitchen. "You might have our last name, but do not think for a second that you are a Hart, Sage." He turns and gives me one more condescending once over before he turns on his heel and begins stomping back towards the front door. "Stay out of our family affairs, lest you wish to end up like some of your meddling relatives."

Some of my meddling relatives.

I know he means my mother, and it stings just the same, but I bite my tongue until I taste blood and watch Andrew Hart walk out of my home.

Perhaps that's where this rivalry originated.

My mother and her meddling.

I was only eleven when she met her swift death.

Old enough to understand my father was in a dangerous profession, but too young to grasp that it would ruin my life.

When people put hands on things that don't belong to them, the men they steal from tend to take something back.

It could have been me.

Sometimes I wonder if it *should* have been.

Andrew Hart's right-hand man came in the night. I woke to him standing at the end of my bed, bloody serrated knife still dripping.

The scream lodged in my throat went unheard when the pillow was placed over my head.

I still remember how the knife felt when it dug into my skin.

No matter how much I thrashed and fought, I couldn't stop it from happening.

A permanent reminder that I would forever be marked.

The X branded into my wrist is proof alone that Andrew Hart believes I'm nothing more than his family's property.

Now I'm stuck.

Fifteen years later, and here he is, haunting me all over again.

I might have lived that night, but my mother didn't.

All because my father's men couldn't keep their hands out of a candy jar that belonged to the Ledgers.

The poor attempt at a whisper draws me back to the present, and I freeze, straining my ears to pick up on every little word that might get shared.

He thinks I don't hear it, but I do.

His hushed order to both guards to watch and report on my every move.

I wonder which one of the guards I can get to crack first, if either of them.

If I had to place a bet, it would be Aaron.

And yet... right as the door begins to close, I meet eyes with Dallas Ward through the entryway.

He wears that carefully controlled mask of indifference, drilled into him during his service in the military.

But it slips.

As if suspended for a moment in time, I see it slip when we lock eyes.

I was *wrong*.

It won't be Aaron who cracks.

It will be Dallas.

Because none of his carefully crafted expressions can mask the hatred that I just saw in his eyes.

After all, I had the same look on my face when he met my gaze.

I go back to wiping down the counters when the door slams shut.

Andrew Hart thinks that I'm a pretty thing to be controlled.

But I've been waiting for this.

It's ten steps earlier than I thought it would arrive, but that just means I need to be more proactive.

If I'm going to dismantle this family, I've got to stay ahead of Adrian's father.

I have to understand how he operates, and then I have to learn to do it better.

Only then can I bring them all to their knees.

9

ELLISON

S leep in a place like this is fleeting.

It evades me even now, when I've exhausted myself with hours of reports and sparring sessions.

I've spent days trying to tire myself.

But nothing makes sense.

Nothing can calm me.

This restlessness isn't something that can be burned out.

It's wound tight within my blood cells, clinging like a plague with no vaccine.

I've known since early childhood that my compulsion to fixate on things might distract me from being a high-functioning adult, but it's never taken hold of me quite this bad.

Now it festers.

It infects.

Like something cancerous that's eating its way into my skull.

We all have our vices.

Most men drink. Some smoke. Some cheat.

But mine?

Oh, mine is Sage Ledger.

Only the sickness isn't something I'd like to rid myself of.

No, this exhaustion, I will gladly let it linger.

I want even more.

I want it to contaminate me in every way that it knows how.

I want to feel it burn me from the inside out. To feel it drain me dry until all that's left is the burning that I feel in my chest.

Nobody knows the lengths that I will go to welcome it in.

Nothing can calm this.

But I take another lap around the compound until the sweat is dripping down my spine and irritating every part of my soul.

Showering doesn't rid me of it either.

I'm restless.

Frustrated.

Miserable.

It's been days since I heard her voice.

Days since it imprinted itself into my mind and I haven't found a way to extract it yet.

But I don't want to.

Do I?

This can ruin your life, Ellison.

That's what I keep telling myself.

Even as I drill it into my thick fucking skull that this is a terrible, *terrible* idea, my heart fights with my head that I will gladly succumb as it consumes me.

Sage Ledger has sharp edges, and my fingers are ready to bleed for them.

I don't want to rid myself of her.

No, I don't.

I don't.

Not one fucking bit.

I tell myself over and over again that I don't want it to end.

It's just started.

I want to savor it.

I want to keep it.

To embed it into my bloodstream.

To flush it into my system.

It's too late to save me now.

It's too late to save *anyone.*

My sights have been pre-set against my will, and there's no way to extract the data and reset the target.

I still hear her voice dripping like honey and clogging every part of my skull.

It pulses behind my eyelids, that sickly sweet anger, rich like caramel as she repeats it back to me. "Why can't you just listen to me?"

I've no way to tell her that I am listening.

That I *did* listen.

I've no way to express to her my desire to hear every inflection of her voice and every breath that she takes.

And so, my longing manifests in ways to drive me slowly insane.

Even in my dreams, I can't seem to escape her.

She comes to me much softer than she did through that pixelated computer screen.

The image of her before me is both intoxicating and nauseating because I know that it cements my fate.

I know that there will be no return from this.

Our lives are now tangled, and I'm going to take what I want.

I'm going to take and take and drain her dry, just to taste this image in front of me.

Her eyes are half-lidded as she looks up at me like she feels the same desire that I do. It drips down my throat, how badly I want to taste, to touch, to bite.

But I pull it back as I gently brush my thumb over her parted full lips.

How incredibly soft. How supple.

Every part of her bends to my touch.

It's almost cruel, the way she tilts her head, resting her cheek in my palm like she knows I will protect her.

As if I'm not the very monster that wishes to sink my teeth into her flesh.

Even the way her throat moves when she swallows makes me burn with it.

I don't take her right away.

I want to.

I want to give in to every sick desire that runs through my head during the daylight hours, but I don't.

She doesn't deserve that.

No, she deserves only good things.

But I still circle her.

Like a predator testing the boundaries of its cage, I turn circles around my prized possession long enough to make her dizzy with it.

The air between us seems charged, or maybe I just want it to be.

There's no telling how deep my delusions have embedded their hooks.

Every time she meets my gaze, her breath seems to catch, and I want to touch.

So *badly* do I want to touch.

But I'm good.

I don't lunge for her. I don't nip at her skin. I don't bite.

I bare my teeth, and I breathe her in.

She smells like rich vanilla, and I have a sweet tooth that cannot be satiated by scent alone.

And still, I wait to touch.

My sweet Sage sits patiently on her knees, looking up at me with ice-blue eyes that still seem to warm me to my very core.

There is no amount of frigid indifference that can douse the heat in her gaze.

How delicate such a creature like this is.

How breathtaking.

She should have never been left alone.

Not someone like her.

She doesn't run from me even though my teeth are bared. She doesn't flinch as my boots scrape heavily across the floor.

She waits, like prey left unattended.

Someone left this beautiful, dangerous thing alone in the middle of nowhere, just waiting to be devoured by some monster like me.

I crouch down before her and still, she doesn't run from me.

Her lips part in fascination. Perhaps with anticipation.

Perhaps with fear, even though she conceals it.

I am still an animal, after all.

My hand brushes a strand of onyx silk back from her shoulder, and she shudders when my fingers graze the column of her neck.

"Do you even know what I could do to you?" I murmur. My mouth ghosts over the shell of her ear when I ask the question, and her breath catches. It's warm against me, something that makes my fingers itch to dig into the thickness of her thighs. My hands tremble with the need to caress her. Still, she tilts her head further to the side when my breath touches her skin.

She smells like something unholy disguised as sweetness, and I know that I will let her drag me to the pits of hell just to get a taste.

"You weren't meant to be saved, were you?" I whisper as I trail a finger down the slope of her neck, across her collarbone, until I can feel her pulse stuttering beneath my thumb. "No, not you. You *want* me to devour you."

She shivers at my words, and I strain to keep myself from giving into my own selfish desires to give her what she wants. For a second, I think she agrees with me.

"This whole thing was a trap, wasn't it, baby? Not for you, but for me."

When I press my lips against her throat, I feel the vibration of her sigh against my lips.

It's deafening, so hungry for more, and almost gentle.

Almost.

She tilts her chin up, silently offering what I long for so badly.

And I take.

She gasps when my hand curls around her nape and drags her in.

Her tongue against mine is the sweetest sin I've ever committed, and I want more.

I don't give her the decency of undressing her slowly, but she doesn't seem to care either. She makes a small noise in the back of her throat when I drop her onto my bedsheets.

The gasp she lets out when I sink into her is quiet, a soft sort of tremble that feels more like an earthquake to me.

It's enough to pull a groan from my own chest, and I know that I'm forever tainted by this woman.

I've been starving my whole life and finally found something worth tasting, and I'll starve again if it means she'll feed me once more in the future.

Her nails dig into my back, leaving trails of fire in their wake, and I don't know how I ever thought I could resist her.

She stares up at me, pupils blown wide, and I can't tell if she's terrified or entranced by the way that I take her apart.

Her lips part around another gasp, breath shaking as she tries to speak, and I want more.

I *need* more.

The look in her eyes mirrors the same one in mine, and I know that she's right there with me.

The weight of my cock dragging against her. The way she squeezes me tight. The sounds she makes.

It's all beyond dangerous.

"Give me more," I rasp against her throat, and she tugs painfully at the hair against my nape, exhales coming quicker against my skin.

There's no greater ecstasy than how it feels when she moves her hips in time with mine, and I'd kill for it. I'd ravage for it.

I feel her lips part against my throat, the hitch of her breath as she tries to make out words.

And then...

"Adrian," she whispers around a sharp breath.

My world shudders to a stop.

My entire body freezes.

That name...

His name...

It crawls up my spine like ice water.

Her hands are covered in blood from the wound she just inflicted upon me by saying his name.

She's still so beautiful, even covered in my blood.

And it stings.

So fucking badly does it sting.

My pulse slips into a state of emergency, and I feel my throat clogging up from the pain.

Why would you call me that, Sage?

Why would you say his name when you hate him? When we *both* hate him?

My thoughts scatter along the floor of my brain, but the damage is already done.

I can't even breathe with how fiercely my heart is pounding against my ribcage.

I jerk away from her touch, hands fisting in the sheets, but she's already fading away from me.

Her warmth dissolves, her breath evaporating like mist against my skin. The room fades around me, and I'm left with nothing but the echo of that fucking name.

Adrian.

I wake with my hands shaking, my body slick with sweat, my pulse screaming in my ears.

The word still burns on my tongue, poisonous and full of bitter fury.

I taste blood from where I bit the inside of my cheek.

And I realize, somewhere in the haze of my hatred and my desire, that it isn't enough just to hate him.

In order to take what belongs to me, I need to be him.

I'll forgive my sweet girl, knowing she never meant to bring me any harm.

But I cannot say the same for her husband.

Adrian Hart and I are going to know each other intimately by the end of this.

And it won't be my fucking blood that's spilled this time.

10

SAGE

The house doesn't echo anymore.

It seems to bend to my will, locking down my every command as if it's never heard another voice.

When I speak, the sound doesn't ricochet off of the sterile walls and instead it settles easily.

That's because it knows who it belongs to now.

The clock ticks like a lullaby in my new office, the black marble and dark oak desk are exactly what I wanted them to be.

Adrian's pale-colored wishes are long gone, and I'm all that's left of him.

Now it screams that it has power.

My pen drags straight, sterile lines through columns of numbers.

All of Adrian's allowances, stipends, hush-money... all of it, he's tried and failed *miserably* to hide it.

The paper trail is so comically clear that I can't help but chuckle as I look through it.

Every single thing he's ever touched leads a neon blinking light saying, "HEY!!!! THIS IS MY FUCK UP!!!!"

It's like he couldn't help but get himself into trouble.

But that's okay. I plan to steamroll it, erasing every trace of his failures as I go.

I'll admit, Andrew's visit threw me off a little.

I hadn't expected him to come barging in like he had.

But it added all the more fuel to my fire.

He's playing checkers, thinking a naïve little girl like me is too fragile and scared to keep up.

All the while I'm playing chess.

I tap my fancy new intercom and call for Aaron to pay my new office a visit.

He shuffles in two minutes late and four foot taps too nervous.

I never really cared for Aaron.

Maybe it's because he looks like a fucking pug and doesn't understand proper personal hygiene.

He's tall and lanky in a way that lacks both finesse and muscle.

And he always, *always* smells like stale coffee and body odor. Not to mention he looks like he's spent too much time sitting at a desk playing detective rather than actually learning how to survive in a place like this.

"Close the door," I order, and he does.

If he knows what's good for him, he'll do every single thing I say.

If he does, then the urge to stab him to death when he's least expecting it might lessen.

Of course, he immediately makes me discredit that notion.

He doesn't sit when I gesture to the chair.

So he's teachable, but only when he wants to be. How fitting.

"How long have you worked for my husband, Aaron?" I lean my head into my fist like I'm bored and stare at the dull man sitting across from me.

"Uh, three years, ma'am."

"Ma'am makes me sound so old," I sigh, and his discomfort doesn't seem to ease any. I lean back and cross one leg over the other. My heel taps once against the oak desk, and Aaron seems to reposition anxiously. "Three years," I hum in contemplation. "Long enough to know a lot of secrets. Long enough to call in a lot of favors. Hmm," I tap my pen on the edge of my desk and stare at him.

After a moment, he swallows.

It seems to strain his throat when he does.

There it is.

The tell.

"Andrew told you to watch me." I don't ask it like a question. I heard it with my own ears. Now I just need a confirmation.

His eyes shift to the camera in the corner of my office, newly installed by my own hand and guaranteed to catch every little thing happening in these four walls.

"No, ma'am, that's not-"

"If you want to keep your tongue in your mouth, then don't fucking lie to my face right now," I don't let my mask of boredom drop when I say it, and I can tell he's scared of me.

Perfect. That's right where I want him.

"He... wanted updates," his eyes move again to the camera in the corner and then back to me.

"Updates on what?" I ask again, holding his gaze despite all of his fidgeting.

"Your movements. Spending. Visitors." Each word seems like it's peeling his throat raw with how much it pains him to say them.

"And what did you tell him?"

The silence goes on for far too long. "Nothing," he lies again.

I tighten my hand on the edge of my desk until it whines under the pressure.

His pulse hammering in his throat betrays what his tongue attempts to hide from me.

I let the silence continue until he swallows again and shifts his posture uneasily from one foot to the other. Then I nod, slowly, controlled, so much so that it makes him shift again, back to the other foot.

"Thank you, Aaron. Keep sending your reports."

"You want me to... to keep sending my reports? To Mr. Hart?"

"Precisely," I give him a practiced smile as I tap my pen against the desk again, and he flinches at the sound. I slide a manila envelope across the desk and tap it with my fingertips. "With these edits."

He hesitates to reach for it, inching closer as if it might bite him before he takes it back.

For now, I let him leave with his heart still safe behind his rib cage.

Fear is his leash, and I know he'll run straight back to Andrew with the lies clenched between his teeth. That's exactly what I want him to do.

"Dallas," I tap the intercom again. "Come in, please."

Dallas doesn't waste time like Aaron does.

He's prompt. Punctual. Always dressed professionally.

He fills my office doorway like he's eclipsing the sun. His posture stays straight, hands behind his back.

Military written all over his form.

"Shut the door," I order, and he does.

He doesn't look at the camera.

No, he only looks at me.

"Sit," I offer, gesturing to my fancy new desk chair.

"I'll stand," the response that comes back is curt but not disrespect-ful.

"Suit yourself," I give him my practiced smile all over again.

We stare at each other like two blades aiming for the same target.

"How long have you worked for my husband, Dallas?" I ask the same question that I asked Aaron, but this time, the answer doesn't hesitate to come.

"Six years."

"Why so long?" I question.

"Because I'm good at doing my job," he responds shortly, like it's self-explanatory.

"And your job is... what exactly?"

"Protection."

"Of whom? My husband?"

"Of whoever hires me," he doesn't even hesitate as he answers.

"And who hired you to protect Adrian? My husband? Or Andrew Hart?"

"Your husband," he simply says.

"My husband is away, Dallas. He doesn't seem like he needs much protection at this current moment. So tell me again," I lean forward and cross my hands over my arms. "Who exactly are you protecting?"

"Protection would extend to the spouse of my protected," he says in a no-nonsense tone.

"Andrew Hart told you to keep tabs on me," I point out, and he doesn't bother denying it.

"Yes."

"And how often are you reporting to Mr. Hart?"

"Whenever necessary."

"And what constitutes necessary?" I challenge, and he doesn't even wait a breath.

"When you become a problem."

That almost brings a smile to my lips.

"Hm," I hum and tilt my head in contemplation. "And am I a problem?"

"Not yet," Dallas answers rashly.

I lean forward on my desk and place my elbow on the dark oak, assessing him from head to toe.

"Tell me, Dallas," I stare at him for a moment and he holds my gaze unlike that spineless leech Aaron. "If you had to choose, where do your loyalties lie? With the man who signs your checks? Or the one who's trying to rewrite them?"

"Loyalty is earned, Mrs. Hart," he doesn't hesitate to answer.

The name stings, but it tells me everything I need to know.

I wasn't the only one listening in the day that Andrew came by unannounced. Dallas heard every word Andrew said to me too.

Andrew said I wasn't a Hart, but Dallas addresses me by my title.

That's the slip-up I saw at the door that night. That drop in the mask of certainty.

It's not obedience. Nor is it defiance.

It's a preference.

"Good. Because I don't play well with people who try to sway those that are loyal to me," I casually say as I lean back.

Dallas' brow furrows just a fraction.

He's interested in the bait.

I turn my desktop towards him, and he glances at it and then back to me before he takes a hesitant step forward.

"The Harts deal in drugs. The Ledgers deal in guns." I tap the next page and a spreadsheet pulls up with glaring red marks all over it. "And what do we deal in, Mr. Ward?" Dallas glances at me for a moment before looking back down at the spreadsheet. "Both families rot the very hands that keep them fed."

"I'm aware," Dallas deadpans. Everyone in this city knows how our families poison everything they touch.

"I'm not here to play with powder, whether it be guns or drugs." I stand slowly and circle the desk, and my heels clack against the new marble flooring. "I'm going to invest our money elsewhere. Something quiet, and something clean on paper, but dirty where it counts."

Dallas tracks me without turning his head.

Professional.

Predatory.

I like that.

"Intelligence... Protection... A firm with a name that looks good on a business card but knows the ins and outs of both families and the business. You get it?"

"You want to... hire men that have worked for both families?"

"Ah, an intelligent man, you are," I quip, and his brow furrows further. "I need a backbone made of men both families were too afraid to keep. Men that aren't afraid to get their hands dirty when it counts. Not the loudmouth ones that want more than they know how to handle. I want the ones who know when to question things and when to shut the fuck up."

His jaw ticks, and it's almost subtle enough that I miss it. It's the look of a hunter scenting prey.

"You know men like that?" It's not a question.

"I might."

"You know them," I respond, because I'm not guessing. I know he knows them. He probably even *is* one of them.

"I know a few."

"Discarded by the Harts for having more than one brain cell. Discarded by the Ledgers for having a conscience." I let the words linger for a moment. "I want them to work for Adrian and I."

"To do what?" He looks me over and my smile is slow to build.

"To see what no one else can see. To hear what no one else seems to hear. To build me a path to the top." I stop just shy of where he stands and tilt my head back to look at him. "And to keep me alive while I do it."

"And what happens... when Andrew Hart asks where this money is going?" He asks, and I smile even bigger.

"Then we'll show him the books that won't lie."

"And what happens when he asks where all of his control is going?"

"Then you can tell him to check the barrel in the backyard," I deadpan, letting my smile drop. "It's either that barrel or a different one, and out of the two options, I'm certain which one he'll pick."

There's a certain recognition there when Dallas registers what I'm referring to.

The cold calculation I'm letting linger between us. A secret I'm letting him in on.

I don't just want the money or the power or the control.

I'm willing to kill for it.

Even if it means I have to kill Andrew Hart.

"I want names," I level him with a no-bullshit stare. "Skills. Locations. I don't care who they hate. I care if they have a brain and know how to use it."

"And if they refuse?"

"They won't."

"And if they do?" He asks, and I tilt my head again.

"Well, then, they might find themselves taking a very long, far away trip from the empire I'm building."

The silence stretches until finally, Dallas nods. "I'll see who I can locate."

"I want discretion, Dallas," I warn him, moving to sit back at my desk. "No tails. No calls that can be traced. No strings leading back to me or Adrian. Discretion. If anyone finds a trail, I want it stitched up so tight that whoever is hunting it thinks they reached out to me first and I put a bullet in their skull for their treasonous ways. Understood?"

Dallas dips his head in agreement.

Like a good boy.

"Anything else?" He asks.

"Yes," I lean back in my chair and make sure my eyes show how serious I am. "From now on, you report to me. Not Andrew. If he asks you for an update, you give him a version of the truth. I don't want you to lie. I want you to edit the truth."

"Understood."

"And Dallas?" He pauses at the doorway and turns back to look at me.

"If I find out you've betrayed me, you'll end up in that barrel in the backyard as well. Are we clear?" I ask, and there's a ghost of a smile on his face.

"Crystal."

Dallas leaves without much fanfare, and I watch him on my laptop as he goes. My new security system is freshly installed, all locks in place, all cameras rolling to watch how my future will play out.

The house is quiet when I dim all the lights.

Quiet, but not so dead and hollow like before.

I'm not just going to burn this empire to the ground.

I will.

But first, I'm going to build something that's worth watching crumble.

And with it, everything that Andrew Hart and Ian Ledger worked so hard for.

What they killed for.

What they'll die for.

It doesn't start with a match or a lighter.

It starts with me.

11

ELLISON

I t's hard to explain just how infuriating it is hearing Adrian's voice even during my sleep.

I already have to babysit him from sun-up to sun-down, and it seems even at night, there's no reprieve from his grating, childish antics.

When his voice drags me out of my sleep, I nearly throw back the blankets and storm into the hallway to put him out of his misery.

I've been seriously contemplating if I could cover up his murder in some way.

I even thought about rolling one of our Humvees over, but that fucking prick wears his seatbelt 24/7 and I knew it'd be a lost cause.

But now that he's woken me up, I might just fucking shoot him and take the jail sentence. I'd probably get better food if I did it that way.

Then I remember I'm not Adrian, so I can actually *use* critical thinking skills.

Why would Adrian Hart be sneaking around in the midnight hours when no one else is around to hear it?

You can learn a lot when you just keep your fucking mouth shut.

It's near silent as I cross the room to listen through the door, and of course, it's Daddy dearest on the other line, not my darling Sage.

Eavesdropping isn't very nice, nor is it decent.

But decency isn't common in this line of work.

It's why I find myself leaning against the cold metal, inhaling the rancid cigarette smoke bleeding from Adrian's lips with every exhale.

It's also why I clench my fist as Adrian's father rips his wife apart like she's the only goddamn problem in existence.

"She's reckless and defiant, Adrian-"

"You knew this going in, Daddy, we both did!" Adrian practically whines. Fucking pathetic prick. They knew what Sage was all along, and now they wish to change her because she won't lie down and take it.

"She's doing things behind your back, son. Behind *our* back," Andrew snaps back, venomous and full of disgust. He hates Sage. It's so clear in his tone, no one could doubt it.

Adrian doesn't defend her. Of course he doesn't. He just sighs, like the very thought of having to entertain anything but alcohol, drugs, or pussy is exhausting to his core. "She can act like she's ambitious all she wants, but these renovations and mysterious errands are nothing but a front, son."

"Maybe she's just trying to prove herself," Adrian sighs. "You know it's-"

"Prove herself?" Andrew barks out a bitter laugh. "She's staging a fucking coup right under your nose and you're either too fucking stupid or too fucking blind to see it! You need to cut her off, Adrian! No more entertaining this nonsense. Take away her funding. I don't give you an allowance so she can use it to pull the rug from under us. Let her run wild long enough to hang herself and I'll take care of the rest."

My head lolls to the side, thudding against the door softly as I take in his words.

They sting as I digest them.

He'll take care of the rest?

No. I don't think so.

Andrew Hart is just as delusional as his bastard son.

I won't let either of them lay a finger on her fucking head.

There's the faintest hum of hesitation from Adrian on the other side, and I hold out the tiniest shred of hope that he'll defend her this time.

He doesn't.

Instead, he maintains that blatant disappointment that he's had since the moment we met.

"I'll handle it, Daddy," he finally mutters.

"You better," his father warns, and the line goes dead with a deafening click.

I stand there for a long while after that, staring at a crack in the flooring, wondering how Sage managed to be born into a family that would allow her to be tethered to a bloodline so wretched and deceitful. The silence on the other side is heavy, and I wonder if Adrian is staring at the same thick crack under his feet, wondering if it's widening or if it's just the floor beneath him caving in under the weight of his father's heavy burdens.

And I realize, I'm not the only one carrying the burden of trying to navigate Sage's future.

But unlike Andrew Hart, I've no desire to watch her crumble.

And unlike Adrian, I have the spine to make sure it doesn't happen.

I promise myself, no matter what it takes to see it through, I'll peel the flesh from my own bones before I allow either one of them to steal the breath from Sage's body.

Even if it means I have to clip Adrian's wings and watch him plummet, it'll be his own unraveling conscience that caused this. His own spineless limitations that will bring him to his knees. I'll set him up to make sure he falls from the highest point imaginable, and when he does, I'll be there to catch the remains of what's left over.

Not only will I catch it, but I plan to latch on and swallow it whole.

There will be nothing else but acceptance left by the time I'm done devouring Sage Ledger.

The next morning comes as slow as dripping honey.

I spend the majority of the night facing Adrian Hart's sleeping back, wishing I could rip his spinal column out while he slept.

By the time we're in the training room, I've already concocted a perfect plan to bring down the entire Hart family, pulling one string at a time.

It starts with Adrian.

He's the weak link, already separated from Sage with a wedge shoved between them. He's out of his father's grasp too, perfectly placed in front of me so I can ruin him.

We have nearly identically set eyes. Nearly the same nose. Nearly the same lips. Only when Adrian smiles, it feels syrupy sweet, like a child that's never known malice. His teeth are perfect pearl white and carved with composite bonding that must have taken hours to perfect.

My teeth are much different.

Mine are set to match my claws, perfect little points that crave to dig into flesh.

While we may have the same soft eyes, I have the teeth to rip into those that I despise.

Adrian Hart will be no different.

––––––––––––––

The training room harbors a certain stench that clings to you.

It smells like sweat and blood and rubber mats that burn when you slam too hard into the flooring.

Aiden, John, and Kent throw punches and banter like raging idiots, and I let myself blend into the mess of it all.

I've always been the quiet one of the group, perhaps also the most deadly. While I do like the guys and find them all palatable, it's never been easy for me to bond like they have with each other. Perhaps it was being an only child. Or perhaps it was growing up in an orphanage. Regardless of what the tragic reasoning may be, I feign my interest in their lives and play the role of their quiet brother in arms who doesn't talk much but always listens.

"Jesus, E," John laughs as he wipes the dripping sweat from his hair line. "You and the kid really could be twins. Look at you," he huffs and leans to sit his water bottle onto the bench beside us.

I look at Adrian just like he said. We are similar. I can see it. The dark hair, the dark eyes, same set facial features. Today, we're even practically wearing the same clothes. "Same build, same haircut, same resting bitch face," John snickers and I push him away with a playful shove to his shoulder.

"Yeah," Aiden snorts. "Except Ellison actually wins his fights."

Adrian flips him off in good-nature, and the guys all laugh, but it's enough to make my jaw tighten with unease.

Twins...

Yes, we could be twins. Bound by blood and of the same flesh.

I've no intention of being tethered in such a way to Adrian.

But I do have intentions of being a Hart.

By the end of this, only one Adrian Hart will remain.

When the others finally head out, I stay behind to train the kid, trading a few lazy hits with Adrian, pointing out weak spots and instructing him to guard his face and stomach better. The space slowly empties, but I notice Adrian's distraction now that it's quieting down. His form is worse than usual, his learned rhythm all gone.

"You good?" I ask, feigning concern for our newest little brother. I wipe the sweat from my jaw and take a step back, and Adrian finally drops his gloves and reaches for his water bottle on the bench.

"Just tired, man," he shrugs and takes a long swig of it. There's tension in his shoulders, a strain in the column of his neck. He's stressed.

"Yeah," I pretend to hesitate until he looks at me. "Hope you aren't too pissed, but I kinda heard your conversation last night," I unstrap my own gloves and Adrian's eyes snap up to meet mine.

"You were listening to my private conversation?"

"I wasn't intentionally listening," I scoff and fold my arms. "You woke me up in the dead of night when you opened that heavy ass door," I roll my eyes.

"It's nothing," he averts his gaze and I snort again.

"Come on, man," I push again, keeping my tone casual. "Out here, we're brothers. Might as well talk to one of us. We're twins after all," I chuckle, and Adrian seems to hesitate, but I see the very moment he drops his guard, like he can't stand not to. I've got him right where I want him.

"It's my fucking wife," he admits. "It's always my wife."

"Sage, right?" I smirk at him, and he narrows his eyes as he looks me over.

"How'd you-" he frowns, and my smile only builds.

"We share a room, dude. You fucking talk in your sleep," I lie easily, and he buys it.

"Figures," he huffs out a bitter laugh. He slowly gets to his feet and we trade off a few more soft punches, circling each other but not really committing to training anymore.

"She's just so fucking cold, dude," he continues feeding me bullshit, and I catalog every single sentence while he talks. "She wants to control every aspect of my life, and my father does, too. They both think they run this shit when it's my life."

"So tell them both to fuck off," I lightheartedly tell him, and he shakes his head.

"You just don't get it, man," he sighs. "Neither one of them are the type of person that will just fuck off because I tell them to. My father runs a fucking business dealing coke."

"Tough break, that," I whistle like I'm impressed, and Adrian smirks at that, like he had any hand in running his father's business affairs. I wouldn't be surprised if he's been snorting his Daddy's coke. Fucking prick.

"Tell me about it," Adrian laughs. "Sage is just.. I don't know, man. She's literally the last fucking person I would have wanted as a wife, and she thinks she's so much smarter than me."

I know she is. I could have told him that the first second I ever heard him speak.

Any woman is smarter than this leech.

"My father fucking hates her. Like, actually hates her. Like, wants her dead hates her, and I'm stuck in the middle trying to get them both to chill out so I can breathe."

"So this is like a vacation for you, huh?" I chuckle, and he's quick to agree. He thinks he's venting but he's feeding me all of the ammunition I need.

"I mean, she doesn't sound terrible," I offer, "but yeah, I get the frustration."

"That's because you don't live with her," he laughs dryly.

Won't be long now.

"Maybe she's just never been put in her place, man," I shrug. "You know how women are. They think they run everything when they don't. You know, if it were me, I'd just cut her off."

"It's not that easy, dude," Adrian's brows knit together.

"Why not? Didn't you say you have cameras in your house?" I nudge the conversation where I want it.

He looks wary at the mention of them, but still, he keeps running his mouth.

"I mean, I don't. Sage put those cameras up, and it took all of two fucking seconds for my Daddy to have access to them. He's so paranoid. Has the whole house wired just to keep an eye on Sage. Says it's about keeping shit secure and making sure she isn't leaking any information out."

"Can you actually see her on the cameras?" I ask in a conversational tone, and he shrugs.

"I mean, I check sometimes. Not very often, though. She's fucking boring honestly. Can't figure out half the shit she's doing, though."

Bingo.

I let out a sympathetic chuckle and sit down on the bench. "If it were me, I'd cut that woman off, for sure. Let your old man deal with it. Sounds like she's just waiting to burn out."

Adrian looks uncertain, so I pat his shoulder and encourage him towards the door. "Come on, man. You're out here serving your country. Chicks dig that kind of thing. You deserve a little freedom. Have some fun. I saw you have a thing for blondes and there's plenty of them in this hellhole. Get a little pussy and just chill out. By the time you're home, your father will have her handles, and you'll have your life back."

Adrian thinks about it for a long time before he's slowly nodding.

"Yeah," he murmurs. "Maybe you're right. Keep the conversations limited to text so she can't get on my ass. Maybe that'll keep her off my back."

"Exactly, dude. Now come on," I grin at him and he narrows his eyes at me. "We're getting wasted tonight."

Later that night, after the whole team has dragged the kid out to the bar, the hours blur until they're loud and hazy, reeking of whiskey and sweat in the building.

Music pounds through the walls, laughter muddles down all of the tension, and I play my part perfectly.

Old brother wanting to have some harmless fun.

"To freedom, boys!" I raise my glass, and the others let out various calls and whistles in agreement. "And to the kid letting loose like a man!" I yell, and the guys all slap Adrian on the back and cheer, all of them drunk on liquor and arrogance.

Adrian's been half gone since he walked in the bar, grinning stupidly as we shove woman after woman into his waiting hands. He acts like he's never been inside of one before, like a child learning warmth for the first time in his life.

But I see exactly what kind of man Adrian is.

He has no regard or thought of his wife waiting at home for his safe return.

The second the blonde bombshell waitress leans too close when she drops off another round of shots, the guys chant his name, and Adrian's smirking, his hand splaying wide on her lower back while I sit back watching.

It's the perfect distraction he needs.

While Adrian's drowning in her arms and whispering sweet nothings in her ear, my hand slips under the table until I find his phone.

He won't notice, of course. The fucking drunk.

I pocket it easily and lean back in my chair to take another sip of my drink.

The taste of whiskey burns my throat, sharp and heady, but it's never tasted so sweet.

Freedom, we toasted.

For me, it's not my freedom that I'm searching for.

I'm doing this for Sage.

To unburden her with this life she's been dealt. To ease the things she's been having to carry all alone.

I'll help her free herself from the Hart family, both father and son alike.

And once she's mine, she'll never sit up wondering where her husband is and if he's keeping his hands to himself.

I'll show her every second of the day that she is the only object of my desire.

The only woman worth my attention and affection.

The one who controls me.

I'll show Sage that I can be trusted.

The barracks are quiet when I return back early, slipping out before any of them can even notice that I'm gone.

The only light comes from the screen in my hand. The glow of Adrian's phone is almost offensive.

There's not an original bone in his body. The passcode's 1234. Of course it is.

I scroll through his contacts until I find it.

Sage Hart.

I grit my teeth at his last name tainting hers.

But her picture glows faintly in the dark, and with it, my heart does, too.

I stare at her for a long time, my thumb hovering over the screen, wishing I could truly touch.

But then I connect his phone to mine, siphoning the feed. Messages, photos, every camera in the house, I catalog it all, tangling our lives even further together.

Every message.

Every photo.

Every camera image throughout their house.

My house.

Her voice.

Her world.

Her entire fucking life.

All of it presses against my fingertips.

I shove Adrian's phone under his pillow. He isn't back yet, but he'll stagger back in some time late in the night and find it, too drunk to put together how it got there.

The next morning bleeds in like a bad hangover. My head throbs, echoing inside of my skull, doing nothing but pissing me off further.

The barracks are quiet, most of the guys sleeping off the excitement from the night.

Adrian's phone sits on the nightstand right where I left it after last night's little field trip.

He had slipped back in some time in the night, stumbling drunkenly into bed. I had watched him check the time on the screen, unknowing that it had been touched by my hands, rewired by my curiosity.

When I force myself to get out of bed, I stare down at him for a moment, taking in the stench of alcohol and the sweaty sheets.

The way his mouth hangs open, the drool on his pillow.

We may look similar, but we are not the same.

Adrian is vermin.

Swine.

A pathetic waste of space.

Space that I'll soon fill.

I drag my feet into the bathroom, knowing I need to get there first before Kent uses up all of the hot water.

The water is scalding once I twist the knob, and the steam glides up the walls, dripping wet and glistening against my skin.

The shower is the only place I can think without someone breathing down my neck.

No eyes. No Adrian. No fucking rules.

My phone practically hums in my hand, like it knows what I'm about to do.

I probably shouldn't look just yet.

But the payoff is right here in my palm, digging into my skin like a solid temptation.

I tap the screen until it lights up, and then I start digging.

The house is massive. Poor Adrian's father must have paid a pretty penny for it. It's all marble and glass, every surface screaming money, like his paranoia is polished into every corner of it. But she's there, somewhere. I know she is.

I navigate from camera to camera, checking the space, cataloging, memorizing, seeing which rooms that she seems to be re-modeling in Adrian's absence.

Click, click, click, click, and I pause.

My finger hovers over the button, eyes laser focused in an instant.

The very moment that my blood cells alter themselves to attune to one need.

Clear as daylight, like the gods themselves decided to hand deliver me to Heaven, Sage appears on my screen.

She's beautiful. Absolutely otherworldly and haunting.

She's delicate in the soft light of the morning as she moves through her bedroom.

Before, when I saw the way she looked at Adrian, her face was tense, the bitterness pressed tight into her brows. Her lips were set in frustration then.

But not anymore.

Now she seems relaxed... so gorgeous in an effortless way.

She moves through the room with an air of elegance, fingers trailing along the bed as she pulls the comforter up to make the bed.

The sight of her in the own home, in a room she has redesigned, makes my stomach twist with pride.

Here, she seems to call to me like a siren.

Even without hearing her voice, I would drown in the depths for her.

The soft cotton nightgown barely brushes the midpoint of her thighs. Dark nail polish brushes her fingernails in a way that's entrancing as they skim her sheets.

She looks like my every wish wrapped up to bring me to my demise.

She looks like everything Adrian will never deserve.

And everything I'll destroy myself to have.

I know this is wrong.

I know I shouldn't be seeing her like this, but it's dizzying.

She's so close and yet so far away.

I freeze as she pauses in front of the bathroom. She glances around and purses her lips, but then I see her reach for a hair tie on the bedside table.

She pads into the bathroom, and I sit, drenched in my own running water as the camera feed follows her every movement.

There.

This is the moment I should cut the phone off.

This is the moment I should leave her be.

But I can't.

She's mine to see.

Mine to long for.

Mine to need.

My thumb traces her outline as she ties her hair up. It still cascades over her back, inky black strands softly wavy and enticing as it skims the column of her neck.

It feels like the glass between us might melt from the heat in my skin as I watch her. My pulse hammers in my chest when she exhales and stretches, the nightgown sliding higher up her thighs.

And then she does something not even I should be privileged enough to see yet.

I know that I haven't earned it, and yet I cannot force myself to look away.

Her fingers skim her thighs until they curl around the fabric resting there, and my breath catches as she pulls the nightgown upwards and over her shoulders.

It hits the ground just like my heart does, and I bring the phone to my face like that will get me closer.

Sage is the most ethereal creature I have ever laid eyes on.

The light in the bathroom bleeds from the opaque windowsill behind a large oval bathtub.

It highlights every curve of her body.

I know I shouldn't look.

I know I shouldn't.

My eyes trace the curve of her hips as she turns away from the camera and saunters over to the shower to turn it on.

I hear it echo all around the room and the heat quickly begins steaming up the room, but I still see her in crystal clarity.

There's delicate black ink tattooed from her nape to her spine, and I strain to make out what it says.

Time will realign.

Beautiful.

Everything about her is beautiful, even the words on her skin.

Yes, time *will* realign. Time will realign everything. I will make sure of it.

When she turns to look at herself in the mirror, I feel my heart stop altogether.

Her breasts are full and perfect, soft and supple enough to make my mouth water with anticipation to taste. There's a little weight on her bones that makes me want to dig my fingers in to leave the imprint of them. I've seen the women Adrian lusts after, young, thin, and lacking anything to grip. That's not Sage. Sage is a woman, the kind of body you ache to hold. A woman made of nothing but heat and temptation. I crave to worship every inch of her. I will, once she lets me in.

For now, I hold my breath as she skims her hands over her lower stomach.

No, my mind screeches to a halt.

No.

I shouldn't see this.

I shouldn't look.

I know I shouldn't.

I drag a wet hand down my face, forcing myself to breathe through the rush of heat clawing up my throat. The tiles around me feel too cold, but the air feels too hot.

I can't tell where one ends and the other begins.

Her fingers skim lower and lower, and somehow, mine mirror the action.

I can feel the warmth of the hot water as my hand follows that path lower and lower.

Sage braces a hand on the counter and leans forward, almost like she can't help it. Her eyes flutter shut, breath stuttering and my chest tightens.

I could help.

I could do this for her.

I could touch her just like this, draw sounds from her lips that could bring men to their knees.

I could pleasure her so she wouldn't have to.

My hand wraps tight around my cock when I hear a strangled little whimper fall from her lips.

My sweet Sage squeezes her thighs together as her perfectly polished fingers move between her legs.

I have to bite back a god damn groan like a teenager when I see it. She clenches her eyes tightly shut and her head falls forward, long black hair skimming her breasts as she works herself up into a frenzy.

"I could do this for you, Sage." I whisper as my hand works faster, too. Sage's breathy little whimpers drive me mad, and I thrust my hips forward, fucking into my fist with enough force to make my bite my tongue.

"I could do this for you. I could fucking-oh, fuck," I shudder when Sage begs *please* into the empty bathroom, like she says it just for me to hear. Her breathing speeds up, her chest rising and falling rapidly as she tenses up and holds pressure in that spot that seems to bring her the most pleasure.

My mind starts getting hazy when I watch her bite her bottom lip to keep quiet, mind spinning with all of the possibilities we could have.

All of the pleasure I could bring her.

I didn't even know I could want someone so much, but I ache with it.

So badly.

So badly, I want to taste her.

I want to touch her.

I want to have her dripping from my lips. I want her hands pulling at my hair. I want her dragging my tongue closer, thighs choking me as they squeeze around my head.

If I were there, I would plant her on that pretty marbled countertop.

I would drag her to the edge and bury my lips between her legs. I'd lap and suck and take as much as she's willing to give me. So willingly, I'd drown in how wet I could make her. I'd leave bruises with my lips, dragging them up her thighs and over her hip bones.

Her pretty pussy could sit right on my face, and I'd choke on it.

I have no choice but to squeeze my cock tighter at the influx of images running through my fucked-up head.

But I know I could give it to her just how she wants.

I know I could.

Whatever her husband has been doing, I know it's not enough. I know it could never please her.

I would bury my fingers inside of her until her hair was slick with damp sweat and sticking to her nape. I'd work her hips against my hand and watch her fuck herself senseless just so I could learn just how she likes it.

My fucking gorgeous, dripping wet, needy Sage.

My sweet creature.

My future wife.

I know that if I sunk into her, she'd wrap me tight in warmth, dripping like sweet honey around my cock, and I'd beg for her to cum. I'd beg for her to let me have it. To let me have everything. To give in to me so wholly. I would give her anything, *be* anything, to please her.

I would.

I will.

My vision blurs as I release onto the tiles, hearing Sage whimper and shudder as her hand slows. She leans over to rest her head on her arm that's supported by the countertop, and I work to match my breathing to the way her chest moves.

Her hands are shaking as she slowly drags herself to stand back up, and I can barely see how they glisten through the small screen of my phone.

Still, the instinct to suck those slender fingers clean makes my heart continue to race.

Just a little longer.

Just a little longer, Sage.

I'll give you everything you want.

I will.

I promise.

12

SAGE

The distance was slow to creep in.

At first, I didn't even realize it was there.

It seeped in like mist rolling through a graveyard in the early morning air, quiet as all the thoughts I wish I didn't have.

Adrian stops answering the video chats first. Then he starts declining all of my calls. Then I get those ominous text messages informing me he's supposedly so busy he can only communicate through messages for a while.

There's no explanation. No expectations for how long that might last. Just a swift wall shut between us that I can't seem to knock down.

We weren't close before. Not even remotely, and still, the anger bleeds into my every thought.

He has got to be kidding me.

Seriously.

No one else in the world could be this audacious.

The fact that Adrian is the one freezing *me* out, like he has any right to, is infuriating.

He's the one who cheated on me.

He's the one who betrayed my trust, and yet it's my phone screen that seems like it has grown a thick layer of ice.

I can't even say why it bothers me so much. It's not like we're close. It's not like I want him to act like my husband. But he *is* my husband.

He's the one I'm supposed to be stuck with for the rest of my life, side by side, for better or worse, until death do us part.

Or, well, okay, not for the rest of my life, because death was scheduled to part us sooner rather than later, but still, the audacity of this man to ice me out when I was the one keeping him afloat in the first place.

I give him a few more chances. I call. I text. I ask how things are doing and if he knows when he's coming home.

Home.

It seems like such a trivial word.

And yet, this isn't his home.

This is a shell that his father bought him, and I'm the one making it into something. I'm the one giving it life and crafting it into my dream.

Adrian should be an afterthought.

And yet, it still stings.

It still feels like poison accepting it.

There's no simple texts asking how I'm faring. There's no question about our Friday dinners or the house or me.

I scroll up through our old messages and somehow still feel foolish for expecting warmth when there wasn't any between us to begin with.

This new silence only makes the old silence feel louder.

The knock at my office door saves me from cycling through a hundred different reasons about what could have changed.

Dallas fills the entryway with that same neutral expression that he always carries.

"Mrs. Hart," he addresses me by my title, and I both hate and love it, because technically, I am a Hart, as much as Andrew Hart fucking hates to hear it. "You had told me to collect you to go get groceries this afternoon," he says, and I know at once that something is off.

Dallas and I have never once spoken of going to get groceries, let alone me asking him to take me. I always drive myself, and a guard always follows. They know I like my privacy. His eyes flicker over to the camera in the corner, so briefly I nearly miss it, but suddenly it connects.

Ah. Of course. We're being watched, aren't we?

Dallas seems to understand the look in my eyes, because he subtly nods his head.

I open my desk drawer and pull out a notepad with some of my earlier scribbles on it.

"Right. Can't forget my list," I mutter and slam the drawer back shut.

It's quiet as I gather my things and follow him out to the sleek, blacked out SUV.

Still, we wait until we're further away from home before he glances into the rearview mirror.

"Your home system is being monitored," he suddenly tells me, confirming my suspicion. I had a feeling before today that I was being watched, but still, it hurts to hear it out loud. No part of my life is ever private. I knew it wouldn't be when I chose to enter this marriage, but my pulse skyrockets at it so blatantly being pointed out.

"By?" I rasp as I look away from his gaze in the mirror. The light turns green, and he scans the intersection before proceeding forward.

I avert my eyes to the window to watch the glass and steel filter by as we pass through downtown.

"If I had to guess, I'd say Mr. Andrew Hart," he answers after a moment of thought. "I hope you don't take offense, but your husband doesn't seem capable of implementing some sort of tracking system."

"No offence taken, Dallas, but let's speak candidly, yes? By doesn't seem capable, you're referring to the fact that Adrian is a spoiled, ill-educated idiot who can barely feed himself, let alone know how to work a security system from across the country," I snap in response, but Dallas' eyes flick to me one more time before they slide back to traffic.

"To put it plainly, yes," he responds, and I can't help but snort. "Has he done something to upset you?" He asks, and my fingers tighten on the strap of my seatbelt. Boy, has he ever.

"Dallas," I sigh.

"Yes, Mrs. Hart?"

"Adrian Hart is a pathetic loser who throws hissy fits and has no spine. He has no respect or manners, has never worked for anything in his entire life, and I fear he only has two functioning brain cells that he sometimes loans out to his friends when he's bored. He most certainly is not a man that I ever would have willingly chose to marry, and while we're being honest here, I would like to also add that I wholeheartedly believe he has never touched a woman before a day in his life, because whereas he lacks in most things in life, he also lacks in the bedroom," I scoff and fold my arms across my chest. "Yes," I tack on. "He has upset me. And he also apparently is no longer speaking to me," I point out.

"Well," Dallas clears his throat and lets his hands glide over the steering wheel as he enters the parking lot of the grocery store and maneuvers into an open spot. "I will not agree nor disagree, as my

employment contract restricts me from expressing my heartfelt griev-
ances with the Hart family."

"Remind me to edit your employment contract," I mumble as
I unbuckle my seatbelt, and I swear I hear the ghost of a chuckle.
My eyes snap up at the sound and Dallas is quick to look down to
unbuckle his own seatbelt. He turns and looks at me over the center
console.

"Mr. Hart, whether it be Adrian or his father, is operating in poor
taste if he has decided to ignore you. If I were in your shoes, I would be
so inclined to focus on my own personal efforts, whether they benefit
Mr. Hart or not." He clears his throat one more time and looks me in
the eyes. "Now, we have a bigger problem."

"Of course we do," I suck in an exhausted breath and gesture for
him to continue.

"The camera feeds. I monitor them all, and forgive me for saying so,
but I don't always trust that my employers have appropriately secure
security systems. When Mr. Hart was sent off to.. well, wherever he
was sent off to, I piggy-backed my own feed on top of it to monitor
your safety better. I get motion alerts, door alerts, and all window
alarms. Whoever is watching, they're not watching twenty-four-sev-
en, but they could if they wanted to. For now, it appears to be just
summaries. They're watching when you're coming and going, when
you're home, if you have visitors. It flags anything out of pattern, and
your feed is out of pattern," his jaw tightens as he speaks.

"Good," I reach over to unlock my car door. "Let's keep him looking at the wrong things."

We talk in the grain aisle like we're discussing which rice is more
suited for the household. I put a bag in the cart, and he takes it out
and puts a different one in, feigning that we have this practiced and
cemented.

"I filed the LLC," I murmur as he reaches past me. "Name's clean. We need a front that sells privacy and sells it well."

Dallas pretends to scan the ingredients of a granola bar box while I look up at the top shelf like I'm contemplating which ones to pick out. "Security and intelligence sells fast," he murmurs. "The public front will be most important for liability purposes. We need quiet clients and confidentiality."

"We'll need people we can trust," I push the cart further down the aisle and watch as Dallas quickly scans the store to make sure no one is listening or watching too intently.

"I have names," he grabs the olive oil I usually buy since a woman is standing just a few feet away. "You need to set up a private offshore account. I can assist with that. This needs to be a slow drip," he says suddenly as he reaches for some coffee. "Not a heavy pour," he continues and leads us further from the woman. "Move two thousand here, four thousand there. No patterns, no dates. Let it grow out of reach."

"I'll need tech, too," I mutter.

"I can get that. Men too. You'll need to stay hands off as much as possible. Deniability when you're building an empire is most important."

"Isn't that having others do my dirty work?" I question with a furrow in my brow, and Dallas levels me with an unimpressed stare.

"How do you think men like your father and Andrew Hart got so deep into this? There's always a fall guy, Sage."

Hearing Dallas say my name makes me feel like I can trust him a little more. It makes it all seem a little more real. A little more honest.

We check out with an entire assortment of things that the cameras will catch. He holds the door and I step into the mid-afternoon sun, cursing Adrian's name as I send him another text telling him we need to talk, as soon as possible, now preferably.

My text is read.

No reply comes.

I stare at my message until the words seem to blur, and then I cast my gaze out on the cityscape as it passes.

It would be almost easier if he just wrote back that he's done with me.

At least that would cut the fragile strings of hope that it's us against his father, and not just me.

The days blur together in a dull haze.

Twice more I meet with Dallas. The second time cements the start of my future.

"I blocked your camera so we could speak freely."

The slim folder he hands me has nine vetted names in it. Nine people who all hate Andrew Hart. Nine people who are willing to follow me, not a misleading man who thinks he's a God.

"Nine is a good start," he tells me, and I choose to believe it. "There are others in the Hart ranks who could be turned. Given the right circumstances," he points out.

"Double agents?" I look up sharply and Dallas hums.

"Potentially. We'd have to funnel them false info to see what leaks, but we can patch those up with some lead if need be."

Lead.

A bullet.

Dallas is telling me he can kill them if they betray me.

Trust.

It's such a fragile thing I hope to build.

But I'm laying the bricks one by one and hoping it continues to solidify.

As the days pass, no responses come from Adrian. He ignores my every call and text, and finally, I simply stop.

Contractors come and go. Walls change their color. The house blooms under my direction.

I sign things. I burn things in the barrel in the back yard. I move money, quietly, like Dallas suggested.

I learn which ones of Andrew's men flinch when I enter the room and I learn which ones stare at you when they think you're someone they can walk all over.

Those men get fired, and the ones that flinch stay. I can use them.

After a full week of radio silence, I put my phone on silent mode and tell myself it's better this way.

Adrian Hart was always meant to die, but I didn't know I'd have to fight not to feel something at the end of it.

I thought we were in this together.

Or at least *trying* to be in this together.

But even if I'm on my own, I know I can do this.

I have to.

"There's something else," Dallas hesitates.

"Just say it," I order.

"Aaron reports to Andrew." He watches my face as he says it. I already knew that. But it still throws me off when he continues speaking. "And so does Robert."

"Robert?" The name makes my mouth water with the need to be sick. I thought I was watching carefully, but apparently, I'm not. "I rarely see him. Are you sure?"

"You're not supposed to see him," Dallas points out. It doesn't make me feel any better. "He's been tailing you for weeks."

Pure anger slices through my vision, and I feel my hands shake. "Should we fire him?" I ask, and Dallas shakes his head no.

"No. We need to keep him at least under some of our control. If he's on our payroll, we at least can keep him somewhat close. If we fire him, he'd still likely follow you, but it'd be harder to keep him on a leash."

"Then we keep him," I rasp and push the folder away in frustration. "We'll have to poison all of the information he gets, and keep him out of our business." I unlock my bottom desk drawer and pull it open, reaching for a folder of my own to hand to Dallas. "I've been looking at office buildings. I want a place that says respectable from the sidewalk but unreachable once you're inside. We need to make sure if we're ransacked or searched, it takes a while for whoever it is to reach our real business."

"I'll go through them and vet the owners. I can get tours scheduled under a false name so Andrew won't recognize it. Once we have the space we can secure it from the inside out, get security soundproof and locked down."

"How can we market this? I have so many ideas and don't know where to start," I sigh, leaning back to rub my eyes.

"Tell them to me. I'll tell you what might work."

"Maybe start small?" I question. "We can market neighbor-hood watch contracts, plaster our name in commercial districts and small subdivisions. HOA patrols. Executive protection. Door services. Whatever we need to do to market a legit business. All of the clients will be real. The *money* will be real. But we'll take the big clients underhand. Escorts, deliveries. I don't care what it is. Andrew controls the drug market, and my father controls the gun market. Who controls delivery? No one. It's fair game. We can control imports and exports. Find ways to muddle their deals. Take control of their shipments and ports. If the product goes missing, they won't know where to look. But we will, because we're the ones who can take it. It's bad business on both sides, and no one will suspect we will have a hand in it."

"You want to sabotage both families?" Dallas deadpans, and I click my pen once before giving him a controlled nod.

He stares at me for a moment and I can almost see the gears turning in his head.

But then he drops his hands and lets out a long breath.

"Fuck it, I'm in," he shrugs, and I sit up further.

"Really?"

"Yeah," Dallas shrugs. "We can do it if we do it right. We can't rush or panic. We have to stay slow and controlled."

"Yeah," I rapidly nod. "We need to keep it quiet for now. You're the only one I've told."

"I'll take it to the grave, Mrs. Hart."

We've taken to doing weekly shopping trips together.

Whatever it takes so we can get some more privacy without the cameras reporting our every move.

Each time, I cement more plans to build my future.

Dallas escorts me back to the house, sweeping his eyes throughout each room in a way that tells me he takes my protection seriously.

He carries in all of my groceries and sets my alarm system on his way out, and then I'm left once more in the silence of my home.

I unpack the groceries slowly, letting myself breathe for the first time in months. While I unpack, I work to make myself dinner as well.

The maids used to cook bland dishes that had no excitement to them. But cooking has always been a safety fall back of mine. Something that brings me comfort.

The pasta comes together easily, flavor filling the kitchen and soothing my soul. The red wine is a little bitter on the way down, but it's one of the few bottles Adrian had stored away somewhere. One of the only ones I kept from his many stashes.

I eat dinner at the kitchen island in my robe and my fuzzy house slippers, and I tell myself this unease is only temporary. I tell myself that everything is temporary, even my uncertainty for the future.

I think about Dallas and whether I can trust him. Whether it even matters I do. Trust is a luxury in my world, and time tells all.

Time will realign.

The words are embedded into my skin, but I feel like it's branded on my spinal cord.

Time will realign. It always does.

Dallas wants what I want, at least for now. We have a common goal. A common thread of understanding. That's enough for now.

Against my better judgment, I also think about Adrian. The way he used to at least tell me to get some rest. To keep him updated on how things are going here. The way he used to at least check that his father wasn't breathing down my neck.

Now I'd settle for even less if it meant I'd get some sort of explanation or response.

Something has changed.

Not the distance. That I always expected.

Not the marriage. That was always a lie.

This is something else.

A voice behind his voice.

A hand on the back of his neck steering him away from me.

There's a kill switch somewhere, and it seems the hand has finally landed on it.

What might have been there at the start isn't always there in the end.

I know that.

It's fine.

I'll let him turn away. He can go if he wants to.

Andrew can watch my cameras with his face glued to the glass. Robert can track me all he wants to. Aaron can report the timing of my dinners and my nail polish for each week.

I'll let them run themselves in circles while they try to figure me out.

I take another sip of wine, and this time it stings my throat a little bit more.

Or maybe it's the moisture building in the back of my eyes.

I look around this kitchen.

My kitchen.

Not his.

And make the decision so quietly that it feels like smoke slipping through my synapses.

If Adrian wants a wall between us, then I'll build him a city.

I clean the kitchen until it shines. I rinse my dishes and turn off the lights.

I walk through my silent halls with my head held high and my feet steady.

At least when I look myself in the mirror, I can say I did my best.

They can watch me all they want, but they won't see a thing.

There won't be fireworks or speeches or screaming.

When I move, it will be like dusk, like the fog, like the tide deciding the shore belongs in its iron grip.

And by the time they feel the water at their throats, it will already be too late.

13

ELLISON

The mirror doesn't lie.

Unless you make it.

I stand in front of it and cock my head to the side, slackening my expression until it morphs into one that I want.

Adrian Hart's reflection stares back at me.

The same dark hair, the same eyes, the same vacant expression. But my eyes are darker. My eyes are storm-gray, with a hint of blue. They glint menacingly, like lightning in a rainstorm.

I've been told my eyes are calculative and cold, but I ease them into something softer until I get it right.

Now I look like a man who grew up with a silver spoon.

I look like the only things that have haunted me are my father's bad decisions and the shadow of powder clinging to my bloodstream.

I look like a man who gets into trouble.

I tilt my chin down further, seeing a boy with no confidence but the audacity to face it. Adrian Hart is clean-shaven, and now, I am, too.

His smirk is nauseating, lazy, meant to charm people into forgiving his stupidity.

It looks wrong on me at first. Too calculated. Too practiced.

I shake my shoulders out and try again, slower, heavier on the arrogance, leaning into the slouch, and for a moment, I almost believe it.

Almost.

"Good morning, Sage," I murmur to my reflection, testing the weight of his voice on my tongue. It settles bitter in the back of my throat.

It's too low the first time.

It's too smooth on the second.

Too rehearsed.

The third time I try, it's perfect, but I loathe the way it sounds, and I know Sage will too.

I smile into the mirror, and Adrian Hart smiles right back at me.

"Good morning, Sage," I say it again, and this time, I sound like the perfect mirror of him.

Adrian Hart.

Even the name sounds fucking stupid.

But I need it.

It's a means to an end.

One that I plan to grasp hold of.

I grab my phone from the countertop and pull up the video feed of my soon to be home.

My sweet Sage stands in the bathroom curling her long dark hair at the double sink.

She looks tired, and I hope that she's getting enough rest. I hope that Andrew Hart isn't shadowing her every move.

Sage's hair is beautiful.

It cascades in thick waves down her back, standing out against her cream-colored robe. The morning light still pours into the room from that window over the bath, and it makes her look just like the angel she is, silver and soft, but deadly.

She tilts her head to the side, and her hair falls forward, streaming over her shoulder and down to the bottom of her breasts.

I swear, for a second, I forget how to breathe.

Sage can't hear me when I wish her good morning, but when she reaches up to tuck a strand of hair behind her ear, I feel the compulsion climbing up my throat.

"Good morning, Sage," I whisper again, and she looks up and at her reflection in the mirror.

Like some small part of her knows that I'm here for her.

Something about the way that she brushes her hair back from her eyes, the way her lips move as she hums like she's lost in her own world.

I've seen thousands of women from all over the world.

But none of them hold a candle to her.

None of them could ever compare to her natural beauty.

I tilt my head and mirror her movement.

She brushes her hair back and my hand follows suit. She exhales, I breathe in.

We're in two different worlds, but Sage has my heart in an iron grip.

She has locked it up and thrown away the key and I wish for it to be lost forever.

For a second, Sage sighs and her eyes flick over to the camera in the corner, and our gazes meet through the layers of glass, metal, and static.

It shouldn't feel like we're connected.

But we are.

God help me, I know that we are.

I'll make sure she knows, too.

When the time comes for us to be united, I'll make she knows that it's me who adores her. That it's me who loves her. That it's me who provides for her.

Everything that Sage touches will bloom. I know it will. I just need to figure out how to help her while I'm stuck in this hellhole.

I've been feeding Adrian nothing but bullshit for the past three weeks, and he's been eating it up like it's a fucking delicacy unknown to mankind.

Every lie I slip into his mouth becomes his own.

It's harming Sage. I see it. I know it is.

But it's necessary.

For right now, making Adrian stay away from her is the only thing that I can do to make sure that she's focusing on herself and her goals.

Adrian only adds stress to her daily life.

He only makes her suffer more, and I won't let him widen the gap where hatred has settled between us.

So for now, even though I can see that Sage dislikes him pulling away, I see her doing better, and I see her reaching out to take control of what she wants.

I'm going to make sure it happens.

Perhaps it starts innocently enough, but I overhear Sage through the cameras speaking to one of the contractors.

She wants a dark stained oak entertainment center for the living space, and they are giving her every excuse in existence why they cannot provide it for her.

No doubt Andrew Hart attempting to ruin her every plan.

I won't let them keep her from the things she wants.

I'm not rich by any means. All I know is how to kill, but when you live my kind of lifestyle, money becomes irrelevant when you have no home or roots.

So paying the twenty thousand dollars and scheduling a delivery for it to the house is nothing to me.

Especially when I tell them to deliver it to her name.

Especially when I see how she falters when it arrives.

I watch as she brushes her crimson stained nails across the wood grain. I see how her chest seems to pause before she releases an unsteady breath.

Sage thinks Adrian isn't paying her any attention, but *I* am.

It's easy enough to override Adrian's phone.

I've had access to it for nearly a month now, and he still doesn't suspect a thing.

I waited until week two, allowing Sage to stew in frustration, allowing her to write him off as inconsequential, and then I sent a text from my phone.

Sage thinks Adrian can't speak with her anymore, and perhaps he can't.

I'll make sure of that.

When I send it, I watch through the screen as she glances at the text, and then her breath catches as she snatches it from her desk.

It was simple enough, but I'm certain that Adrian has never apologized to her a day in his life.

I apologize that we aren't speaking. I'm not trying to hurt you, but I'm trying to get better, Sage.

I hope the entertainment center was the one you wanted. I know that I have a lot to make up for, and I'll try to do better.

I won't have phone privileges until the end of next month.

Until then, I hope Daddy isn't giving you too much trouble.

This is my new phone number for now. I dropped my old phone during training and they couldn't fix it.

I'll speak to you next month.

Until then.

Adrian.

Calling Andrew Hart Daddy makes me want to vomit, but I need to maintain Adrian's disgusting way of life to make sure my plan works.

And I know it will.

I can tell, as soon as Sage finishes reading the text, she reads it again.

And then she reads it a third time.

And then her hand drops to her side and she stares at the marble flooring for a moment.

I know that she probably has a thousand thoughts racing through her mind, but this is only the first step in altering her mindset of Adrian.

She doesn't respond to the text, and I don't expect her to.

I expect to work for her forgiveness to right the wrongs of Adrian Hart.

Sage is simply too intelligent to fall for sweet words alone.

She's going to fight me tooth and nail, picking apart every sentence.

She'll look for my lies and half-truths, trying to decide if her husband suddenly grew a conscience overnight.

She'll probably tell herself it's too little, too late.

But then she'll read it.

Again.

And again.

And again.

As long as it takes for the message to sink in.

And each time she sees the words, that seed that I planted will grow a little stronger.

Each time she questions if Adrian is really trying, even if it's a lie, she'll start to soften.

I can tell she doesn't want to feel it, but I see it.

The relief.

A tiny shred of peace that I've given her with one text message.

That's the thing that Adrian doesn't understand.

His life could be so fucking simple if he would appreciate the things that he has.

All Sage wants is simple reassurance, evidence that she is most important, because she is.

All she wants to know is that Adrian is in her corner, even against his fucking father.

It could all be so simple.

When I finally take my rightful place, Sage will understand that all of his hurt had to happen for me to take care of her.

I want her to look at me and see the man she always deserved.

Not Adrian's ghost.

Not Andrew's pawn.

Me.

The one who keeps her safe. The one who strips her bare and takes care of everything for her.

The one who learned every habit, every want and need, every fucking dream.

Even the ones she doesn't voice.

That's love, isn't it?

Doing what's best for someone even when they don't understand it yet.

Everything that I do, I do for Sage.

To better her life.

To make sure she thrives.

To show her she's loved.

I thumb the screen one more time, and Sage is smudging lip-gloss across her plump bottom lip.

"Soon, sweetheart," I murmur, and the faintest smile ghosts over her lips.

I'll take care of her.

I vow it.

The afternoon heat is stifling.

We're all dripping sweat by lunchtime, bound together by joint efforts to drain our energy dry.

The mess hall is alive with noise, all of it getting lost against the commotion of it all.

I sit across from Adrian, watching him shove food into his mouth like he's been starved of manners for his entire fucking life.

Knowing him, he has.

This will be one habit I won't be able to indulge.

He laughs too loud at the table.

He chews with his mouth open.

He doesn't seem to notice everybody glancing over at his obnoxious behavior like he's embarrassing even them.

But I notice.

I notice everything.

"So," I huff, leaning back and dropping my fork into the tray. "What do you usually do back home when you're not, ya know, pretending to serve your country?" I cock an eyebrow at him and Adrian laughs like we're old friends.

"Party. Drink. Fuck," he grins like a schoolboy and I want to mash his teeth in. They're too white. Too polished. All fake.

"Yeah," I chuckle darkly. "That checks out, dude." The words bait him just like I want them to. "Ever get into your old man's stock? If you catch my drift?" I waggle my brows and his laugh is hesitant this time. That's the thing about men like Adrian. They don't know how to hide their tells. Every thought he's ever had crosses his face.

"Uh, sometimes," he admits after a moment. He reaches up and rubs the back of his neck and his eyes dart around to see if anyone else is listening. "Why?"

"Man, you're more badass than me," I shrug and take a swig of my water and Adrian tilts his head in contemplation. "I've always wondered what that rush feels like." I lower my voice and look around too, conspiratorial like it's just between us. "Never had the balls to try it myself though, man. Too chicken shit, I guess. Probably not man enough to handle it honestly; I can barely hold my fucking liquor," I laugh.

I see the exact second that the idiot latches onto the bait, and I snatch the reel back.

Adrian's shoulders roll back like he's the most confident man in the world. His chest puffs up, posturing and he throws his head back and laughs all too loudly. "Are you kidding, man? Coke's the best. It's a fucking headrush in seconds. Everything just feels elevated, you know? The world finally makes sense for five goddamn minutes, and once you've had a woman on that high, you know you've lived!"

He's a fucking liar.

He doesn't know a thing about sense and clarity.

But he likes hearing himself talk, so I let him.

He rambles on and on about how his father doesn't notice shit. How the blondes he likes to bang are delectable. How his wife isn't his type, but she's still a good fuck when he's high.

I want to wrap a rope around his slender fucking neck and kick the chair out from under him.

Pathetic, evil piece of shit.

Sage is a good fuck, that I know he's right about.

But not his type?

Sage is everyone's fucking type.

She's gorgeous.

Nothing like these ditzy fucking blondes Adrian likes to fuck around with. He only likes those because they're impressed by Daddy's money.

Unlike Sage who knows how to use her fucking brain and sees Adrian for what he really is, a pathetic little man with bigger balls than he has brains.

Fucking selfish prick.

I hate him.

I hate him so badly.

I wish he were fucking dead already so I could-

"She keeps redecorating the house," he says with a scoff. My mind instantly zeroes back in at the mention of her. "You should've seen what she did to my fucking office, man. Painted over the walnut paneling with some fucking dark shit."

I laugh on cue, shaking my head. "Man, that's rough. You know women have no taste. You can't let her run the place like that. She's gonna turn your mansion into a fucking emo dollhouse."

Adrian laughs, thinking I'm on his side.

But I know the exact shade she chose. Down to the very last detail, including what light fixtures she uses.

"Show me," I say casually, and he's too fucking senseless to say no. He pulls his phone out and flips through photos, showing me angles of the house, some half-finished rooms, one of the newly painted areas.

Her touch is everywhere. It's so obviously hers and gorgeous.

I can see her style in every single line, every detail. It's completely hers.

"What the fuck," I exclaim, feigning disgust. "She's fucking everything up."

"Right?" Adrian grimaces and locks his phone. "She doesn't even tell me about the shit she's changing. Like it's her fucking house or something."

"I bet you're real tired of that," I chuckle, and he solemnly nods.

"Yeah," he sighs again and taps his fingers against the back of his phone. "Yeah, I really fucking am."

That night, the barracks are wild again. The guys are drinking and playing cards, being loud as usual. I play along for a while, smile when I'm supposed to, cheers when they hold their drinks out.

I know we've still got a few weeks until Adrian's ready for assignment, but I'm ready to be out of this hell.

Adrian is right in the middle of it, soaking up the attention like a fucking dish sponge. He's half drunk before I finish my first beer, cheeks flushed, eyes all glassy and speech all slurred. When he throws his arm around my shoulder and calls me big brother, I nearly laugh in his fucking face.

He doesn't know that I'm already picking him apart one thread at a time.

Around midnight, I tell them I'm going to shower and turn in for the night.

No one even notices when I slip away, all too drunk.

In the quiet of the bathroom, I lean against the shower tile and pull my phone out again.

The feed pops open like a hand delivered string of fate.

My Sage is asleep.

The sheets are pooled around her waist, and one hand is stretched wide, resting across the pillow beside her. Her lips are parted just slightly, hair wild across the silk pillowcase.

She's fucking beautiful.

"Goodnight, sweetheart," I murmur and brush my fingers across the screen

Right as I say it, she shifts in her sleep.

She rolls, tucking her face into the pillow beside her and pulling it into her chest.

Like she heard me.

Like she wants me, too.

Like she's ready for me to come home.

I watch her for a long time. So long that the water starts to chill.

So long my chest starts to ache.

"Soon," I whisper.

Soon, I'll go home.

Soon, I'll make sure she sleeps peacefully beside me.

"I'll be home soon."

14

SAGE

Dallas listens.

Not like most men do where they say they heard you and then you say tell me what I said, and they stare at you like they have rocks as braincells.

Dallas listens to every word I say.

Not only does he listen, but I can see the gears turning in his head as he processes the words I say and generates an intelligent response that won't get us both killed.

"I just don't understand how he can just-just fucking disappear like this," I huff in frustration, pacing in front of the kitchen island.

Dallas has watched me stare at my phone off and on for days now.

I think I've picked it up and put it back on the counter two hundred times today.

Each time, the text message doesn't magically alter itself in any way, and still, I seethe with anger at his audacity. "He sends one fucking text about trying to get better, and now what? I'm supposed to just accept it? How could he even get better? Rehab? Because that's what he fucking needs. God damn alcoholic child. What else could he need?

Church? Fucking space?" I scoff and Dallas leans against the counter, cocking his head to the side as he studies me.

"I mean, come on, Mrs. Hart," he reaches up and loosens his tie before he rolls his sleeves up and reaches for the knife I have lying by my cutting board. I had meant to start cooking but I'm just so frustrated over this entire thing. "You said it yourself. He's never been reliable, and I've known him for nearly ten years."

"That's not the point," my voice cracks with shame. "He's my husband, Dallas. I mean, he owes me something. I don't know what, but he definitely owes me *something*. How can he just... just do this to me? Ugh!" I exclaim as I slam my hands on the countertop.

Dallas doesn't seem very impressed with my meltdown.

"He owes you nothing," he responds, understanding but still somehow firm. "And you need to focus," he points the knife at me lazily. "Plans require execution. Don't worry about Mr. Hart. Worry about yourself."

He's right.

He's always right, damn Dallas!

I take a slow breath in and press my palms flat to the counter, nodding to myself.

"And for now," he sighs and starts cutting up the zucchini I left laying out. "You need to eat. I'll cut these this time, but I'm not your maid, *Mrs. Hart.*" He says my name like a slur this time, and I petulantly stick my tongue out at him.

"I was going to let you take some to go, but not anymore!" I huff and stomp to the refrigerator.

When I turn around, I see the ghost of a smile on Dallas' normally cold face.

I catch it before he can hide it, and it makes my chest warm a little bit.

It's stupid.

Maybe I'm just starved for some kind of stability.

But I have no one in my corner.

There's no one that helps me. No one that cares. No one that's willing to have my best interests at heart.

Dallas is grounding me right now.

He's the tiny sliver of hope that I have left.

The one thing that convinces me that we can do this.

"I don't like vegetables anyway, Mrs. Hart," he shoots back, and I have to fight the urge to roll my eyes.

"Fine," I mutter under my breath. "But if you burn my zucchini, I'm docking your pay."

He doesn't even look up at me, but I hear a breathy sound from under his breath. "I'd like to see you try, Mrs. Hart."

God, I hate how that stupid last name sounds when he says it, all condescending and clipped.

But he's the only one who says it like it's my actual name.

By the time we finish dinner, I'm a little calmer.

Dallas pretends not to notice me scrubbing the same pan twice, and he finally leaves me be after sweeping through the house, checking all the doors and windows before setting the alarm.

Once he's gone, I move to my office and pull up my desktop.

It's been an awfully busy week, but each time I complete one more task, my heartbeat speeds up and threatens to run right out of the front door.

I finally cemented my LLC registration, making sure to choose something that isn't glaringly obvious that it belongs to me.

Eden Intelligence.

It's nice and clean, bold, and looks good on the new business cards I've ordered.

The sleek imprint and new logo I designed looks good on my desktop background.

My planner and notebook are slammed full of things to do and people to meet.

But it's all coming together one day at a time.

Dallas and I have done the final walkthrough and selected a location, a sleek warehouse that looks non-descript and professional.

The keys felt like a loaded gun when Dallas placed them in my hand.

But now the real work must begin.

We're gearing up for operations, field work, tech analysis, logistics.

The whole works.

We've got a plan to execute it perfectly, and I've got Dallas in my corner keeping me from falling out from exhaustion.

Every line I type on my computer makes me feel less like Adrian Hart's waiting wife and more like Sage. Not Sage Hart. Not Sage Ledger.

Just Sage.

A woman with drive and a plan, and the means to choke the life out of men to get what I want.

The house is quiet as the night winds down, and I move through and re-check the same locks and windows that I know Dallas already secured, just for my peace of mind.

But that's when the doorbell rings.

I freeze when I hear it.

No one comes here this late. Not even Dallas, and if it were an emergency, he would have contacted me.

I make my way quickly down the stairs and peer through the glass, catching the tail end of a delivery van at the edge of the circle drive.

He shouldn't have even been able to make it through the gate unless someone either buzzed him in, or he had the code to enter.

Which tells me someone sent him.

I open the door cautiously, heart slamming against my ribcage, just in time to hear the truck door shutting and the engine revving back up as the truck pulls away from the curb.

I pull the door wider and step out, fastening my robe tighter across my body.

That's when I see them.

They're dark.

Not the kind one would send to win someone back.

But they're perhaps the only ones I would choose for myself.

A bouquet of deep-wine colored roses are staring up at me. Velvet smooth, almost black tinged at the edges. The kind of flowers you may send to a funeral, or the table of a very dangerous, powerful man.

There's no card, just a folded note tied to one of the long stems with a thin black ribbon fastened tighter than a noose.

My hands tremble as I pull the end and unravel the fabric.

I appreciate you, Sage. The house looks good.

There's no name.

No return address.

But I know who it's from.

I stare at the handwriting.

It's sharp and neat, almost too perfectly engraved into the card.

Adrian?

I try to remember what his handwriting looks like, but I threw out all of the bullshit from his office, and I don't have anything to compare it to.

I try to think of the way he signed his name on our marriage documents. This doesn't look like that. His handwriting always leans lazy just like the way he walks. This is confident and controlled, etched with intention.

I turn my head slowly to look up at the camera in the corner, and the tiny red dot blinks red just once, almost like it's taunting me.

He couldn't have sent this, could he?

Adrian's never done anything for me.

First the entertainment center. Then the text. Now the roses.

My pulse is beating like it means to harm me.

I can't tell if I'm flattered or terrified, and for a moment, I feel rage build inside of my chest.

How dare he!

How fucking dare he!

I hastily make my way to the kitchen, chest rising and falling in anger, and I slam my foot down on the pedal of the trashcan. The lid slaps against the island when it opens forcefully, and I lift both hands with the intention of throwing the bouquet in the trash.

But my hands shake wildly.

My chest moves far too fast for my body's own good, and I just can't.

I can't.

My hands slowly lower, and I feel so conflicted as I set the flowers down on the island and step back.

It makes a small clang when it meets the surface and I feel like my heart shatters with the force.

Adrian has no right.

He has no right.

He fucking left me here to deal with this shit show all by myself.

I've done my best to erase him in the two months he's been gone, and now he's trying to what? Win my affections? Apologize by drowning me in gifts?

It's more frustrating that I can't figure out his angle.

He cheated on me.

Adrian fucked another woman in the wedding dress my father picked out.

He doesn't care about me.

He did his *best* to make my life hard.

And then he went and fucked everything up and got sent off to God knows where while his father pulls his puppet strings.

I'm not going to lay down and accept his apology when he's done nothing to earn my forgiveness.

That night, I dream of my husband for the first time.

Or maybe what my mind wants my husband to be.

I dream of Adrian Hart's hands on my waist, his breath hot against the column of my neck.

His touch is slower this time.

Not selfish.

Not limp.

This time he grasps hold of me and whispers all the nasty things he wants to do to me in my ear.

This time, he whispers my name like he actually cares that I'm tethered to him until death do us part.

This time, he tells me that I'm beautiful and that he's sorry, and he wants me.

Adrian's lips trail down my spine, licking up the delicate strokes of my tattoo in a way that's dizzying.

I turn my head when his lips meet my shoulder blades, and his face is concealed in the shadows.

I wake up gasping, the sheets tangled between my legs, hand clutching my chest.

I don't even remember what my husband's voice sounds like, and yet the ghost of his voice rings in my ears.

Or was it my own voice?

Was it him or me whispering the things they want?

My throat feels dry, and my pulse skitters away like a stray cat slinking back to the shadows of night.

It wasn't Adrian.

I know that.

But my body doesn't seem to know it.

I don't want Adrian Hart.

I don't want to want him.

Even if he is my husband.

My one goal is still to bring an abrupt end to his life, and I'll see to it that it's done.

By the time the sun is forcing its way to daylight, I've made my coffee, showered, and stared at those fucking flowers ten times over.

The petals glisten, fresh and rich, like they were delivered straight from the florist, delicate and brand new just for me.

They still sit right where I left them the night before.

I tell myself it doesn't matter.

I tell myself that I don't care.

I'll focus on my business.

Adrian and his fucking flowers can rot for all I care.

But every time I close my eyes, I see his hands.

And I hear that whisper brushing the shell of my ears.

If this is what the distance does, I'll sever it clean and put myself out of my misery.

Adrian Hart will regret ever signing his name alongside mine.

I'll make sure of it.

15

SAGE

The world looks different when you build it yourself.

It's been two weeks since I received the flowers.

Two weeks of trying to push Adrian out of my head.

Eden Intelligence looks like nothing from the sidewalk, just frosted glass, a matte black door, and a tasteful plaque that's discreet.

My new warehouse still smells like fresh paint and rain-soaked asphalt. The concrete floors still gleam from the new sealant, and the glass offices upstairs make everything glow with a perfect shine.

Seeing my hard work brought to life cements my future.

This is mine.

Not my husband's.

Not my father's.

Not Andrew Hart's.

Mine.

Dallas paces the main floor, talking to the contractor about my brand-new security system. It's from a foreign company. One that can't be bought by the Hart or Ledger heads.

Despite the importance of today, he moves through my new building with a confident glide, hands steady, and voice certain.

I'm learning he's the type of person who never needs to raise his tone to get the results he wants.

Already, I've started to trust him more than I should, but he hasn't led me astray yet, and I need someone like him in my corner.

He gives me a tight nod and I turn on my heel to follow him.

It's finally time to bring my plans to action.

The meeting room is small, glass-walled, and spotless.

But though you can see everything on the inside, it's soundproofed and private.

Any word that leaks through these walls won't come from the cameras.

It'll come from one of the men in the room.

The large oak table fits six chairs, and five of them are occupied.

Dallas sits to my right, always to my right, like he's permanently fixed there.

Across from me are the men who we've hired to help me build an empire that no one will expect my iron grip to have a hold of.

Anderson stands behind me, my newest shadow. His posture is always straight as a blade. He doesn't talk much, but Dallas says he trusts him with his life.

Samuel, Trevor, and Peter have all been handpicked and vetted, loyal each for their own reasons. I can't tell yet if they're loyal because of the money or if they simply want to follow a new hand in the game, but I'll take it either way.

We've got money moving in every direction, but mostly sweeping in.

On paper, we've made sure it's squeaky clean.

We've got neighborhood watch contracts in three affluent subdivisions, two executive protection accounts, hourly patrols in HOA communities, and officers that we've flipped to our side.

Off paper, the cash is swept up in a tangle that can't be undone. It's disjointed, slow, uneven, innocent enough to be boring if anyone peels back the wrong layer.

Every man is paid twice, once on paper, and once off.

Our real work leaves no breadcrumbs for others to snack on.

I made sure of it.

This warehouse is a maze of my own creation, brought to life by Dallas' expertise.

There's two-factor authentication at every door. Keycards assigned to every man. A guest entry that dead ends into a pretty lobby with nothing but free water and a nice oak reception desk.

The real heart of it is all on the second floor, behind airtight doors that won't open for just anyone.

"Alright," Dallas' voice is like gravel when he speaks, but I keep my gaze level on the men in front of me, searching for weaknesses. "Now that we've got all your contracts secured, the front's airtight. So listen closely. We aren't going to repeat ourselves."

I lean forward and open my folder before taking a deep breath. They've all been given copies, and I've gone over the plan so many times I could probably do it myself on zero sleep and a good coffee.

"We're done waiting," I clear my throat, looking around the table at each and every one of them. "Two of my father's idiots have been sloppy. I've had Samuel tailing them for almost a week now, and they're sitting on a warehouse full of product. Product that we're going to take. They think no one's been paying attention, and they think everyone is blissfully unaware of what they're pushing."

Samuel nods once and slides a paper to each of the men, showing photographs of my father's two fuckups, and the location. "Four guards rotate on every hour. I've already looked them over with Dallas, and trust us, they're pieces of shit, so don't worry if you end up having to pop them," he deadpans, and a few of the men chuckle. "There's one camera on the front, and one on the rear that's only on at night. Tomorrow, they have a shipment coming in, and one drop ready to go out. The place will be full for at least forty-eight hours before it's moved again."

Fucking perfect.

Dallas glances over at me and we seem to hold a silent conversation before he glances at the others. I turn back and tap the folder in front of me. "We hit it this weekend. I'm done waiting around for the perfect time. It just needs to be done. You'll go in, kill the power. I want every inch of your skin covered. Nothing should trace back to us or I'll kill you all myself. Understood?" I wait until they all agree and then take a deep breath. "You'll take everything that you can get your hands on in a fifteen minute window, and then I want you out of there. Guns, money, drugs, paperwork. I don't care what it is. Grab it and load it up into the vans and bring it back here. Use the rear entrance. We can worry about what's inside later. For now, we grab it, stash it, and lay low until the heat simmers down."

"You..." Trevor carefully interrupts me, sitting up a little straighter in his chair. "You want to rob your father?"

"I want to take down his empire. And not just his," I lower my voice conspiratorially. "His, and Andrew Hart's."

The silence that follows is so thick that for a moment, I've worried I fucked up.

But Trevor claps his hands like he's delighted, and Peter is smiling broadly like I've just handed him the keys to a candy shop. I hear

Samuel muttering about how I've fucking crazy, but they're going to make it work.

It's the only reason I can let the anxiety in my chest loosen a little.

"The vehicles are unmarked. I've scrubbed the plates. Two of our PD contacts-"

"We've got PD contacts? Sweet!" Peter beams even harder.

"We've got two," Dallas steamrolls over his excitement. "Ramos and Kline will make sure all traffic is halted at each intersection. They can't keep the lights red forever, but don't speed and draw attention to you. Stay calm and collected, and everything will look clean. By Monday, the product will be in our storage, and their warehouse will take a major hit."

"And if there's anybody in the way?" Peter smugly crosses his arms, and my stomach drops a little, but I know what goes on in this kind of business. I signed up to take on my own sins when I decided to push into this market. To get to cleaner water, I've got to swim with the sharks first.

"Then they're not by the time you leave," Dallas retorts calmly. His tone stays casual, like he isn't instructing them to fucking kill anybody who gets in their way.

The men all nod, and Anderson remains quiet, but he straightens his spine when I look over my shoulder at him.

"This is how it starts," I cut in calmly, nodding my head like the understanding is finally settling in. "We're going to take small bites until there's nothing left to chew on. By the time they realize what's happening, or who is happening, they'll be crippled."

"I'm always hungry," Peter claps again, and I think I like him. He has a certain ruthless tenacity that lightens my mood inch by inch.

"We'll get it done, boss," Dallas's lips twitch with something that looks like pride, and my heart swells with it.

"I can't do this without you guys," I murmur, and they all settle down a little to look at me. "This isn't about getting revenge or being a menace. These men.." I shake my head and look down at the table. "Both of them have dictated every part of my life from birth to now. But it's not just my life. It's everyone. Everyone in this town has been harmed in some way or another. They are nothing but rot, and they've infected this city from one side to another," I pause to let my words sink in, and I hear Trevor clear his throat. My eyes glide over, and he seems a little hesitant, but he opens his mouth and holds my gaze.

"Forgive me, but," he clears his throat again and I brace myself to hear something terrible. "You want to take down the Hart family, too, but aren't you married to one?"

My eyes snap down to the ring on my finger.

The ring I didn't ask for.

The ring I never would have chosen for myself.

I don't want to defend Adrian.

I don't.

I'm not even sure that Adrian would defend or protect me if the roles were reversed, but I think back to his text message. To the flowers and the entertainment center and the way that little morsel of hope has slithered into my heart valves and threatened to bleed me dry if it nicks one.

"Adrian is... difficult to navigate, at best," I level him with a stare that tells him we both share sentiments about my husband. "I didn't ask for Adrian to be my husband. He didn't ask for me either. But we're stuck together now. He's tethered to me, and I'm tethered to him, and the only way to sever that is to cut it clean down the middle."

My insides feel ice-cold with the thought of what I know will likely happen in the end, and I know I don't do a good job and controlling my face.

"Adrian is infected just like the rest of them. He's spoiled and childish, and he's... he's incredibly pathetic, all things considered. But until he's rotten from the inside out, too, he could be useful to us. Everyone is a pawn in this game. Even me. But people, given direction and power, can bend. They can heal and resurface from the cancer clinging to them. I'm... trying my best to carve it out of him. And if I'm not successful," I suck in a breath and feel the weight of acceptance rush into my lungs. "Then I will remove him from the chessboard myself, and we will make our next move."

"You'd kill him?" Trevor rasp, narrowing his eyes at me. It's not quite disbelief etched on his face, but something skeptical rests there.

"I'd kill anybody that gets in the way," I answer calmly. "Even you," I tell him, and this time, it's shock that bleeds into his eyes. "That goes for all of you," I gesture around the room. "Trust is incredibly hard to come by. Right now, in this room, there's only one person I truly trust." I can see Dallas shift his stance from the corner of my eye and I know my words have brought him pride.

"But I could learn to trust you all as well. For now, we have a task to complete, and this will be our first bridge of trust. If you show me that you can be loyal to me, then I'll treat you all well. The Harts, the Ledgers... they don't care about the people that they use. They don't care who they trample over. But I do. I do, and I don't want to use you. I want you to join me. To help me, because I do need help, and I'm not too stubborn or prideful to ask for it. So I'm asking. Help me, and I'll continue treating you well. Betray me, and I'll make sure you have a swift death," I tell them all seriously.

"This is the only warning that you're going to get. I need you to prove that I can trust you."

"Well, alright then, Ma'am," Peter smirks as he looks around. "You heard the lady," he slaps Trevor on the back and Trevor lurches forward with the force of it, muttering under his breath that Peter is a fucking dick. "Let's make sure our shit is airtight, boys. We've got some shit to do."

The meeting ends not too long after that.

Dallas goes over entrance and exit routes, timing, contingencies in case things go south, and I soak it all in.

"-moved from the warehouse to Pier 3 around 0130. Five-man crew, all armed but can't shoot for shit if going by how they did at the range last Thursday. Cameras on the outside are dummy cameras, and we'll hit it with a blocker when we get there."

"Power?" Peter asks, and Trevor taps his fingers repeatedly on the document they're looking at.

"Snipping it," he shakes his head. "Single feed from a utility box on Port Avenue. Sloppy job honestly. I can kill it in thirty seconds, maybe less," he shrugs.

"Clean exits to the expressway. Maybe four if we need to swing down the Riverbend. PD can loop these two traffic cams, maybe the four just for the sake of it. We'll hit green the whole way down."

The way these men slip into different people... deadly people, I should cower away from it.

But I can't.

Seeing how they navigate, how they slide into a completely different mindset, a soldier mindset, it's fascinating.

The playfulness is gone.

The hesitation is gone.

All that's left is cold determination.

A common goal tethering us all together.

I meet Dallas' eyes over the table and he nods at me.

"You did well," he mouths at me, and I can't help but smile at him while the others draw out the path they plan to take out of the city.

We're doing this, and I'm not alone.

Dallas is in my corner.

And these men... these men are also in my corner.

My back is no longer against the wall, and I'm going to take what I want.

I'm going to take back control of my life.

Even if I have to squeeze so hard I break my fingers.

When this is all said and done, I won't be in anybody's shadow.

Not Mrs. Hart.

Not my father's daughter.

Not Andrew's mouse, still stuck while he swats at me with filthy blood-soaked paws.

Just Sage.

The woman who is going to ruin them all.

16

SAGE

The night feels suffocatingly still.

Too reckless. Too aware of what we're trying to accomplish.

It's like even the air around me knows I'm leading men to their possible downfall.

A quiet before the storm outside starts raging.

I know these men are capable.

I know they're military trained and they have drilled the plan over and over until they could recite it front to back with not an ounce of hesitation.

And yet I can't keep my hands from fucking shaking.

I try to keep my movements soft and slow, to make them look natural, like I'm not panicked and trembling from the inside out.

The cameras can't know I'm listening.

Dallas drilled it into me.

"Act normal, Sage. Keep your head on straight and let us do the heavy lifting."

I know that's what he said. I know that's what he needs me to do so they can get this done without worrying about me spiraling or getting into any trouble.

So I try to move through my kitchen like I'm not a criminal mastermind playing house while a warehouse is being raided in my name.

I try to keep a loose hand on the wine glass in my hand. Each sip is bitter and burns with the knowledge that if this goes badly, I could get my men killed.

They're meant to trust me. To trust that my plan is going to work, and that everyone will make it home safe and sound.

The spoon clinks the bottom of the pan as I stir food that I'm not even hungry for.

It bubbles quietly, and the silence is stifling and uncomfortable.

I've no choice but to click on the sound bar that I have mounted under one of the cabinets. The hum of my Spotify playlist helps to calm me just a little bit, and I hum along as I move around my kitchen.

Everything needs to look calm and convincing to anyone that thinks to check these cameras.

Just a lonely wife on a quiet night cooking dinner for herself.

Nothing unusual or out of the ordinary. I do this all the time. This is just another standard night for me.

But the earpiece tucked deep in my ear hisses with faint static, and I stop breathing for nearly a full minute.

The words aren't meant for me.

I'm not even supposed to hear them.

But I do.

"Shots fired!"

I freeze with my hand tight on my wineglass, half raised to my lips and swirling like blood in the glass.

Blood that could be spilling out on a floor while I'm getting ready to enjoy a nice hot meal.

I can't respond.

I can't even fucking ask what's happening or if someone is hurt.

It's one way communication, and I can't even pick up my cell to call and get a status update or it will give me away to whoever is watching on the other side of the camera.

So I calmly set my wine back down and take a subtle breath before I lick my lips.

I stir the sauce like nothing is happening and I force myself to continue humming along to the radio like I'm fine. Like I'm not two seconds from falling apart.

And then my phone rings.

It blares so suddenly that I nearly drop my spoon in the pot.

The ringtone slices straight through my nerves, sharp and shrill as it screams at me to answer.

My heart feels like it's lodged in my throat and I almost start hyperventilating where I stand.

Dallas wouldn't call.

He knows better.

So it has to be bad. It has to be. Someone has to be dead.

I snatch the phone from the counter and bring it slowly to my ear.

"Hello?" I practically whisper.

"Hi, sweetheart."

My entire body goes cold, and this time I do lose grip on my spoon. It clatters against the edge of the pot, and I suck in a ragged breath.

The voice is low and smooth as it swirls around my head. So calm that for a second, I think I might be fucking hallucinating.

"Adrian?" I whisper.

He's not supposed to have phone privileges for another two weeks.

He's not supposed to. He told me. He-

"I pulled some strings so I could call you," he says lightly, like he can read my thoughts from wherever he is in the world. The way his voice rasps in my ear rolls down my spine and I shudder. "Couldn't stand the silence anymore. Just needed to hear your voice."

No.

Something is wrong.

Something isn't-Adrian would never say that to me. Adrian doesn't care that there's silence. He even initiated it.

I grip the countertop harder, staring at the black and gold marble like it holds all the answers to what the fuck is happening right now.

"You... you sound different," I whisper it before I can stop myself, but I can't push down this feeling that something isn't right. The alarm bells are sounding at full volume, and my ears are ringing with it.

He chuckles, so low and sultry in my ear, so certain. "Yeah, you'll probably say I look different, too. I'm sure you'll see that later when I'm able to video call."

"Oh," I murmur. My head is starting to throb with how tense my face is.

Something inside of me is festering like a slow-moving poison. Confusion. Unease, maybe. Distrust.

But something so fucking traitorously warm, too.

Something I push deep down and hope will drown before I hang up this phone.

"Got my nose busted up pretty bad," Adrian swallows audibly, and my heart is beating a thousand miles per hour at the sound. "Looks like shit now, honestly. Nothing I can do about that, though."

"That's... I'm sorry," I murmur, unsure what else I could possibly say. Adrian's always been vain when it comes to his appearance, so even him shoving off the fact his nose is different makes me second-guess him even further.

"They, um-" He pauses for a moment and I hear him sigh again. His voice goes a little quieter when he starts back up. "They're working us like dogs out here, and it's hot as hell. I'm trying to bulk up a little and build some muscles. Lay off the drinking. Hopefully it's working a little. The guys say I'm getting bigger."

I can't imagine it.

I can't imagine Adrian any different from the one that left me here. From the raging, whiny alcoholic that can't control himself.

The silence stresses so thin that I can hear his breathing on the other end, slow and calm.

But his voice shifts into something a little more rough. Into one I've never heard from him before. It grows heavier when he says, "Sage, I'm sorry."

My throat goes incredibly dry, and my head is so muddled, but still, I can't help but think that even the way he says my name sounds different.

All of Adrian's past apologies have been practiced. Carved into whatever convenient explanation he could think of on the fly.

"I know this marriage isn't what you want," he says, and it sounds so strained, but so honest, like it hurts him even to admit the very words to me. "I know I haven't been good to you. I fucked up, Sage. I broke your trust, and I probably ruined it beyond repair. But I want to try and earn it back." He takes a deep breath and I find myself mirroring the action, trying and failing to reboot my brain from the lack of oxygen supply.

"I've been learning a lot out here. Being away from home and Daddy and that environment... I'm learning about life and myself, and mostly about the importance of appreciating people who see when you're trying and want to be better, even when you don't deserve it."

My heart is slamming against my ribs so hard I can barely breathe.

I never in a billion years thought I would hear Adrian Hart admit any wrongdoing. I never thought I'd hear anything remotely close to the words he's saying to me. Or how heartfelt they sound.

Adrian's only been gone for nearly four months.

Two months.

That's it.

Can he really have changed so drastically in that little amount of time?

He continues, softer and a little sweeter as I take the words in. "You were just trying to make me better before I left, and I treated you like shit. I see that now. But when I make it back to you, I'm going to show you that I've changed. I'll make things right, Sage."

For a long time, I can't even say a single word.

Even as I open and close my mouth over and over again, I can't think of a single logical thing to say.

I don't trust Adrian.

This distance was never supposed to happen in the first place, but a foundation of mutual trust was never built. All we have are lies and secrecy and deceit.

I don't know if I believe him, and I don't know if I ever will.

I don't know if I'm even capable.

And still, I can feel my pulse everywhere. In my throat. My wrists. My ribs.

"If you're lying to me," I finally whisper, "I'll fucking kill you, Adrian."

The sound that comes through next isn't fear.

Not even close.

It's a chuckle, low-toned and husky. Nothing like Adrian's. It's too deep. Too confident. Too fucking smooth and seductive. It drips into my ears like honey and I've long forgotten that one of my men could be lying in a pool of their own blood right in a remote location right now.

"I'll bring you the gun myself, baby," the voice teases.

My heart stops altogether.

I can physically feel it seize up in my chest.

No.

This can't be Adrian.

It can't be.

The tone is all wrong. The personality. The warmth. The sweetness.

It's all wrong.

"Hey, man, we gotta head out. You coming?" A voice calls out faintly and I lean forward on instinct, straining to hear anything else around him.

"Shit," he murmurs under his breath. "I have to go."

I hate that for a second, I don't want him to.

For just a second, I want him to stay.

To show me what other differences there are to pick apart.

"We'll talk again when I can. Do whatever your heart desires, Sage. I'll support you. Just don't believe anything my father tells you. Alright? He wants to keep us apart."

My lips part, but they tremble so fiercely that I can't force any words out.

"Goodbye, Sage," he murmurs so softly, like he wants the words to caress me through the phone.

"Bye," I whisper back in a daze, and the line goes dead.

I stare at the phone long after the call ends.

Even the low-volume music isn't enough to bring me out of my shifting thoughts.

I can't tell if my heart is racing from confusion or fear or something else entirely.

But the phone lights up again in my hand and my breath stutters when I read Dallas' message.

Still buying groceries after work tomorrow? Do I need to drive you?

That's the code.

The message he promised to send if they pulled the job off smoothly.

They did it.

Oh my God, they fucking did it.

They pulled it off.

My knees nearly give out from the weight of the relief I feel.

I have to force myself to finish cooking, and then I have to force the food down.

The wine doesn't sting so bad this time.

And when I'm finally finished, I don't even bother with cleaning up my mess in the kitchen.

I retreat to the one room the cameras can't reach- my bathroom.

The burner phone that Dallas gave me a few days ago is hidden there in one of the bathroom drawers.

By the time my bath water is steaming hot, his message comes through.

One of your father's men shot at Trevor. Peter had to put him down. We got rid of the bodies. Nobody injured. Picked up eight pallets and stored at the warehouse. I'll pick you up in the morning with Anderson.

I type back a simple thank you, but after a moment of thoughts, I send a second text telling him that everything is falling into place finally.

And it is.

It really is.

When I sink into the hot water and lean back against the porcelain, my mind drifts right back.

To the phone call.

To him.

To the way his voice rasped when he said my name.

To that deep, seductive chuckle.

To the promise in his voice when he said he'd come home an entirely different man.

Home.

That word belongs to me now. To the world I'm building myself here.

Can I share it with him?

Can I ever truly trust or believe him?

Could I still kill a man who suddenly sounds like he means every word I've ever wanted him to say?

Adrian is my husband.

Whether he wanted to be or not, he's legally my husband.

I was sent here to kill him.

But I don't know if I can kill a man who makes such promises and declarations to me.

I don't know if I can follow through with my father's bidding.

I close my eyes and take a deep breath.

The memory of his voice fills my head, rich and dark, and so different from what I remember.

It's only been two months, but now I'm starting to second guess if I even remember what he really sounded like before.

The hatred had burned so rapidly in my mind that now I fear I altered the truth of what I actually knew about him.

That voice on the phone... that wasn't something I remembered.

That was the voice of a man that was certain.

Of a man that made promises that he kept.

That was a voice that might drive me mad if I'm not careful.

And before I can stop myself, my hand trails down, chasing that warmth until my body trembles with it.

And when I finally crawl into bed, my skin is flushed from the heat and the water, my body still trembling and legs a little unsteady.

When I finally drift off to sleep, I dream of Adrian again.

His hands on me.

His mouth whispering promises into my skin in that same tone.

Vowing to take care of me.

Vowing to make it all right.

17

ELLISON

The satellite feed looks like a bleach-stained catastrophe.

It's bright, white, and makes it glaringly apparent that our next op will be a shit show from start to finish.

I couldn't care less what the names of the men on the screen are. They all become another faceless moving target once we're sent after them.

The briefing has been droning on and on for ages, but my eyes keep trailing back to Adrian.

The little shit isn't listening to a word that's being said.

He'll be the first to get blown up if shit hits the fan.

The coordinates aren't anything out of the ordinary, just another hole filled with nothing but heat and more dust. Plus the usual nameless assholes we're supposed to shoot once we get there.

I sit at the end of the table like usual, trying to force my gaze to stay straight, but I can't help but cut my eyes slightly to the left.

Adrian's not built for stillness.

He practically trembles in his chair, knees bouncing, fingers picking at each other. Everyone else is focused and listening, but not him.

He simply can't stand it.

I couldn't imagine what he's like when he's high. Surely he can't get much better than this, but I've been wrong before.

Right now, he looks like he'd rather be anywhere but here. That's to be expected considering his father sent him here as punishment. Apparently, Adrian didn't realize that meant he could potentially fucking die.

The rest of us were born for this.

We signed up for it, choosing the only legal way to get our hands dirty.

Murdering under the guise of following orders is simply something we do best.

I watch him because I've been through all of this a hundred times before, and I've got nothing better to do than catalog the other men's bullshit in my brain.

After hours of looking at the surveillance the intel team has collected, we hit the mats just like we always do. Nothing better to do in this hellhole but beat each other up.

Sparring is a language of its own.

It's easy to get lost in it, though I can't say Adrian gives me much of a challenge.

He's gotten better since his arrival four months ago. I can at least admit that. But for someone on my level, after years of putting in work to craft myself into a living weapon, it's almost laughable how many times I've bested him.

I start off light today, working at him, prodding like I'm having a bit of fun, but I can tell his head's not in it.

Older brother Ellison is here to save the day. I internally roll my eyes.

"You're off today, man. What's going on?" I ask between hits. "Is it the upcoming op?"

He brushes his fist against his jaw like he's trying to wipe the feeling of my fist off of his skin.

"Daddy called me this morning." He says it too casual, and I hate the gnawing feeling that begins to simmer in my gut.

I've only talked to Sage twice more since our first conversation, but I've been watching the camera feeds nightly.

Sage doesn't trust me.

I can tell.

She keeps me at a verbal distance, not giving away too much information about what's happening back home. I can tell she's skeptical when I speak, and her responses usually stay clipped, but I know I can wear her down. It's just a matter of time.

"Let me guess. More bullshit about keeping your wife on a leash?" I chuckle even though the rage builds within me. The trick with a man like Adrian is to make him think you aren't too interested in what they have to say, and then they'll fill the silence with all of their secrets because they can't fucking stand not hearing themselves talk.

He lets out the most profound sigh.

"He wants me to... cut things off with Sage, is more like it," he murmurs like it's a secret between the two of us, and he sweeps his eyes around the training room when he says it. The other guys are scattered throughout, so I know they can't hear us, but the fact that he thinks he can trust me over them makes me feel a little victorious.

Hearing him say Sage's name makes me want to cut his fucking tongue from his throat. But that would be a bit dramatic, I think. So instead I just say, "Oh yeah?"

He hesitates to nod his head, like the very gesture is admitting he likes to kick puppies for fun in his spare time.

"What, did he give you an ultimatum or something?" I prod further, and he nods again. I think of Sage. The house, the money, the whole fucking mess of deceit going on around her, and my gut tightens. "Is he gonna take away your allowance or something?"

Adrian exhales long and slow before averting his gaze. That's when I know that whatever comes out of his mouth is going to piss me off.

"He... I found something out a few months ago," he drops his voice even lower, still circling me under the guise of exchanging a few light punches.

"Something bad?" I tempt him to admit it, and just like I expect, he purses his lips and swallows back the thickness in his throat before he nods again.

"Sage..." he starts, and I have to brace myself for what's coming next. "Her mother died when she was a teenager," he says it like he's ashamed. "Her father is just as bad as mine. One of his runners stole some powder from my father's docks," he whispers, and I tilt my head to the side as I analyze him.

He's too fidgety. Too nervous. Too fucking ashamed.

He better not say what I fucking think he's about to say.

"My father sent men into their house when her father was away." Don't you dare fucking say it, Adrian. Don't you fucking-

"He had her mother tied up and drugged. And then he... he had her tortured and killed," he whispers the admission. "Sage was home at the time, and one of his men stabbed her so she'd quit fighting them."

I don't mean to do it.

Well, that's not exactly true.

I don't regret it in the slightest, but perhaps it could have been better timed.

My hand moves before the thought even finishes.

I misjudge the weight I put behind my next fist.

It lands hard.

Hard enough that the runt staggers backwards, and he rears away from me as his hands fly up to grab his face. The sound of my knuckles connecting to his jaw is enough to draw the attention of the others.

For a second, I think I broke him.

I almost wish I did, but I can't deviate from the plan.

Shit.

I've got to control my fucking hands better.

Shit, he looks like he's going to cry.

"Oh, shit, Adrian! I'm so sorry, dude!" The apology lodges in my throat like a bitter pill. I'm not sorry. Not sorry at all. The fucking prick deserved it. He deserves to burn in hell like his piece of shit father.

"Let me see it, man!" Adrian chuckles, but it trembles as it falls from his lips. He waves me off with that stupid laugh that he gives when he's overwhelmed and uncomfortable. "Oh, shit, we need to get you some ice!"

"Don't be a drama queen, Gray. I'm fine." He laughs again, but his eyes are a little watery from the burning he likely feels in his nose.

I still drag him into our makeshift locker room.

Up close, Adrian always smells like cigarettes and teenage-boy cologne.

No wonder Sage can't stand him.

He tries to knock my hands out of the way when I press ice into his cheek and apologize again, but I make him sit down while I doctor him up.

"I'm really sorry, man," I tell him again and he shakes his head, making me nearly drop the ice. "I honestly thought you were looking, and you turned at the last second, so it landed harder than I meant it to," I breathe out in a rush.

"It's all good, dude, really," he shrugs.

"I also didn't mean to cut you off. Your dad is brutal, dude. Do you think he'll go that far with Sage?" I try to get him talking again, and he easily accepts the bait.

"Honestly, yeah," he murmurs and leans his head back. He closes his eyes and soaks up the feeling of the ice on his face and I have to resist the urge not to wrap my hands around his windpipe.

"I think he'd do it in a heartbeat. He wants her gone. I mean, I get it. Things would be so much fucking easier if she was out of the way. He'd probably just stage it to look like some accident or something."

My hands actually start shaking with the urge to kill him.

It's all I can take just to keep it contained.

Control your fucking hands, Ellison, I tell myself.

"You okay with him, ya know?" I make a gesture like I'm slicing my own throat and stick my tongue out, feigning dead, and Adrian laughs.

The sound makes me want to bury him ten feet underground.

"I mean, it would make my life a hell of a lot easier," he smirks. He actually fucking smirks. I asked him if he was okay with his father killing Sage, and he actually fucking laughed.

I'm going to kill him.

I'm going to kill him, and I'm going to kill his father.

I'll make sure they both die a horrible, painful death.

It's what they both deserve after how they've treated Sage.

Their bones will rot at the bottom of a deep well where no one will ever find them.

I vow it to myself.

"I've got this girl I've been seeing. Real smokin' hot," he smirks again. "I'm talking model body, long legs, fit. She plays beach volleyball, too. So hot."

"I'll fucking kill him," my brain keeps repeating like a mantra.

"We've been fucking around for like two years. I mean, it's not serious or anything, but having a wife makes it a bit of a bummer, dude," he laughs at his own joke and doesn't even realize that he's digging himself into a hole that he'll never be able to crawl out of.

"Well, I mean, it was good at first because she'd let me roleplay and all that. I even got her to wear Sage's wedding dress one night," he snickers and beams at me like it's his greatest accomplishment. "But she got tired of that pretty fast and backed off a little. And Sage only gives it up to me on Fridays," he snorts. "Like some fucking ritual or something. She's probably got it marked on her calendar or some shit."

They only have sex on Fridays?

My mind starts racing with the new information I'm drowning in.

For starters, now I have more information about why Sage might hate him. She probably distrusts every single word I'm saying because she knows about Adrian's affair. Of course she does. She's been re-modeling their entire fucking house. I'd be surprised if she didn't find out every secret about him in the process.

And no wonder she hates his guts. What kind of man cheats on their wife and is this smug about it? What kind of man thinks inflicting a wound this deep on the one person they've vowed to love is okay? I might be a cold-blooded killer myself, but even I have somewhat of a moral compass, and this motherfucker is crossing lines that have trenches waiting on the other side.

Second, Sage only has sex with Adrian on Fridays? That is definitely an unexpected piece of information, but I can probably use it to my advantage later on.

If I remember correctly, Sage and Adrian weren't together long before he was sent here. Just a few months. Which means they've probably only had sex a handful of times before he was shipped off. That'll make it easier for me to convince her I'm him.

If his skills in the bedroom are anything like his other skills, he was probably terrible, and I'll have to beg on my hands and knees for Sage to let me touch her.

I fucking hate Adrian.

If this line of work hadn't taught me a little bit of restraint, I think I would have already strangled him with his own bedsheets and left him dangling for one of the new recruits to find. At least then, they'd get some real-world experience and Adrian's existence would have benefitted someone.

"That's just cold, man," I finally force myself to respond to him, trying and falling just a little short of convincing him that I think it's funny. He falters for just a moment, but then I can see him second guess himself before he sees my smile and barrels on.

"Man, Casey wanted to pretend to be my wife for a few nights. A man's got needs," he grins like his mistress playing dress up in his wife's wedding dress isn't a mortal sin that deserves eternal damnation.

"You're a charming sociopath," I sigh, and he only smiles harder. "I'll give you that."

"I learned it from my Daddy," Adrian laughs as he hops off the bench.

He tosses his ice bag into the trashcan beside the door and I stare at him as he rolls his shoulders back and reaches out to clap me on the shoulder.

"Let's go, man! It's almost lunchtime!"

I stare after him for a moment as he walks through the door.

I pretend I'm not imagining his blood evacuating his arteries when he turns back and waves for me to follow.

18

SAGE

The warehouse still smells like paint days after our heist went down.

I've been pacing it every day, burdened with the weight and fear that any second now, my father is going to walk through the doors, somehow knowing it was his own daughter who took from him.

The pallets lay untouched still, locked down behind dozens of security measures, one floor down where no one will find them.

But today is the day.

Dallas and I have it all planned out.

We've been waiting, feeding false information to the other guys just to see if anything slips from loose lips that don't know how to stick together. They haven't failed or slipped up yet, and Dallas assured me they could be trusted, but still, we agreed that we would need to keep giving out false leads until everything calms down.

My father has been frantic.

Four of his men are dead, and while I didn't shoot them, my chest still burned as I lit up the bloodstained clothes in the barrel in the backyard.

It's a heavy burden to carry, being the one who gives the kill order.

We've been monitoring Andrew's movements.

He's been tailing me, and yet, I've had Peter tailing him even more viciously.

It's happened so fast that I didn't even realize it. Somehow, I've become just as venomous as the men I want to take from.

I don't want to be like them, but you reap what you sow. There's no way for me to stay innocent when the blood has saturated well past my wrists.

For now, I try and fail to wash them clean.

No matter how much I scrub, the knowledge that their deaths are on my hands makes my future feel like it's dimming right before my eyes.

I told Dallas that I needed to speak to him today without the others present.

My personal office at the warehouse is soundproof and secure, but I still can't help but feel like someone is listening. This time, what I have to admit out loud is the least damning thing I've done, and yet it feels like it's heavier than anything else I've owned up to.

"I think we have a problem."

The words come out quieter than I intend for them to, but Dallas hears them all the same.

He knows how to read my cracks by now, and this one has been growing deeper with each passing day.

"Spill it." He leans back in the chair and watches me with that same patience I wanted when we first spoke in my home office.

"It's... it's Adrian," I admit, and I feel my cheeks warm when I say his name. "He's... he's been calling me again."

"Did you answer?" Dallas asks.

"Yeah," I solemnly nod. "Yeah, I did."

"And?"

"And... we've got a problem."

"Spit it out, Sage," Dallas spits the words out, crossing his arms. We've been getting more comfortable around each other these past few weeks, but it's still odd for him to talk to me so informally. He's the only one that could probably get away with it.

"Adrian is... he's different," I whisper.

"How so?"

"Just-just *different*, Dallas," I breathe out. I lean forward and prop my elbows on the desk so I can rub my temples. "He called me a few days ago and apologized to me. He said he fucked up, and that he is learning and working on himself. He... he said he quit drinking and that he's been working out and focusing on being a better person. And that he wants to work on us."

"Do you believe him?"

"It's stupid, isn't it?" I whisper back, even though the hope still simmers in my chest. I've answered two of Adrian's calls since the first one, and he did sound different. He sounded almost optimistic. Like he wanted to be better. Like he wanted to come home to help me.

"I wouldn't necessarily say stupid," Dallas mutters, but it's not very convincing. "It's certainly not expected. Do you think his father put him up to it?"

"I don't know," I admit, leaning back again. Dallas cocks his head to the side like he's trying to sift through all of the potential outcomes that this could bloom into. "He seems like he's sincere. But I don't think I can trust him. I didn't... I wasn't necessarily forthcoming about it before, but Adrian was having an affair when he left. He doesn't know that I know, but he alluded to it when we spoke. I know we weren't close before and I know this marriage wasn't our decision, but it still hurt," I whisper, and I have to look away from him to hide just how much.

"I don't really actually fucking like your husband," Dallas grits his teeth, and I keep my eyes focused on my hands to avoid the look on his face. "No offense, Sage, but he's not really screaming husband material," Dallas sighs like it pains him. "But it could work in our favor."

"I-Dallas, I don't really want to just use my husband," I push down the shudder at calling him my husband again. "We can use him, yes, but I don't think I'll ever fully trust Adrian. He's told me to stay away from his father and to keep guards with me. I think... I think he knows something he isn't telling me, but he doesn't want to have the conversation over the phone. He almost sounds like he's trying to get out from underneath his father's boot, but I just don't see the Adrian I know as being capable."

"What does your gut say?" Dallas asks, and my eyebrows knit together in contemplation. "Come on, Sage," he prompts me further. "You have a strong gut, and you're in charge. What do your instincts say?"

"My instincts," I whisper and cut my eyes back to his, unsure if I even want to say it out loud. "My instincts tell me that if he's being honest and if he means what he says... then we could build this together. We could work together to put an end to all of this. But... this is a war, Dallas."

I can tell he doesn't get what I'm saying, and I knew he wouldn't because I've never told anyone this before.

"Adrian's father killed my mother," I quietly tell him, and he takes a deep breath as he watches me work through my thoughts. "I don't know if he knows, and I don't know if he even cares. But his father killed my mother. And what's worse... is that my father knows, and he never did a damn thing to avenge her. And I know... I know that this isn't about revenge. This isn't about getting even. But it's gone on too long. Both of these men are evil, Dallas. They're evil, and nobody is ever going to stop them. They have haunted this city since before I was born, and they'll continue to do so unless they're stopped."

I have to take another steadying breath to keep my voice from shaking, but I can tell that my words have gotten to Dallas. I can tell that he's on my side and in my corner.

"This is a war of attrition, Dallas. I plan to eat away at them until there's nothing left to nip at. I've been sharpening my teeth for my entire life, and I'm tired of waiting. I want to end them. Both his father and mine. And the truth of the matter is that I'm going to do it whether he's with me or not. It was always the plan."

"What do you mean it was always the plan?" Dallas rasps, and I can see a thousand lifetimes of worry in his eyes.

"My father arranged this marriage because he wanted me to get secrets. He sent me here to use me as a weapon. To kill Adrian. And I planned to. I really did plan to, Dallas," I admit shakily, but then I slowly shake my head. "But if Adrian is redeemable... if he's moldable... I don't know if I can go through with it. The Adrian I've been speaking to doesn't sound like the old Adrian. Not at all. And I just-I just don't know if he's that person anymore. I can't trust him completely, but I've started to wonder if he's even the Adrian that I once knew."

"Sage, he can't possibly have changed that much in only four months," Dallas pushes back, but I can tell he's conflicted too. "I get that he's still young, and I get that he isn't always awful, but let's look at this realistically," he splays his hand wide on my desk and thinks for a moment. I can tell he's trying not to hurt my feelings.

"Just say it," I whisper.

"Adrian is an alcoholic and a drug addict, Sage."

It stings.

God, does it sting to hear it.

"You and I both know it. These people," he shakes his head and gestures towards the door. "These men are not going to follow someone that they don't respect or trust. Adrian's an addict, and we both know he isn't stable. He may be doing well over there, and he may claim he's trying, but this environment is deteriorating to him. It keeps him crippled because he has no will. He has no self-control when the coke and liquor is dangled in front of him. I understand you, Sage."

I close my eyes tight because all of this makes my heart ache terribly and I'm not sure I can hear much more.

I know that killing Adrian would be the most logical path to take, but I don't know if I could do it.

I don't think I can if he's a new man when he comes home.

I don't love him, but I won't become like his father. I won't just eliminate those that wrong me.

I won't become a monster.

"Sage, look at me."

I slowly open my eyes and meet Dallas' gaze from across the desk.

"I understand you, and I get it. We still don't know each other well, but I'd like to think we have an understanding of each other's character. You and Adrian don't love each other. I know that. But you took vows. For better or worse. And Adrian's been at his worst for a long time. You want him to be better, and that's great. That's wonderful. But don't lose yourself trying to craft him into something palatable. Do you get what I'm saying?"

"Yeah," I whisper.

"Trust your gut, Sage," he tells me earnestly, and I nod my head in understanding. Trust my gut. That's what I've always done. That's how I've always survived. Now I just need to see if I can survive my husband.

Time will realign.

It always does.

"Trust your gut. But remember what kind of man Adrian is. Changed or not, he will always be a Hart, and that means he can never truly be trusted. Just because he doesn't have a spine doesn't mean he's harmless. You can train him to be obedient, but even obedient dogs can be dangerous."

How fitting.

I once thought of Adrian as a dog, too.

I thought I was conditioning him. I thought I was training him.

And all it got me was the burn of betrayal when I learned of his wandering hands.

"I know it's hard to swallow, and I'm not telling you to abandon your morals. Just use your head. Think smart. If it feels wrong, then trust your gut. Don't let him waltz back in here and take what you're working so hard on. Make him work for your forgiveness, and make him work for his place in your business. He's not his father, but he isn't in charge, either. Make sure he remembers that."

My shoulders finally loosen after my talk with Dallas.

He's right.

I know he is.

But I still don't know which direction I plan to take.

It will all depend on if Adrian keeps his word.

For now, we have business to attend to.

Dallas follows me down the long hallways until we reach the elevator.

It doesn't have a down button, but it has a key code that only he and I currently have access to.

I type it in, and the arrow flashes down instead of up.

I turn my head and look at Dallas, and he's the perfect picture of ease.

One day, I hope I can master that same look of calm indifference.

For now, I'll let him do it for me.

The guys laid it out nicely.

It's clean and cataloged by number and type.

But God damn it all, we hit the jackpot.

"This is... this is just fucking insane," I murmur as I hesitantly lift my hand to run it along the first pallet.

The foam almost feels poisonous to touch, and I don't even hide that my breathing has sped up.

It's stacked high, foam boards and plastic wrap keeping it all tight together, like an assassin's birthday present just waiting to be unleashed on the world.

"We're going to wipe the serial numbers, grind them down so we can use them ourselves or redistribute," Dallas calls out from behind me, and I don't even turn to look at him, too much in awe at what I'm looking at.

The pallet is slammed full of guns. Pistols, rifles, you name it and it's there. The metal gleams under the overhead lights, like it knows it's a shiny new toy meant to cause trouble.

But that's not as impressive as the three stacked pallets of cash.

More money than I've ever seen printed. It's piled high, shrink wrapped and menacing.

My hands tremble when I reach out to run my fingertips across their surface.

"How much?" I whisper, and Dallas's boots scuff on the hard flooring as he steps up beside me.

"We're estimating at least ten million," he answers, and my head snaps to the side so fast that it cracks. "You're in the big leagues now, Sage," he tells me, and now I understand.

Now I understand what it means to feel powerful.

To have money like this at your disposal.

To want for nothing.

I stagger back like the green paper burns my palms.

"See to it that this money is cleaned," I practically whisper the order. "I don't want anything tying it back to my father."

"I'll see that it's done," Dallas agrees at once. "What do you want to do with it?"

"I-this is a lot of fucking money," I force out, looking at him helplessly.

"Yeah, no shit, Sage," he deadpans and then reaches up to pinch the bridge of his nose.

"Don't sass me, Dallas, I'm freaking out a little here," I huff and throw my hands up in the air, and this time there's no mistaking the chuckle he lets out. Of course, this is the time he decided to show he has a sense of humor! "Men are so fucking rude," I mumble, and he outright laughs at that.

"Oh, shut up! You give me an idea for it then! I've never seen this much money in my entire life! Forgive me for not knowing what to say!"

"Alright, alright," he relents finally, still chuckling under his breath. "How about you give the guys a small cut for helping out. Money keeps mouths closed."

"How much? A million?" I ask.

"A mil-Sage, a million?! Why the fuck would you give away a million dollars to each of them?"

"I don't fucking know, okay! One of them almost got shot and they literally had to kill people! I don't know how much shit like that costs!"

"Oh my God," Dallas groans and rubs his temples. "Okay, dial it down," he points at the money and then at me. "We need to have a crash course in criminal empires because we can't have you just handing out money. 200k will suffice. How about this? We can flip the guns to our guys, keep the rest as back stock. I also want to sneak some into your house. I doubt they're that stupid, but I want you to have some in case anyone ever breaks in. We can launder the cash through the HOA programs and fake a security upgrade, so no one catches on. We'll keep the paperwork clean and make sure no one comes snooping. Then we need to cut a payment to the cops we used for the job. After that, the rest needs to go into your offshore account."

"Dallas, I can't just put this much cash-"

"I know a guy for that, Sage," Dallas cuts me off. "I can meet him and have him wire the money to your accounts. He owes me a huge favor anyways, and I've been dealing with him for years. He won't care where we got it. Just that he gets a cut."

"Okay," I rapidly nod, trying to cover all of our bases. Dallas' reassurance makes me feel a little better, but my heart is still beating hard enough I feel it in my throat.

"Okay," I repeat, finally calming down. "We'll move the guns to the south bay tonight. Wait until it's dark and take the guys with you. There's no cameras but make sure no one sees you. And then we'll do what you just said. My father is freaking out. We need to keep him that way. He'll likely suspect that Andrew had a hand in this, and that's exactly what we want him to think. He can't know we have it, so we need to keep this as quiet as possible. We'll work on clearing the serials on the guns this week, and then we need to keep our men armed at all times."

"I think that's the ideal plan," Dallas nods. "I can keep you updated while we work it all out, but don't say anything over the phone or text. Keep it in person like this. We're watching both Andrew and your father, but fingers are flying with accusations, so we need to lay low and keep moving on like nothing is going on. Alright?"

"Alright," I nod a few times and Dallas finally sighs.

"Alright," he agrees finally. "Now, go home. Cook some dinner and eat. Play it cool. It's Friday, so I better not see you at this office until Monday. I'll keep checking in and you keep laying low."

"Okay," I sigh, long and exhausted. "Just keep me updated."

Dallas nods and I turn on my heel to head back towards the elevator.

But right when I enter and scan my key card, Dallas turns back to look at me.

"Remember what I said, Sage," he calls out. "Trust your gut. If you decide to trust him, then trust him, but lay down the law. Understand?"

"Understood," I call back.

The elevator dings and the doors start sliding shut.

I hold Dallas' gaze until they fully close.

19

SAGE

By the time I finally changed out of my work clothes and pulled on something warmer, the entire house smelled like lemon, butter, and thyme.

I was mentally exhausted by the time I walked in the door, but I still needed to eat and maintain my calm composure.

I set the chicken back into the skillet to finish, breathing in the savory lemon sauce swirling around the pan, and forced myself to function like normal. One deep breath in and an even longer one out.

I never realized how draining it was balancing a double life on the tip of my finger. Everything felt like a heavy burden to carry lately, no matter how small the task was.

Cooking at least gave me some sort of relaxation. It was the one thing my mother used to let me help with before she met her untimely death at the hands of Andrew Hart.

I can remember the purple stepstool that she used to drag into the kitchen so I could see above the countertop. The smell of her cooking was always better than mine, richer and warmer. If she were still here with me now, the silence might not be so full of my screaming thoughts.

It should have been a calm and easy night; one wrapped in quiet cooking and maybe a glass of wine.

But Dallas' words were still swirling in the back of my mind just like the sauce in my pan.

We'd finished cataloging all of the pallets and getting them separated up. The contingency plans were in place, and no secrets had slipped out yet. The money was stashed away.

Everything was fine.

So why does it feel like I'm still drowning with worry?

I poke my fork into the sweet potato that I just pulled from the oven, and it slips right through. The broccoli is all steamed up and seasoned, and my wine glass is full.

If anyone looked at the cameras, this would just look like another night of domestic bliss for me. A nice, long dinner followed by a peaceful night of rest.

Dallas had coached me to keep my cool, to keep my head on straight, and I'm trying. I'm trying so hard, but the inner turmoil has been taking its toll on me for days, and I feel like I'm spiraling out of control.

I try not to think of the blood that wasn't actually mine. I try not to think of the four bodies that the earth is currently draining dry as they rot away. I try not to think of the bloody clothes that I burned up in the backyard. All because I told men to point and shoot instead of ask questions.

Most of all, I try not to think about the phone calls from my husband, who suddenly sounds like a man I could actually stand to be in a room with.

The wine in my glass is crimson and dark, sweet like temptation and heavy on my tongue.

It reminds me a little too much of the blood staining my hands.

It leaves a wet ring on the marble and I keep moving it to a new spot like it can erase the evidence of what I've done.

I take a few bites of my chicken, but it tastes like iron in the back of my throat.

Bloody.

All the time.

Everything.

Just covered in blood.

I take a deep breath and will the thoughts out of my head, but none of them will leave.

I promised myself I wouldn't.

I promised I would leave it alone.

He told me he couldn't talk, that there's no special privileges where he's stationed. Like the rules were something he suddenly actually followed. But all night, my mind keeps reaching for something to hold, and everything keeps slipping straight through my fingers like smoke.

I dry my hands on the dish towel next to me and then reach for my phone.

It feels like a loaded gun in my hand, and I worry that I'm about to be covered in even more blood – this time my own.

I glance at the security camera above the pantry.

Is he watching?

Does he wonder what I'm doing? Does he care?

Does he see me living my mundane life without him and plan to adapt to me?

I can't stand the not knowing.

I know he's told me over and over again throughout our last few phone calls, but I need to hear it again.

I need to hear the sincerity in his voice when he promises to give himself to me.

I can't stand one more minute without hearing it.

My fingers tremble when I unlock my screen and scroll until I find my contacts icon.

Tapping the button feels like pulling the trigger, but I press it and ignore the panic that flares in my chest when it immediately filters through to the voicemail box.

That felt worse than getting shot.

I knew this would happen.

I knew.

He told me he couldn't talk, and I know he's not on vacation. He has a job to do there, an important one, and there's more pressing things to focus on than nagging wives.

Act normal, Sage. Act normal. Put the fucking phone down.

I dial again.

This time it rings twice before the line connects, and I sit up straight on the barstool, clutching the phone like it was a lifeline.

I barely hear the sound of breath over the voices in the background.

Is he at a party? Is that what this is? Is he back to his old ways already? Is that why he didn't want me to call?

"Hello?" His voice sounds breathless enough that I imagine he snatched it up as soon as he saw it ringing.

There's a lot of static in the background and a handful of male voices barking out instructions and following up with some laughter.

"Adrian?" I ask, and I hate how soft it comes out. The rolling nerves in my stomach make me feel sick.

There was a last-second sharpness in his hesitation, like he needed to get a hold on himself before he could respond to me.

"What are you doing man? We're in the middle of a briefing."

"Family emergency," the rough voice on the line breathes into the receiver, and I can tell he's annoyed. I can also tell that isn't a voice I've ever heard from Adrian before.

"Sorry," I whisper. "I know you told me not to call-"

"No, it's okay," he responds. "Hang on-" There's some muffled scraping as another man starts droning on and on about some kind of exit path and radio signal, and I strain to pick up on anything that might sound out of order.

There's a chorus of groans and a few frustrated men barking for the others to pay attention, but I hear a door creak on its hinges, and then it falls a little more quiet.

"Sage," Adrian breathes into the phone, and it's a lot warmer than the tone he had when he spoke to those men. "Hey."

"Hey," I whisper back. "I'm-I'm really sorry. I know you told me you couldn't talk and I called anyway."

"No," he says immediately, a little harsh sounding before he quiets down into something softer. "No, it's okay. I want to talk to you."

"It didn't sound okay," I respond after a moment, glancing up at the camera in the corner. "I don't want you to get in trouble."

"I'll live," Adrian chuckles darkly. The sound alone made my chest tighten and I looked down at my wine glass before reaching out to take a big swallow. "But why did you call?" He asks in a softer voice, gentle, like he might scare me off if he pushes too hard. "It's usually the other way around with me calling you."

I stare down at my new marble countertop, all that gold splitting into the black like a map leading to a version of me that didn't know how to merge together with this current version. "I keep thinking," I whisper into the phone, like saying it out loud will make it real. "And I hate the things I think about."

"And what's on your mind, Sage?"

I hate the way my heart races when he says my name. Like it holds weight and relevance just by existing.

"You. Us." I force the words out through the tightness in my throat. "About the things you said when we last spoke, and the-just the way things seem to be changing. Like you're-you're just..." I trail off in frustration, clenching my jaw to keep from spilling all of my thoughts onto the countertop.

I don't know why I feel this way. Why I can't just push it down and let things happen as they've been happening. To let time work it all out for me. To realign what's meant to be cemented in my future.

He doesn't get aggravated or snappy with me like the old Adrian would have. He doesn't rush to tell me to stop beating around the bush. He doesn't try to fill my silence with anger.

"Sage," he says in a low voice, a little rough around the edges but still cautious. "Ask me what you want to ask."

I don't mean to ask it.

It wasn't even the question most present on my mind.

But it's the one I spit out as soon as he finished speaking.

"Why did you cheat on me, Adrian?"

This time the silence doesn't get filled.

Time feels like it stands still.

The old Adrian would have laughed at me. He would have pushed the question to the side or thrown it back in my face just to hurt me for questioning him. This time he doesn't do that.

This time, he seems just as shocked at my question as I am.

"Before you left, I-" my words get a little choked up and I have to take a deep breath to calm myself down. "I know you didn't want to marry me, and I know things weren't great, but I thought we were trying to adapt to each other. I thought we were-I thought we were at least trying to be in each other's corner."

I hate the way my voice breaks on some words. How I sound so defeated when it was me who brought the topic up in the first place.

When he finally answers me, it comes out much smaller than I expect it to.

"I was a coward, Sage," he quietly tells me, and I suck in a ragged breath at his admission. "I was-" There's a long sigh on the other end and what sounds like some rustling as Adrian sits down. "I was a fucking junkie," he says it in nearly a whisper, like it pains him to say it. "I was a spoiled brat, just like you said. I don't have a solid answer for why I did the things I did. There's no easy way to say it and no grand excuses, Sage. I was just a piece of shit that didn't have my head on straight. I didn't even have it on at all, honestly."

I reach up to rub my eyes with the heels of my hands, and stars bloom behind my eyelids, proving my intuition that a migraine is coming on from all this overthinking and worrying.

"I don't want to hurt you in any way, Sage," he continues, and the rasp in his voice cuts straight through me this time. I feel my eyes watering before I can tell them not to. "I know I've done a lot of damage, and I'll own up to it. I know I was cruel and disregarded you and our marriage, and I'll be honest; I didn't realize how much damage I was doing until I got out here. I'm learning a lot, and I get it now, how important having someone in your corner is. How important you are. I know I did something that broke your heart, even if it was never truly mine to break. But I want to fix it."

I lean over onto the counter and rest my face on my forearms, trying to breathe through the tightness in my lungs.

"I don't know how to believe you," I whisper back. The confession hung for a second too long, enough for me to second-guess saying it. But Adrian didn't let it linger for too long.

"I can't prove it overnight, Sage. I'll have to show you with my actions. I don't expect you to just trust me right now, but I can work to earn it. I can promise to be honest with you, and we can work together to find a level of trust that feels solid."

The heat pooling behind my eyes made me feel weak. I loathed letting him see me be vulnerable in any way, but this conversation needed to happen. This honesty needed to happen.

"You were the first person that showed me any kind of push back," he murmurs softly. "The first person who treated me like I wasn't some helpless head-case. I hated you for it, Sage, so I hid from you and I kept doing what I did before you came into my life. And I thought I could get away with it, but it took a toll on me, too. I didn't realize I was digging myself into a hole I might not be able to climb out of."

A traitorous tear slips cold and fast down my cheek, and I hastily reach up to wipe it away, not wanting there to be any evidence the words affect me.

"I'm not just a project, Adrian; we're *married*," I stress, and he immediately jumps in to soothe me.

"I know, Sage. I know," he answers quickly, like he needed me to hear the truth behind it. "You're the person I made vows to. Not my father. Not the money. Not myself. You're the person I made them to."

"Vows," I whisper, and my hands tighten against the marble edge before I force myself to relax them again. "They were made for all the wrong reasons, Adrian."

"They were," he softly confirms, and I close my eyes tightly to keep any more tears from spilling over. "But we can remake them, can't we? We can redo things. Make them for the right reasons this time."

"Do you even want to be married to me?" I whisper, and Adrian doesn't hesitate.

There's not even a breath before his answer comes, firm and unyielding.

"Yes."

My breath catches at the weight the word carries.

It's one word, and yet it feels like something damning and healing all at once.

A word that makes the anger in my chest evaporate in an instant.

That warm feeling I experienced whenever he said my name had been drowning, and now it rose up like it finally found a pair of lungs.

"I haven't touched a drink since I left, Sage. Not one," he tells me without hesitation. "Haven't touched a line. I've been eating everything they give us regardless of how fucking disgusting it is. I sleep when they make me. I work out until my hands shake. I hate it and I love it, but it's making me better," he tries to reassure me. "I don't know who I am right now, but I know I'm better than I was, and I know by the time I make it back to you, I'll be even better than I am right now."

He swallowed so thickly that I could hear it, and I braced myself for whatever was about to fall from his lips.

"I think about you a lot. Mostly in stupid ways. Whether you're skipping breakfast still or if you're sleeping on your side of the bed or mine. Whether you'll let me in the house when I'm finally out of this shit box of sand."

That draws a small, breathy laugh despite how wobbly my emotions feel, and I can hear the warmth in his words when he speaks again.

"I like that sound," he softly tells me, and my heart kicks into overdrive at the gentle affection I can hear in his voice. "I'd like to hear it again some time."

"When will you be able to call again?" I ask in a small voice, and I hate that it sounds needy.

But perhaps I do need him.

Perhaps, being on my own is what's making me crazy. Maybe I need Adrian here to scream at so I can feel like myself again.

"Soon," he answers, and I can practically see that smug smile that I always want to knock off of his face forming. "I can't promise when. There's a mission coming up soon. If it goes the way they think then I may be able to talk again soon. If not, it may be a few days."

The cold springs from the center of my chest, spreading into my limbs until my fingertips are shaking. "Something dangerous?" I ask. It's a stupid question, of course. Everything the military does seems to be dangerous. And I know he can't tell me.

"Yeah," he answers quietly, and I can tell that he wants to say more. "I can't," he whispers. "I'm sorry, Sage, but I can't say more about it."

"Okay," I whisper, and then I force myself to take a deep breath.

It flashes through my mind. For just a moment, I try to imagine being one of those wives, the ones who sob on their front porch as uniformed officers deliver news of their spouse's demise.

Just yesterday, my sobs would have been ones of relief, but now I'm not so sure.

"Just don't fucking die or anything, because I'm already too stressed to plan a funeral on top of everything, and caskets are expensive," I huff, and Adrian's returned laughter is nearly a groan.

"Yes, ma'am, I'll try not to inconvenience you," he deadpans, and my lips pull into a smile against my will. "I have to go, baby. They'll come looking if I don't."

Baby.

That's new.

"Okay," I murmur. "I'll talk to you later?" I ask, and he hums into the receiver, low and soothing.

"I'll call as soon as I can," he promises. "Goodnight, Sage."

"Goodnight," I whisper back.

I stare at the phone until the screen times out and finally goes dark.

My own reflection looks like it's mocking me.

It's almost a version of me that I almost can't stand. Someone weak and reliant. Someone who gives in and trusts too easily.

But maybe this version of Adrian is one that I *can* rely on.

Maybe this version of Adrian is one that I can trust.

I replay our conversation over and over again in my head while I clean up the kitchen. If anyone looks at the cameras, they'll probably be able to tell how much my conversation with Adrian settled my frantic heart.

And as much as I hate to admit it, it did settle my heart.

When I crawl into bed, the tv playing in the background muffles the quiet of the room, but it can't muffle the thoughts in my head.

I close my eyes and try not to imagine a man with my husband's name but a stranger's voice.

ELLISON

The briefing ends without me. They'd find me later like they always do.

I made sure the room was empty before I finished my conversation with Sage.

Sage.

My sweet darling wife.

I'd told the guys I was talking to family, as if I had any left. Like I hadn't spent a lifetime without one and recently found it in the shape of a woman who might put a bullet between my eyes when she finds out I'm not the man who put that ring on her finger.

I didn't move when I hung up the phone, not for a long while.

I'd stared at my right hand and watched the tendons flex under my skin, remembering the way that hers had shaken where she rested them on the countertop three thousand miles away from me.

I rolled my neck and shoulders and brought the phone back up.

My reflection stared at me through the dimmed black glass.

My face.

Not his.

Taller by just a touch. Shoulders cut harder by work instead of money. Nose a little rougher from dealing with nineteen-year-old me finding out I had a decent right hook. Eyes a little darker, a little grey.

No camera in the world could convince a man who raised Adrian.

But a screen? A distance? Some hope?

I thought of Sage in that kitchen. I thought of the way she had said *vows* like it was sharp on her tongue.

Training taught me to keep the people you use at arm's length. You don't reach. You don't pull things closer. That's how things get messy and people get hurt.

But I needed to bring Andrew Hart closer.

I needed to step into his world if I wanted to have Sage. If I wanted to keep her.

I straighten myself up when I hear boots coming down the hall.

The door swings open and one of the guys peeks their head in, eyebrows waggling. "Done with your crises, loverboy?"

"Bite me," I throw back without any heat.

"Ready? Looks like we'll be getting some action. We're on deck tomorrow morning for recon," he grins, and I slap him on the shoulder as I step past.

This may be my only opportunity coming up.

Adrian's my mark, but I think of the first time I heard Andrew Hart order his son to kill her.

To kill Sage.

The woman that belongs to me.

I think of the way Sage whispered for me not to die.

And I know that soon... very soon, Adrian will cease to exist, and Andrew will be my next target.

If there's one thing that's certain, it's that bodies tend to drop around me like sand in an hourglass, and there's two more about to fall.

20

SAGE

The house feels awfully quiet tonight.

Quiet like a calm before a storm.

Like something is waiting to strike at me the very second I turn my head.

I jerk awake in the middle of the night, restless and heavy-eyed.

There's a storm raging outside. I thought it was all just a dream, but the lightning cuts through the break in the curtains, and the thunder shakes the windowpanes, rattling my bones along with them.

The first thing I do is reach for my phone. There's nothing waiting. No messages. No missed calls. Just an empty screen that reflects the quiet throughout the room.

I try to go back to sleep, but something urges me not to yet.

I felt this way before I slept too. I'd laid there staring into the blacked-out room cursing the very day that coffee was invented, and my father for introducing it to me. Maybe if I dialed back the three cups a day I've been averaging, then I could get a decent night's rest.

I grab my phone before I can think better of it and scroll through my call history.

I'd cut my own throat before I admit that I felt like a lovesick teenager, but my heart has been aching the past few days.

I spoke to Adrian three days ago, and the weight of his words carried with me all throughout the week.

I thought he would lie to me; that he'd try to cover up his mistress and make excuses for my cold-shoulder dismissals and his wandering eyes.

But he didn't.

He told me exactly what I already knew. That he did it and he fucked up.

Maybe I shouldn't have, and maybe he didn't deserve it, but something almost like regret had seeped into my heart from the very second that he'd hung up the phone.

Part of me felt like this was all Adrian and his father's fault.

But I know I'm not entirely innocent.

I've been cruel, too.

Maybe not cruel enough to accept any blame for him stepping out of our marriage. But I *have* been cruel.

I've said hurtful things, and I've tried to force Adrian into a mold that I wanted filled. I can't help but wonder if maybe I should have just encouraged him and let him fill his own shoes.

It's not like I'm falling in love with him. I just want him to recognize that I'm the lesser of three evils. Between me, my father, and his own, I'm the only one that could ever truly care about Adrian. I'm the only one willing to even try.

I just need him to trust me and prove that I can trust him in return.

I know I'm not going to be able to sleep anymore tonight, so I get up and clean my kitchen, soaking up the messes from cooking earlier in the night. Wiping down the counters and washing all of the dishes is the repetition that I need to allow my head to empty and just focus on each manual task.

And it seems like my mind finally goes quiet for the first time all week when the screen lights up and my ringtone starts blaring through the quiet, shrill and daring all at once.

My heart almost stops entirely when I glance over at my phone on the edge of the sink.

It feels more dangerous than a hand grenade, like touching it will make me explode into pink mist and cover every surface in this kitchen.

For a second, I *really* can't fucking breathe.

I stare at the name. His name – Adrian, like it might burn a hole straight through the glass and wiring. He's never called me this late before, and he's certainly never tried to do a video call.

My hands tremble as I wipe them on a dish towel and slide my fingertip across the phone to accept the call.

It takes a few seconds for the image to come into focus. The screen flickers like static, fighting through the signal to bring him to me.

And suddenly there he is.

Adrian's sitting on the edge of what looks to be a bunk. The lighting isn't the best, dim and covering the back half of his room in shadow.

His face fills my screen finally, familiar and foreign all at once.

"Sage," he breathes out, smiling in a way that fits him, but somehow doesn't.

I can't find it in me to speak.

I really can't.

Because my brain is screaming at me that something's not right.

He looks different.

Still Adrian, but somehow also not. His jawline is sharper, the baby fat no longer clinging to him. His eyes are the same shape, but they're darker somehow, and I know it's not a trick of the light.

It can't be.

Even his posture is wrong. It's too straight, too rigid. My Adrian was a slouch, lazy and always hunched. I know that for certain because when I get mad, I always yell that he looks like the fucking shrimp from Shark Tale, whiny voice and all.

This Adrian seems far too aware and much too present.

"You look..." I start, and then immediately falter for the right word. How do I say, *you look like you aren't my husband because you fucking aren't,* without sounding like I'm mentally deranged? "Different," I tack on, and then internally cringe because really, Sage, that's all you could come up with?

He laughs softly, and now that my eyes are finally open, I realize that it's not the condescending laugh that I remember. It's close, but it's not the same. This one is lower. Warmer. Like it's meant only for my ears to hear.

"Yeah, this place certainly changes people," he chuckles, rubbing a nervous hand across the back of his neck before he rolls his shoulders. My Adrian does that, too. "You holding up okay? I didn't expect you to answer so late, but figured I'd try."

I nod automatically, like my brain knows I need to react even though my mouth seems to be tangled up with a thousand different questions. My pulse is hammering away beneath my skin, beating my bones into dust with how violent it feels.

He tilts his head slightly, like he's studying me, and then he leans forward a little more, peering into the camera lens like he can see straight through my bullshit excuse before I can even say it. "You look tired," he murmurs.

"So do you," I whisper before I can stop myself. "Don't they let you sleep in that place?" If I can do anything, it's deflect with humor and sarcasm.

Something gentle flashes in his eyes. It's not surprise, but fondness maybe. It makes my stomach twist in a way that's nauseating.

"I miss you, Sage," he says, and it sounds so easy for him. Too easy. Like he's practiced saying it.

I almost drop the phone into the sink.

The words hit me like an arrow that's been searching for a lost target. I hate that they sound so fucking convincing.

While he's still leaning forward, I force myself to focus on the details instead, all of those small things that don't fit into my Adrian box.

His shirt is rolled up at the sleeves, and my Adrian is somewhat pale, a night owl with pasty skin to match. This Adrian is tanner, sun-kissed from time in the desert. There's a faint scar along his wrist that wasn't there before, something jagged that tapers up his thumb. There's a steadiness in his voice every time he opens his mouth.

He's not twitchy, not like my Adrian who seemed distracted by every little noise and movement. My Adrian couldn't sit still for more than ten seconds at a time, and this one is centered and frozen, like a marble statue that belongs on the living room mantel.

Still, I play along. I match his tone and keep up with my questions.

I ask about the weather there and how much time he's spending in the sun. I ask about the food and if they're keeping him well fed. He answers everything easily, even joking about some of the men stationed with him. He laughs every single time I roll my eyes and leans a little closer like he's delighted by the very sight.

For a split second, I almost forget that this man is a stranger. I almost forget that I'm meant to be afraid. That he's an imposter.

He's charismatic and magnetic, each little reaction so genuine that it almost feels real. The fondness that glints in his eyes when I smile almost feels like he means it.

When the laughter finally dies down, there's a stretch of quiet between us that feels like a question and an answer. Like it's loaded.

He stares at me like he's memorizing, like he knows me and yet fears he won't ever get to see me again.

"You're not wearing your ring," he suddenly notices, and my eyes slide down to my bare hand. I hadn't even realized that I'd stopped wearing it.

"I didn't want to damage it," I lie, but I see immediately that he doesn't buy it.

His lips thin out a little into a somewhat saddened smile, but he doesn't lose that affection in his eyes.

"You don't have to lie to me, Sage. I know I fucked up badly. It's okay if you don't want to wear it," he tries to reassure me, but my heart lurches in my chest and I rapidly shake my head.

"No, it's-" I pause and try to calm myself back down, wondering when the shoe will drop and he'll lash out at me like he used to. Only I remember again that this man is not my husband. He won't revert back to Adrian's old behavior because he *isn't* Adrian.

"It's not that," I choke out, and it falls short of convincing.

"What is it then, baby?"

Baby.

There's that fucking word again.

I hate that my breathing speeds up when he says it.

I hate it even more that I can tell he notices it.

"Just-I-Adrian," I whisper, and he leans forward like it'll bring him closer to the answer.

"What's wrong?" He asks in that same soft voice, and I have to swallow back my hesitation.

"I don't like it," I whisper, watching his face for any slip that might show anger.

"The ring?" He asks, and I slowly nod my head.

"What don't you like about it? It was my mother's," he points out, and again, I falter. How does this man know it belonged to Adrian's mother? Unless he is Adrian. But there's no fucking way. No way. I'm not crazy. I'm not one of those women that fall into hysteria after being left alone for too long. I'm not hallucinating.

This man is *not* my husband.

So how on earth does he know things that I've never even heard Adrian speak of myself?

"It was," I murmur back in surprise. My fingers brush along my ring finger on my left hand and I take a deep breath before I drag my eyes back up to meet his. "But it's not me," I whisper. "This was the ring I was told to wear, but it's not me. It doesn't feel like it's mine. It feels like a prop."

Adrian (fake Adrian) stares at me for a moment, his brow furrowing slightly before smoothing back out into something soft, and he nods his head twice. "Then I will take you to get a new one when I'm home."

"What?" I whisper, and his entire body seems to soften at my surprise.

"We'll get one that you love. We'll go together and pick it out when I get home. Is that alright?"

"Yeah, that's... that's perfect," I murmur, and fake Adrian's smile builds slowly, a little lopsided and charming, like he feels accomplished. It's not smug like my Adrian's. This smile is pleased. Genuine instead of practiced and pasted on.

He leans back against the wall and looks me over once, and I start to panic a little at the intensity in his gaze.

"I should probably go," I finally say. "I couldn't sleep before, so I was just up doing some things around the house when you called," I explain.

"Wait," his tone changes into something deeper. Something a little more urgent. "Please don't hang up yet," he pleads, and I freeze at the earnestness in his voice.

He sighs before reaching up to rub a hand down his face. "Look," he rasps, and there's that tone from before that I recognized was off. Now I know why. It's because he isn't Adrian. "I know things weren't good between us before I left. But I meant what I said before, Sage. How I treated you has been weighing heavily on me, and I just-I just need you to know that I'm sorry. I want to be better. I am better. I just need you to try and trust that. I'm truly sorry, Sage."

My eyes sting with unshed tears at the apology.

I know he's not my Adrian, but I needed to hear that he's sorry so badly.

I'm almost willing to accept it as Adrian's truth just to ease the vice grip of bitterness around my heart.

"I want to," I whisper around the tightness in my throat. "I just don't know if I can yet."

"Just let me prove it to you when I get home," he rasps again. "Please, Sage. Just give me a chance to show you who I really am, or at least who I'm becoming." His gaze holds mine through the screen and the sincerity in his eyes is almost frightening.

"Okay," I say, because it's easier than screaming what I really feel to a man who doesn't even truly know the weight of what the Hart family has done to me.

And he smiles... that same slow, dangerous lopsided smile that feels more like a mask than my Adrian, and bids me goodnight.

When the screen goes black, I sit there for a long time staring at my own reflection.

And then I get up and move.

My feet move on autopilot.

The floorboards creak as I step into my office.

I don't bother turning on the light, knowing the cameras will click to life to follow my motion.

The one in my office is meant only to catalog, not to loop feedback straight to Andrew. But it's still a camera all the same.

I yank open the top drawer where the burner phone has been safely hidden.

Dallas picks up on the second ring, his voice heavy from sleep.

"Kill the cameras," I order in a soft voice.

There's a pause. The kind that carries years of tension and too much history.

"What?" He snaps, attention focusing entirely on me finally. All traces of exhaustion are wiped clean. "Sage?" He asks carefully, his voice turning a little more urgent. "What happened?"

"Just do it, Dallas," I snap back. "Now. And get here immediately."

I hear him mutter a curse softly, then the faint sound of keys dragging as he rushes out of his front door. The red light on the camera in the corner goes dead, and my shoulders loosen slightly.

Only minutes later, headlights sweep across the glass panels surrounding the entrance.

Dallas doesn't even knock before he's barreling in. His shirt's half unbuttoned, hair messy from sleep and eyes wild.

"What?" He demands as he sweeps his gaze over me, looking for a physical injury. I know I'm not dressed appropriately for guests, let alone a man in my home, but neither of us are worried about that right now. "What's wrong?" He barks again, stepping forward until he's dropping his chin to look me in the eyes.

"I just spoke to Adrian," I let out a steady breath, hand tight around my cellphone.

"Okay... and?" Dallas deadpans.

I make sure to meet his eyes, keeping my voice steady even though my heart isn't.

"We video called tonight," I whisper.

"Sage, fucking spit it out!" Dallas snaps, and the words tumble out of me in a rush of nerves.

"I don't know how, or why, or even who..." I whisper again, and Dallas' brows knit together.

"But that man was not my husband."

21

SAGE

Dallas stares at me like I've grown a second head. Or a third. Or eighty-seven.

He looks at me like I cracked my skull open falling down the stairs and he's not sure if I'm hallucinating or if he needs to take me to the hospital.

Honestly, with how it feels having to put this into words, he might need to just check me into the psych ward for a lifetime vacation.

His chest is heaving from the adrenaline of racing over here to make sure I was okay, and now he sees that I'm not.

His eyes dart all over my face like he's searching for evidence that I'm joking, that I've finally lost it, that this isn't one more thing to unravel tonight.

"You-" he shakes his head as he trails off, chuckling uncomfortably like he's not even sure how to breach the topic. "Sage, you're not making sense," he finally says, voice stuck somewhere between disbelief and worry. "What do you mean he's not your husband? Who else would he be?"

I press my hand to my chest, trying to keep my breathing even as I stare at him. The storm outside is hammering against the rooftop, and I feel drenched from head to toe. The thunder rolls overhead like it's trying to break through the walls to hear the secrets being shared between us.

"I mean it wasn't him," I whisper. "It looked like him, and it sounded like him, but it wasn't. I know my husband, Dallas, and that man was not my husband."

Dallas runs a shaky hand through his hair, turning to pace for a moment before he covers his mouth with his hand. When he turns back to me, I know he doesn't believe me.

"Sage," he starts delicately. "You've barely slept. You're overworked and overwhelmed. This isn't-"

"Don't patronize me, Dallas!" I snap, voice cracking sharper than the lightning outside. "I know what I saw, and that man is not my goddamn husband!" I yell, and Dallas glances down to my shaking hands before he slowly nods his head.

He exhales through his nose to steady himself and turns back to look at me full on. "Alright. Let's just-let's just slow down here. Rewind and start from the top. Tell me exactly what happened."

I move to the counter and place my hands on the edge before I curl them around the corners until my knuckles ache.

"He video-called me tonight. Out of the blue. Said he didn't think I'd answer but wanted to try. I-I thought I was imagining things at first but... Dallas, he looked wrong. Not-not like sick wrong but like-like he was an entirely different person. His eyes were darker, his posture still and calm, even his-even his voice, Dallas, the way he said my name-it was all wrong. He was too composed, too practiced and too-you told me trust my gut, Dallas. You told me to trust my gut and my gut is telling me that I know what I saw. My Adrian couldn't fake that kind of calm if his life depended on it."

Dallas studies me carefully, crossing his arms like he's trying to rationalize whether what I'm saying is even possible. "It could be the lighting, the connection," he murmurs and then gestures at me. "Hell, it could just be you've spent too much time away, Sage! Sometimes people misconstrue what they see just to-"

"I know what I saw, Dallas!" I slam my palms against the marble and the harsh slap makes him flinch. "You don't understand," I rasp, nearing tears now. I need him to understand. I need him to listen to me. I'm not crazy. I know what I saw.

"You don't understand," I whisper, feeling wetness build behind my eyelids. "He knew things he shouldn't know, Dallas. He mentioned my ring being his mother's-Adrian's mother died when he was seven, Dallas. He barely even remembers her! He's never once said a word about her to me. Not one single fucking word, and this man knew."

That seems to finally land.

Dallas frowns and his shoulders tense up. "Alright," he slowly relents. "Let's say you're right. Let's say it's not Adrian. Then who the hell is it? Because no one else could have access to his chains of contact or know those details. He'd have to either be someone Andrew planted or someone nearby Adrian."

The thunder clashes so loudly above us the lights flicker almost like they're trying to tell us we're right. For a moment, the entire house plunges into darkness before the backup generators kick on and hum to life. Then everything glows a sickly yellow, and I can't help but think this is what I'd look like if you cracked open my chest.

"He said he missed me," I whisper, and Dallas narrows his eyes. "Dallas, he-he says things that are-that aren't normal for a stranger.

He knows things about me and he's-he seems like he-like he actually means it."

Dallas' mouth opens and then shuts again. "Maybe this is just-maybe this is some kind of-"

"Some kind of test?" I finish for him. His eyes tighten as he looks at me. "From Andrew? Or my father? I've thought of that. But why now? Why send me someone better than the real thing? What could it change?"

"Better?" Dallas questions, and I swallow hard.

"He's not like my Adrian," I quietly reveal. "He's-he's kind. Thoughtful. He listens to me and responds passionately, and he looks at me like-like he's in love with me, Dallas. That's not Adrian. This man looks so similar to him that it's scary, but it's not him. It's someone trying to play him."

"But why?" Dallas paces, rubbing at the back of his neck in frustration. "Alright. Let's assume that this man is an imposter. Why? What's the purpose? If he's someone close to Adrian, then he's stationed, what, overseas? How would someone even fake that? And what's the angle? What do they get out of faking it?"

I don't answer right away. I don't dare voice my fear aloud even though I feel it scraping at me, jagged and sharp enough to maim.

"Unless," I finally say, voice trembling with the weight of what could possibly have happened. "Unless he's not stationed at all. Unless Adrian's already dead."

Dallas freezes mid-pace. "Don't," he warns softly, but I see the gears turning behind his eyes. He thinks just like I do, and we both know it's a logical possibility.

"What if Andrew had him killed and replaced? What if that's his way of keeping me compliant and in line?" My words come out rushed and desperate, tumbling over each other in an attempt to rationalize this. "He knows I'd never betray him openly, but if I thought Adrian was still alive then-"

"Then you'd behave," Dallas finishes grimly. "Fuck, Sage." He drags both hands down his face and plants himself at my kitchen island. "You can't just jump to murder and body doubles. I just fucking woke up."

"Then explain it!" I shoot back at him, pointing toward my phone lying helplessly on the counter. "Explain how he knows details that I didn't even pry from Adrian's mouth! Explain how he knows things that were never said, never written, and never even thought about!"

He's silent for a long moment, the thunder filling the gaps between us as his eyes harden and slowly slide back to me. "What if you're not wrong?" He quietly suggests.

"What?" I blink repeatedly like it'll clear the fog of confusion.

Dallas clenches his jaw and pokes his tongue against the inside of his cheek while he thinks. "What if Adrian is gone? What if it's true and this guy is your husband now? Not legally, not by name, but functionally? What if it isn't a trap but an opportunity?"

I stare at him before I start laughing, half in disbelief and half-horrified. "You aren't trying to-to say I should just go along with it, are you?"

"I think," he carefully starts, "that if this man has Andrew fooled, if he's in deep enough to talk to you, to maintain the act, and truly take over Adrian's life, then he can be useful to us. We can find out what he knows, what he wants, and maybe we can finally turn the tables."

For a long moment, all I can hear is the pounding in my head and the echo of thunder outside.

"And if he's dangerous?" I ask, crossing my arms. I can't help but bite down on my bottom lip until I taste blood.

Dallas shrugs, though his eyes are sharp and calculating like they are when he's working. "Then we do what we always do, Sage. We end the fucking problem."

The generator hum is stifling underneath my feet, housed in the basement and working overtime to protect me.

I look down at my phone again and the dark screen shows only my reflection, my wild but tired eyes, something I can't put a name to. Something scared.

"Dallas," I whisper, and I drag my eyes back up to meet his. "What if-" I falter and swallow the thickness in my throat. "What if I end up getting too deep, too?"

"What do you mean, Sage?" Dallas softly asks.

"What if I end up just like him? What if I get too deep in the lie? What if we-if we play along... if we let him fill Adrian's shoes?"

"Get too deep in what way?" He asks, and I crumble under his knowing gaze, lowering my eyes to the countertop.

"I thought Adrian was changing," I whisper. "Dallas, I really-I really thought he was changing. I had hope that he was. I had-I had a plan and a thought to trust him, but it was never him. It was never even him, Dallas," I stress, and Dallas takes a few steps forward and hesitantly reaches out, placing a hand on my shoulder.

It's terrifying and grounding all at once. It shakes just like my own hands.

"Dallas, what happens if this man comes here... this new Adrian, and I end up falling? What if I-what if it's me that gets caught up in the lie?"

"That's not going to happen, Sage. That's not-"

"I've been dreaming of him, Dallas," I whisper the admission. "Every single night since we first spoke on the phone. I don't even know him, and I like him," I feel like the words might strangle me.

"He's everything I wanted Adrian to be, and also everything he's not, Dallas. I know myself. What if he comes here and I fall for it all and it backfires?"

Dallas stares at me for a moment, and then his hand steadies on my shoulder.

His stillness drags me out of my fear, and I look up at him with wide eyes. "What is it?"

Dallas hesitates, eyes conflicted but calculating, and I urge him to tell me. "What is it? Tell me!"

"What if it's you?" He asks and I nearly take a step away from him.

"What?" I rasp, and Dallas hesitates again, but he looks me right in the eyes.

"What if Adrian and Andrew have nothing to do with it? What if it's about you?"

"About me how?" I whisper. The fear is just as strong as the confusion, and now my brain is conjuring up a thousand different questions and what-ifs to work through.

"What if he wants to be Adrian for you?"

"I don't-" I whisper, shaking my head. "Dallas, I don't understand."

"Sage," he breathes out and sits back down at the kitchen island. "What if he is stationed with Adrian? Like you said? What if he is? You told me weeks ago that Adrian broke his phone. What if he never broke it? What if this man is someone stationed with Adrian and stole it?"

"Why would he steal it?" I question, but I see where his train of thought is running off to. It *is* possible.

"Think about it, Sage," he urges. "What if he somehow found out about you? What if he saw you or heard you when you spoke to Adrian? He could have pieced together that he and Adrian look similar enough to trick others. He probably found out what kind of lifestyle

Adrian lives. I mean, fuck, Sage, Adrian doesn't know how to keep his goddamn mouth shut. We both know it's possible that he's been telling all of his secrets. He's probably been bragging about his life and you and his family. What if this man realized that he could live Adrian's life, but it's *you* he wants."

"Me?" I whisper, and Dallas nods.

"That would explain his escalation in contacting you, the urgency about making things right and keeping you happy. If he was trying to convince you, then he probably hasn't convinced Andrew. We could-"

"We could flip him to be loyal to us, and he could work as a double agent for Andrew," I murmur it so quietly that I'm not sure Dallas even hears me.

"Sage, we could flip him and use him. And if-and I do mean *if*, Sage- I won't have you fucking forcing it if it doesn't feel right or he's dangerous to you... but if he's capable of it and you find yourself falling in love with him... then we might have to call him on it."

"Dallas," I whisper miserably, and Dallas cuts me off.

"I know," he nods, lips thinning out. "It's not ideal circumstances. And I don't want to put your safety at risk either, but Sage, you said it yourself. It seems like he *means* it. It seems like he's the better, smarter version of Adrian. What if he can be? We can make him be. And if you happen to fall in love with him, then that's only more reason for him to stay on your side."

My mind is racing like a speed horse on a track and my chest feels tight, but everything that Dallas is saying makes sense. Every bit of it seems like a logical step we could possibly take.

"I know it's not ideal," he repeats softly. "But a man like that protecting you... a military-trained man smart enough to hack phones and cameras and God knows what else... Sage, it might be safer to have him with us than against us."

"I know," I whisper. "I know."

"Then what do you want to do?" Dallas asks, and I don't think before I answer.

I can't.

Because if I do, then I might be tempted to say no.

I might be tempted to reject it.

But if I say yes, my life might turn on its axis.

My world may shift in my favor.

And the man who claims to be my husband might be the one man in my life that keeps his promises to me.

He might be the only one that I don't have to pay to be around me.

He might be the one exception that I can learn to trust.

The one Hart, who isn't a Hart at all.

"I'll do it."

22

ELLISON

I haven't slept.

Not really.

The barracks have a certain hum that doesn't ever seem to shut off.

And now somehow, it's melted into Sage's voice as it cycles through my mind over and over again.

The fluorescent lights buzz just enough to make my skin crawl with paranoia.

I've been sitting on the edge of the bed replaying her face in my head, that quiet suspicion she tried so hard to keep carefully concealed from me.

It didn't work.

She knew.

I don't know how the hell she did, but she did. The way she looked at me through the screen, like she was trying to pinpoint exactly what it was that made me different than her darling Adrian, it told me everything that I feared.

She wasn't charmed by me.

She was measuring me. Like my worth could be summed up by whatever pixels shone the brightest.

Still, she answered every question. She talked to me. She even smiled at me.

That has to count for something.

There was a certain curiosity hidden underneath all of that suspicion and confusion.

I could see it clear as day, even though she tried to mask it.

She wasn't necessarily put off by me, even though I wasn't the version of her husband that she was used to.

She almost seemed like she was *considering* it.

Like she might be able to stomach it, even if I wasn't the man that she married.

She almost seemed like she *liked* it.

I rub my hands over my face, groaning at the ache in my bones from all of this constant pretending. Even just attempting to stand and sit like Adrian for long periods of time was excruciatingly bothersome. Every word, every blink, every goddamn breath that I take has to sound like him, lazy, arrogant, and unintelligent.

I whisper his name under my breath and then mimic it again and again until it feels right coming from my lips.

I've been listening to the videos I secretly recorded from our conversations. I've studied the rhythm and cadence time and time again, and yet, it's so natural to let it go when I speak to Sage. It's so natural just to be myself, because that's the version of Adrian that she likes.

That's the version of Adrian she deserves.

The version she craves.

"Hey, Sage," I murmur and shake my head. That's not quite right.

"Baby, please," I plead, and that's a little bit closer.

"Did you miss me, Sage?" I ask, and that's it.

Well... almost it. It's good enough, all things considered.

I have half a mind just to give up the illusion.

If she already knows and is deciding to play along, is there even a reason to keep up the charade?

Or maybe she thinks she knows, but she isn't completely sure if Adrian and I aren't the same person. Maybe she's testing it.

Wait a fucking minute.

I sit up straighter and stare at the phone in my hand. It always feels like it's about to morph into a rabid beast and take my arm off.

Wait one goddamn second.

It can't be... she doesn't think that I'm a *plant,* does she?

She doesn't think that Andrew Hart sent me after her... right?

Because I would *never.* I would never fucking work with that piece of shit. I'd never fucking hurt her. Not a single strand of hair on her head would ever feel wronged by me.

Andrew Hart, my puppet master? No, I chuckle internally, shaking my head. No... over my dead body. I'd rather burn in hell than give in to one single command from his mouth.

The phone screen lights up in my palm before I can consider how to rectify the situation.

And of course, I just can't catch a fucking break.

If Sage wasn't waiting for me back home, I'd consider just blowing my brains out to rid myself of having to deal with the entire Hart bloodline.

Daddy shines up at me, like a promise of damnation, and I shouldn't answer. I really shouldn't answer. If I couldn't fool Sage, how am I supposed to fool Daddy Dearest?

Andrew fucking Hart.

My stomach twists into knots and I exhale through it, forcing my jaw to relax and the tension in my chest to loosen.

I shouldn't answer, and yet this opportunity is just too good to let pass by.

I hit accept before I can spiral over it.

"Hey, Daddy," I say, letting the words drag out just long enough to sound bored, just like Adrian would.

"Adrian," Andrew's voice bleeds through, sharp as barbed wire as it forces into my ear. "You sound like hell."

"Haven't been getting much sleep," I easily lie. "We've got a big op coming up and I'm running on fumes."

He lets out a sound halfway between a scoff and a laugh, like he can't believe I'm finding something difficult. Of course I am, because he's spoiled me for my entire life. He thinks me incapable.

"That why your voice sounds different? You finally hit puberty out there?"

"It's just fatigue," I answer, gritting my teeth to keep from saying what I want to say. "Been yelling over all this machinery all week."

There's a pause that drags on long enough to make me uncomfortable, and then he goes and fucks it all up.

"So. Have you decided what to do about that stupid bitch of a wife yet?"

My pulse detonates in my veins.

"Excuse me?" I rasp, and it almost feels like I'm choking on the words. Heat scrapes up my throat, and my heartbeat starts to race.

Andrew's tone drips with that same smug amusement that his son gets, like a petulant child that's never been told no.

"Don't play dumb, son. You think I don't know she's been poking around? She's a liability. You should have gotten rid of her already. Her own father is losing credibility with his product going missing. We don't want to align ourselves with scum like that. How do you want me to dispose of her?"

Something in me snaps.

I can't say what it is.

Maybe my blood vessels.

Maybe my fingers from how tightly I'm gripping the phone.

Maybe my sanity.

"Watch your fucking mouth," I practically snarl. It's the most vicious I think I've ever sounded in my life, but he's deserving of my wrath.

It feels like everything goes still.

"What did you just say to me?" The words are said so low, so disbelieving, that I almost laugh in his face.

"I said, *watch your fucking mouth,*" I repeat. I bite down on my tongue to keep from saying more, and the taste of iron fills my mouth.

"You forget who you're talking to, boy-"

"I'm talking to a man so obsessed with hearing himself talk that he can't see the difference between control and a rotting limb," I snap. The words come out before I can stop them, and he's stunned to silence. "I'm sitting in a goddamn war zone, about to walk into something that might kill me, and you're worried about whether my wife is on a fucking leash?"

Andrew's tone drops into something deadly. "How dare you speak to me like that-"

"Maybe you'll get your wish," I cut him off again. "Maybe I'll die out here and you won't have to deal with me anymore. Or maybe I come home broken. But if I do come home, things are about to fucking change, *Daddy.*" I spit the name at him. "Starting with how you speak about my wife."

There's nothing on the line but static and heavy, venomous breathing.

"You've lost your goddamn mind," he finally says.

And then the line goes dead.

I stare at the screen for a long time, watching my reflection settle back into focus.

My face looks wrong.

I can't remember what it's supposed to look like, but Adrian Hart stares back at me.

"Maybe I have lost it," I murmur to myself.

I don't really have it in me to worry about what catastrophe our little argument will cause later.

The next day, the briefing is a blur of maps, instructions, and barked out orders. I don't even hear half of it.

My mind is still stuck on Sage. On her voice, the way she said my name like she was testing me, the smile that fell on her lips when I made a joke.

Two days left until we get deployed. Two days to decide how far I'm willing to take this lie to get to her.

After the briefing, Adrian finds me near the lockers, chewing gum and grinning in a way that always seems to infuriate me. There's a certain arrogance to him today as he brags to the others about how he "cracked" a fine blonde girl last night at the bar.

"Yo, Gray," he slaps me on the shoulder. "When are you gonna get laid? You're always so uptight!"

"Dude, not all of us want to fuck every woman that moves," Johnny snorts, and Adrian laughs like it's not at his expense.

I don't answer him. I just shove my gear into my bag and drop it on the bench beside us.

"Come on, man," he presses, tugging at my shoulder again. "Let's go blow off some steam!"

"Not in the mood, Hart."

"What? Scared I'll bruise your ego? Come on, let's spar!"

I turn to face him, and he falters slightly at the look on my face.

I can only imagine what he sees in my eyes.

I wonder how apparent the hatred is.

Or if he can even recognize it.

"You really want to test me today?"

"Hell yeah, man," his grin widens.

Fine.

We can test it.

I let him lead me to the mats.

I let him throw the punch like always.

I let him think he knows what he's doing and stands any chance against me.

The first hit I land sends him stumbling backwards.

The second one knocks the wind out of him.

"Jesus, Ellison!" Someone shouts as Adrian stumbles again, clutching at his chest, making a noise that sounds like a wounded animal.

I don't care.

I slam him into the mat so hard that the windowpanes shake. He's gasping for air, blood streaking from his split lip, and the crimson is almost enough to work me up into a frenzy.

I lunge again, and hands grasp at me from all sides.

The others drag me off of him before I can do any serious damage.

My knuckles sting in a way that tells me the blood on them isn't all his.

Adrian wipes his mouth, still swaying on one knee where he glares up at me. "What the fuck is your problem?"

Blood trickles down from my nose and smears across my lips, and I lick it away with my tongue.

Adrian looks ghostly pale, lips trembling and hands shaking.

Pathetic.

He stares up at me like I'm a wolf getting ready to lunge again.

"My problem," I snarl and lick my lips again, "is you. We're about to walk into a mission that could kill us all and you're treating it like a fucking game! You're reckless, careless, and spoiled! You don't respect anyone-not this team, not your life, not even your fucking wife."

The silence after that is deafening.

His mouth opens once, but nothing comes out.

I spit out blood on the mat beside him.

"You can't be trusted," I tell him. "Not with this team or our safety, not with your life, and sure as hell not with hers."

I snatch my bag from the bench and storm out, and the room stays frozen behind me.

By the time I hit the hallway, my pulse is hammering away at my skull.

I lean against the wall, breathing hard, sweat clinging to my sweat-shirt.

The anger doesn't fade any.

It stays right there with me.

My mind is made up.

When I get home... when I make it home, Sage will see.

She'll see *me.*

23

SAGE

Dallas has been sitting across from me for the past hour, tapping the edge of his glass against my desk like the noise alone might shake loose some kind of answer.

I wish it would.

The rain has been relentless this week, and the house feels like it's drowning under constant rainfall and my sorrows.

The windows rattle every time the wind picks up, and I've been on edge with every little noise.

He hasn't said much since I told him my plan, since I said I'd play along.

Not with my father.

Not with Andrew.

With him.

With the man pretending to be my husband.

I keep telling myself it's just a game. That I'll stay sharp and detached, keep my cool and let Dallas see what he acts like.

But my hands keep shaking.

"Are you sure you're up for this?" Dallas asks for the thousandth time today. "If this is a set up, you're walking straight into it and-"

"I know," I stress, eyes still glued to my phone. "But if it's not a set up, then it's an opportunity. You said that yourself."

He doesn't argue with me, but I can feel the doubt. He doesn't like this any more than I do.

The phone finally vibrates against the table and I suck in a ragged breath.

Adrian.

The contact name stares up at me like it's taunting me. Like even the phone knows it's a lie.

Dallas' chair scrapes softly against the floor as he straightens up. "You sure you're ready for this?"

No.

No, I absolutely am fucking not.

"Yes, absolutely."

We both ignore the tremor in the words and I hit accept.

It takes a few seconds for the connection to stabilize. The screen flickers off and on until he finally appears, and it cements my suspicion again.

That same dim light is behind him. The same sharp jawline, same dark eyes that don't quite belong to the man I married.

He's sitting on the edge of his bed, shoulders squared and voice steady like before. "Hey, Sage."

Every part of me wants to hang up.

Every part of me can't.

He says my name like it's something sacred. And the look in his eyes... it's so focused, so affectionate, that my fingers don't even think to press the end call button.

"You look tired," he says, tone soft like it never used to be. "You haven't been sleeping any better?"

"The weather's been bad here, so it's been keeping me up," I lie on autopilot, and then curse myself for letting him pull me further into the deception.

"I'm sorry, baby," he says it so soft, so tempting. I see Dallas' head snap up from the corner of my eye and it takes everything in me not to look over at him.

We both aren't used to hearing my husband call me baby.

"I hope it passes soon so you can get some rest," he says, and I bite my bottom lip to keep from blurting out a million questions. But he leans forward suddenly, eyes a little conflicted before he continues. "Sage..." he starts slowly, and then his lips thin out.

I have to brace myself for whatever is coming.

"You remember how I said we had a big op coming?" He asks, and I tilt my head slightly, narrowing my eyes. My knee is bouncing rapidly under the table and I can't get it under control.

"Op?" I repeat, as if I don't already know what that means. My stomach tightens with nerves. "Like, you're getting sent somewhere?"

"Yeah," he nods, and then takes a deep breath. "It's... more dangerous than I anticipated," he admits, and suddenly my fake fear is replaced by real fear. His eyes shift slightly, like he's trying to watch my reaction closer through the delay.

"Are you-are you worried?" My heart stumbles, and he takes another deep breath before he answers.

For a fraction of a second, he looks like Adrian, more than he ever has before.

"No," he shakes his head. "Not really."

"Why not?"

Fake Adrian shrugs, like a man who has seen enough death that it no longer scares him. "Not worth it being scared," he murmurs. "Gotta go either way."

I just nod.

What am I supposed to say to that when I know it's true?

He leans closer to the camera, and his eyes soften as he takes me in. "You look different tonight."

"Different?" I murmur, and he smiles at me, lopsided and unfamiliar. It still makes my stomach turn, but I can't be sure if it's from fear or curiosity.

"Yeah," he nods his head, his smile building even more. "Your hair is beautiful, Sage. Really. Have I told you that before?"

"No," I whisper, and he hums under his breath, eyes roaming my face.

"I'll try to tell you more often. I'm sorry I failed at that in the past."

"It's... it's o-"

"Don't say it's okay, please," he cuts me off, and it almost sounds pained. His eyes scrunch slightly like he really can't stomach me saying the words. "I know it's not okay, Sage. Let's just-let's try to be more honest with each other, alright? If I'm failing or fucking up, or just-or just being stupid, I want you to tell me. I'd rather know so I can fix it."

My pulse beats against my ribcage, trying to spill through the gaps between the bones, trying to race to my heart.

How earnestly would I have begged for my Adrian to admit these very same words to me.

I would have.

I really would have.

If he could have opened himself up to me, to our marriage, we could have tried to at least be happy with each other.

Maybe then, he might still be alive.

"Have your guards gone home yet?"

The question draws me from my racing thoughts, but I nearly choke on my next breath.

I have to fight the urge not to glance behind me to the camera in the corner.

He isn't watching, is he?

There's no way he knows Dallas is sitting right across from me listening to his every word.

We checked the camera feeds a dozen times before we called, and they're off. He shouldn't know.

"I think Dallas is around here somewhere," I twirl my hand in the air like I'm gesturing towards the house and he hums again.

At least now we know he was monitoring the camera feeds at some point.

"Yeah, I got an alert a few days ago that the cameras had been shorting out," he murmurs, staring at me intently. I can't tell if he's baiting me, but it seems like he knows more than he's letting on.

If he's smart like we think he is, then he does.

If it were me, I would have memorized every pattern, every discrepancy, every little thing that could get me caught.

"Must be the weather," I hear myself mumble.

"Well, make sure he checks it out, okay? My father's been acting like a fucking lunatic recently. I don't want him anywhere near you."

His father? My brain scrambles to grasp just how many clues he just dropped in a few short sentences.

Adrian never would call his father anything but Daddy.

He'd never insult his father like that.

And he certainly wouldn't say that he didn't want me anywhere near Andrew.

"Why not?" I ask, unable to stop myself.

Fake Adrian is quiet for a moment before he looks me over again.

"Sage," he says my name like it's delicate. "I had an argument with my father recently, and it's been eye opening, to say the least."

"What'd you argue with him about?" I push further, and he doesn't hesitate to say me. "Me?" I whisper. "What about me?"

"It seems he wanted me to be married to you before, but now he's questioning it," he points out.

This most certainly is information we didn't have before.

I don't flinch as Dallas skyrockets to his feet and begins pacing the room. I can practically hear the gears turning in his head.

"Why would he question it? He's the one who wanted us married. It was his idea," I throw back, voice rising in frustration.

"I don't know, but look, Sage," Adrian scoots closer to the edge of the bed, and he leans down so he's closer to the camera.

Now I can really see him.

Now the light pulls out the emotion in his eyes, and I think Dallas was right.

It's right there in his eyes.

"Listen to me," he continues softly. "You are my priority," he says, and Dallas freezes in the middle of the room. He slowly turns on his heel to stare at my phone.

Oh, God. Dallas was right.

"You are my priority," he repeats. "I don't want my father anywhere near you, and if he tries anything, then I'll put him out of his fucking misery."

I can't hide the shock and surprise from my face, but he can't hide himself either.

This man is dangerous.

I can see it so clearly now.

The blue in his eyes isn't as sharp as mine or Adrian's. His blue is subtle, shadowed by the storm grey and the promise of death.

"What did he say?"

He hesitates, and his jaw tightens enough that I can tell his teeth clack together painfully.

"He told me to get rid of you," he reveals.

Dallas' hands twitch by his sides while mine start to tremble. "What?" My mouth goes dry.

"I told him to watch his mouth."

He says it so simply.

I don't breathe for a full five seconds. "You *what?*"

"I told him there'd be some changes when I return home, and that it starts with the way he speaks of you. I don't want him anywhere near you until I'm out of this place."

I can't even process what he's saying.

Adrian has never raised his voice to his father. He's never defended me, not once, and now I'm just supposed to accept that this man, this stranger, this *imposter,* was willing to defend me?

"You don't believe me?" He asks after a thick silence.

"I don't-" I swallow audibly and then want to bang my fucking head on the table since I'm apparently unable to form a single coherent thought. "I don't know what to think," I admit. "You just-you just sound so different from before."

Dallas gives me a look that says *he's obsessed with you,* but my pulse is too loud to pay any attention to him.

"I meant what I said last time, Sage," his tone drops into something low and raw. "I'm done letting our fathers control everything. I'm done pretending this marriage is just a deal they made. I'm clean and sober. No more drinking. No pills. No bullshit. I want to start over when I get back, and that starts with you and me."

The words cut through me like a blade dipped in honey.

Sickeningly sweet.

He says it like he means it.

In a way that my Adrian *never could.*

"Why now?" I whisper.

"This place has given me some clarity, Sage," he whispers back. "It took me a while to get my priorities straight, and I'm sorry for that. But I realized I was choosing all the wrong things, and making all the wrong decisions. I don't just want to do it for you, but also for me. I want to be better. I know that I can be. But I also want to be better to you." He pauses and scans my face again for any reaction, and I try my hardest not to give him one.

"You were the only one before that didn't treat me like I couldn't get better, and now it's my turn to take care of you. It's my main priority as a husband, and I want to do it. There's no crazy excuse or reason why other than I want you in my life, and I want to be a better man. I'm trying my hardest. I just hope that with time, you'll see that."

I shouldn't.

God, I really shouldn't.

But something in me twists and softens, even as every instinct in me screams that it's a trap.

When he smiles at me, it's that same quiet, devastating lopsided one.

And I hate that I want to believe him.

I hate that it sounds so believable.

"I'll prove it to you," he says softly, so soft, like velvet in my ears. "When I get home, I'll prove it to you, Sage."

I dig my nails into my palms to keep from shaking. "You better not be lying to me."

He doesn't break my eye contact.

"I'm not, baby."

I don't know what else I can say. It's hard to open my mouth without screaming things that could make this a thousand times worse, so I keep my mouth shut.

"I might come home soon." My world tilts slightly. "If I get injured or if things go bad on this op, they'll send me home. Maybe for good."

"You-" I whisper, the words dying on my tongue. "You mean soon?"

"Yeah," he whispers. "Soon."

I can't tell if it's a threat or not.

I want so badly for it not to be.

The call only lingers for a few more moments. His face, his haunting lopsided grin and lips that seem unable to dampen when he looks at me... I don't know how long I'll be able to keep up this lie.

Not without pouring out my heart and soul.

And maybe I will... if he's the man he pretends to be.

The better version of him.

Dallas stares at me for a long time after the call ends.

"I was right," he murmurs.

"Yeah," I whisper back, eyes snapping from my phone screen to his. "You were."

"It's not Andrew or the money... it's you," he sits down heavily across from me. "He doesn't want Adrian's life. He wants you."

The words feel damning as they fall from his lips.

24

ELLISON

The sun is stupidly bright the morning we roll out.

The kind of light that bleaches color from everything and makes the men squint like they're already halfway to hell.

And we might as well be.

I couldn't tell you how many times I've argued against this mission.

Enough that my hands shook with effort to keep my anger contained.

It's a death sentence.

Not for me.

But for the other guys, it's a death sentence.

I won't say I'm better than they are, but I like the taste of blood, and red is my favorite color.

I've got no plans to die in this desert.

I have a wife to get home to.

The truck engine makes my entire body buzz and it fuses with my adrenaline.

The static coming through the radio becomes an afterthought as I focus on the vibration beneath my feet.

Some of the guys are laughing at jokes I can't hear. Some are dead silent, trembling in their boots.

Just like I do, they know this mission was dead in the water the moment it was assigned to our unit.

We had to take our four Humvees, but they don't do much protecting from the dust that somehow always ends up making my mouth feel gritty.

I'm so fucking jealous of those young guys that get stationed in places like Florida and Korea.

This place is just a never-ending vacation in hell.

I should've joined the goddamn Air Force.

It smells like metal and gunpowder, and somebody's cologne. Who the hell puts on cologne to go get blown up?

I push my kit further into my shoulder and check the chamber again because habit is the only religion I ever learned to practice, and it's hard to shake.

I glance over at the kid, and of course, he's looking right at me.

His knee is bouncing like he's all wired up on his Daddy's coke again. "You alright over there, Gray? Look a little nervous," he grins, all teeth, the kind that's just begging for my fist to rearrange it.

"Always," I easily throw back. It sounds like me, and not him. Thank God. "How's your lip feeling?"

He looks away instead of answering, but I see him run his tongue along his scabbing split lip, and the fact he's in pain brings me joy.

We mount up like always.

The kid is supposed to stay near me.

Higher chances of him surviving, they said.

I take the rear-left in the second Humvee. It's so hot out that the heat from my skin soaks through the seats. Sweat crawls down my spine and finds a home in my waistband.

The convoy lurches forward, tires kicking up dust and gravel, and the city starts sliding past us.

Children watch us with wide, unsmiling eyes of people who've learned too early that the end is inevitable at the hand of a soldier.

"Radio check," Johnny calls, and a chorus of "ready" responses come back.

Adrian's voice is cocky and chipper in my ear. I could cut through it with a dull spoon.

He has no idea what he's about to see.

I tell myself to breathe.

In through the nose, out through the mouth.

Think two days ahead.

Think Sage's hair catching light in that kitchen.

Think the way she said my name.

Just a little longer.

We just need to make it a little longer.

In through the nose, out through the mouth.

I lied to Sage.

Just once.

Maybe I shouldn't have.

Maybe I didn't mean to.

I said I wasn't scared.

But death is always scary.

I know some of these men are about to meet it.

As soon as we step foot outside of these Humvees, some of these men will be doomed not to return.

Some of them will never see the light of day again.

Just a dust-filled bloom clouding their airways as they take their last breath.

In through the nose, out through the mouth.

Johnny meets my gaze from across the truck, and he subtly shakes his head.

Bad deal.

That's what his eyes say.

We both know how this will go.

I turn my head as something glints off of Johnny's visor.

We pass a rusted bus that's been there since the last war that ravaged this place. The smell of fuel and burning rubber clogs my nose and my own leg starts bouncing with anticipation.

The street starts to narrow as we get further in.

Someone on the radio calls for a copy, and then-

-everything flips.

Light, heat, and a force stronger than any God.

The world folds in on itself and slingshots me hard into the roof.

My teeth knock together, and blood fills my throat. My shoulder goes *wrong* with a wet pop, and then the truck descends into a screaming, grinding animal.

Dust becomes a living thing in my throat. Glass becomes stars.

Somebody is shouting *contact, contact, contact,* and my ears are full of the ocean.

I taste copper and dirt.

Everything is sideways.

It feels like my brain is trying to crawl out of my eyes.

"OUT! OUT!" Johnny screams, his voice fading in and out, and I move on instinct because instinct is the only thing that ever saved me. I kick my feet down hard, plowing into the door until the hinge screams and it gives out. My left arm feels like dead weight, and the pain is excruciating.

I hit the ground hard enough that my vision goes black.

The Humvee behind us is a blooming flower, flames licking up to the sky, hood crumpled like decaying leaves, petals of color pouring out of the windshield.

Or is that blood?

I can't tell.

Rounds snap through the air and I flinch, ducking my head even though it's already scrambled.

They're too close, too clean.

I press my cheek to the gravel and return the fire in short bursts, cursing under my breath. The muzzle fights me, blinding me even further, my vision tunneling for a moment.

A figure stumbles from the lead truck, right into the line of fire, and then drops boneless to the ground.

Another crawls out behind him, dragging a leg that won't listen, and I can see his eyes are smeared with blood.

I move to him, because he and I may be the only ones left when this is all said and done.

"Stay with me," I yell, voice carrying over the gunshots and screaming, the way you talk to a dog you refuse to lose. It's Nico. One of our younger guys. His pupils are blown, face a mess of burst vessels, blood foaming from his ears. He's blinking out.

I hook an arm under his and it feels like hot coals raking over my shoulder. I nearly throw up from the pain, but we have to keep moving. A still body is an easy target.

We stagger to the side of a collapsed wall; rounds spray the bricks just inches from my ear and dust grits into my teeth.

"Suppress fire!" Someone yells, and I lean around the edge and paint a doorway with fire until the barrel ticks like a gas stove.

There's a quick barreling rush and then the lead Humvee folds in on itself and the flame flares out. The sound is a freight train rushing in my ears. I don't think. I move.

"Move! Move!" I yell at Nico, and I set him down hard behind the wall. He nods like my word is the gospel, body pushing forward on will alone even though his eyes are clouded over with blood.

I sprint low across the ground as rounds chatter past me.

Heat peels skin from the air and the truck is a furnace.

I grab the rear door, wrench, and it comes away in my hand like a rotten tooth.

Inside is smoke and screams and the rancid, ugly smell of decay.

There's two bodies in the back. One's bent all wrong, face unrecognizable and charred, dog tags hanging on a jag of the seat. The other is a heap of gear and blood and what's left of a burnt-up uniform.

My lungs seize when I breathe in, but I hook my fingers into the first vest and drag.

He's fucking heavy. They're always heavy, even when there's less of them than there should be.

"Come on," I rasp under my breath, and the pain in my shoulder explodes like a supernova. I get the first body out and dump him nearby, and then I go back, because I hate myself and I love someone three thousand miles away.

The tags glint in the firelight.

Hart, Adrian, A+

They cling to the ruined body like a bad joke.

For one second, the world narrows to a point.

One step. One choice. One life.

What kind of man will this make me if I go through with it?

It's too late to find out.

I rip the chain free from where it clings to the body's vest, and it snaps skin from the neck when it lets go.

I don't look at the face because there's nothing left to see.

I jam the tags into my mouth, tasting nothing but ash and salt, then tear my chain free from my own neck.

Gray, Ellison, O+.

It sits like a gravestone in my palm.

But I loop my tags over the charred cartilage.

I pull the kid's chain and wrap it around my own throat, and it feels like freedom.

Someone is firing from above and dust rains from the balcony overhead.

Pain sings through my stomach as a blade slides right in.

I look down dumbly at the handle jutting from my abdomen.

For a heartbeat, I see Sage's hands turning the knife through my skin, and I laugh, short and ugly at how things are going down.

Then training takes the wheel.

I rotate with the force, driving my elbow into the attacker's nose, feeling the cartilage give way. I take his knife out the same way it went in, brutal and ruthless.

And then I drive it back home to where he kept his bad ideas.

Liquid evacuates his skull and drips down my fist as he falls to my feet.

Blood goes warm down my waistband, somehow even worse than all the sweat.

The edges of the world go fuzzy, but I've got someone waiting for me back home.

I stagger off and grab Nico again. Two steps, three, four. The alleyways are tight here, the kind that funnel sound and fear and make it echo off the walls.

I drag him through a hole in a wall into a courtyard shadowed by laundry lines and broken satellite dishes.

My lungs scream and my shoulder feels like a socket full of glass.

"Stay awake, kid! Stay awake! Say your name," I yell out orders to him, and I get a groan in return.

"N-Nico," he stammers, and I snap my fingers.

"What's two plus two?"

"D-don't be a dick, Gray."

It hits me like another knife to the stomach, and I barely hesitate.

"You must have really fucked your head in that blast," I laugh it off. "This isn't Gray. It's Hart."

"J-Jesus Christ, you two look j-just a-alike," he stumbles over the words, and I chuckle again.

"It's just the blood in your eyes, kid. Don't swear it," I rapidly key my radio with blood-slick fingers. "Mayday, mayday, mayday, this is Hart," I say, and the lie fits in my mouth like it was born there. "We're hit. All trucks down. Multiple casualties, need med evac at grid..." I rattle off numbers on autopilot, drowning while the world swims. "Contact still active. Pop smoke."

"Copy, Hart," the voice comes back, strained and focused. "Birds six minutes out. Hold."

Six minutes is a goddamn century. We don't have six seconds, let alone six minutes.

But they find us.

Of course they do.

The doorway spits out two men with rifles, teeth bared as yelling.

They see blood spilling and think we're an easy target.

The first one eats two of my rounds before he can even step in the room.

The second one runs blind and I meet him halfway, my fist flying with a satisfying crack, and then the butt of my rifle ends the conversation.

The edges of my vision cloud and I reach for Nico's shoulder.

"Stay with me," I say again, and I'm not sure if I'm pleading to him or myself.

Rotors blare overhead and every cell in my body wants to scream. The air chops into submission, a vibration that scatters dust all through the wind. The alley turns into a blender. Gunships rake the rooftop and the world flashes white.

The med bird drops low enough to shake my teeth in my skull.

The door gunner yells something that I can't hear and two medics fly out, crouched, like sprinters who never learned how to stand up. They get hands on Nico, eyes clinical and darting rapidly.

"You Hart?" The other one yells over the chopper.

"Yeah," I yell back. Adrian's chain is hot against my skin.

"Your shoulder's out. You're bleeding. Sit tight and we'll patch you on the move."

We hop into the back and I help get Nico situated because I don't know else to be in this world.

The medic shoves me down anyway and I only resist out of principle.

The interior smells like antiseptic and fuel.

I try not to breathe it in while they cut my shirt and pants.

They talk over each other as if my body isn't bleeding all over them.

"What's your name, soldier?" The other medic yells over the roar of the engine.

"Hart," I rasp back. "Adrian Hart."

The city pulls away and my shoulder is a distant planet.

My stomach feels like it's four stories below me and my throat tastes like smoke and iron and a name that doesn't belong to me.

I close my eyes and see Sage on a beige couch that she hates, her knees tucked under her, phone lighting the curve of her cheek.

"Stay awake for me, Hart," the medic says, tapping my cheek. "You with us?"

"Yeah," I slur.

Sincerity tastes strange on Adrian Hart's tongue, but I savor it.

"We'll get you patched up, Hart. You got family back home? What are you planning to do when you're outta this shit box?"

"My wife," I rasp, and the guys chuckle.

"Which one of those questions were you answering?" He jokes, and I groan when I say both.

The field hospital is a fever dream of stainless steel.

Voices ricochet from all sides. Crying sounds but then halts all at once.

They pop my shoulder back in with a force that drags a yell I don't have the conscience to be embarrassed by.

They irrigate the wound in my abdomen, and the cold water is agony, but at least it's fucking clean.

Stitches pull the edges of me back together and Sage's voice is the only thing running through my mind.

The overhead light is stark and annoying. The cot they slap me into is as thin as paper.

A major in a uniform crisper than any I've ever seen comes by with a clipboard and a face that doesn't move much.

"Hart," she places a sympathetic hand on my forearm. "I'm sorry about your team."

KIA, wounded, commendation, report.

She asks the questions and I answer in clean sentences.

In my version, Ellison Gray was in a different truck.

In my version, he burned.

In my version, I dragged two out and kept a third breathing.

The room goes quiet like we're all listening to what kind of man that would make me.

"You've got options," she finally softens. "We can stabilize you here and send you back with the next rotation, or we can fast-track a discharge with honors. You've done your share, Sergeant. No shame in going home."

Home.

A house with cameras I've already learned to kill.

A kitchen with a woman who looks at me like she knows all of my secrets.

A father who will want to put an end to me as soon as I step in the door.

"I want to go home," I say.

My voice is steady but my hands are not.

She nods like she expected that.

"It'll be a few days with the paperwork and debrief, but we'll get you a seat. Just rest easy for now."

She leaves me with a plastic cup of water and a head full of possibilities.

I stare at the dog tags resting against my chest.

Hart.

They feel lighter than mine were.

Or maybe I just feel heavier.

It's hard to say.

Across the aisle, Nico stares at the ceiling with his head wrapped up like a bad Christmas gift. He turns toward me slowly. "We make it?"

"We made it." I don't tell him what we lost to do it. "You did good, kid."

Night comes quiet but my head is screaming.

My shoulder throbs. Every time I blink, I see the charred flesh and carnage.

I press my palm over the new wound on my stomach and feel my pulse beating there.

The morphine's walking up and down my spine like it wants to trample me.

I squeeze the tags between my fingers until the edges bite.

I wonder what it will be like when I get home.

I wonder if she'll accept me.

I could confess.

I could tell her everything and beg and hope she'll love a monster just because I say please.

But my teeth are still sharp. My claws are still out. And there's still blood to be spilled.

One target is down, and another remains.

Andrew Hart is up next.

But it'll all have to wait.

Until I get home to my darling Sage, the world will know no peace.

25

SAGE

I haven't slept since the call came through two days ago.

"Your husband's coming home early, Ma'am. He's been injured but he's alive."

The words were supposed to bring me relief, to sound comforting, but my mind's been a mess ever since.

The not knowing is worse than anything.

I wonder what he'll be like, or which Adrian is coming through that door.

I wonder how badly he's injured and if he's going to change once he gets here.

I wonder so much that my mind starts to cycle into a pit of despair.

I've been counting down the hours, even though I have no clue when he'll be here.

All I know is that he's coming, and I'm not sure which Adrian is supposed to walk through that door, the real one, or the one who claims to be.

The sound of tires crunching over the gravel drive makes my heart seize up.

It's too early for the guards to change shifts, and Dallas is already gone for the evening.

Rain has softened the world outside, and yet the mist still clings to the air. The house is washed in that dim, watery light that turns everything ghostly, and I'm scared when I open that door, it's a ghost that I'll see.

For a moment, I think I've imagined it.

But then the headlights cut across the window again, and I know I haven't.

He's here.

My throat tightens with an unknown emotion.

I can't breathe around the sound of a car door shutting, or the low scrape of boots across the porch.

I want to duck and hide, to run screaming for the hills.

But I don't.

I just stand there staring at the doorknob like it might burst open at any second.

And then it does.

The door swings open slowly, like it's been waiting for this moment too.

He fills the doorway, tall and quiet and wrong in all the *right* ways.

It's Adrian's face. *Almost.*

But not Adrian.

His hair is pitch black like mine, longer than it used to be, falling in uneven pieces that catch against the bandage at his temple. His skin is a little paler now, marked by faint bruising and the shadows of exhaustion clinging to him.

And his eyes... God, those eyes.

They used to be clear blue, sharp and cocky and smug.

Now they're stormy.

Now they're more grey, alive and unreadable, matching the mist outside and glinting with the lightning still lingering close by.

He looks at me like I'm the first thing he's seen in months.

Like I'm the first person.

Like I'm a life raft being thrown when he's been drowning out at sea.

And for a moment... just for a moment, I forget to be afraid.

I forget he's not actually my husband.

"Hey," he murmurs, and his voice is rougher than I've gotten used to. A strained rasp that catches like it's been dragged over sandpaper.

I thought I'd hesitate more.

I really thought I would.

But he's standing here bandaged up and looking at me like I hung the stars in the fucking sky, and I don't know how to take a step back.

He takes a slow step forward, the weight of his body a little uneven. The limp is small but visible, and I can see that he wants to hide it from me, like he's ashamed of it.

The silence stretches until I think my heart might beat out of my chest.

And then he says it.

"Did you miss me, Sage?"

The way he says my name is maddening.

It's soft, almost tender, but the same exact tone he used on the phone. The same cadence. The same practiced intimacy.

He says it like my name tastes good rolling off of his tongue.

My stomach twists into knots.

Because he sounds exactly like him and nothing like him all at once.

"Y-you're back," my throat burns, and I want to bang my head into the door for how unintelligent I sound. You couldn't think of anything else to say, Sage? Really? Nearly six months, and that's all you've got?

"I said I'd come home," he murmurs, and the faintest smile ghosts across his lips, but so does the exhaustion and sincerity. The shadows under his eyes give away just how tired he really is, even if he tries not to show it.

He reaches for me before I can back away, his fingers brushing down my arm, and I shiver. It's just enough to feel me. Not enough to hold or trap. Just a touch. But his skin is burning hot and makes my skin flush. And I can smell him now.

Cedar, vanilla, smoke, and something darker underneath. Something feral that makes my chest hurt with how good it is.

There's no cigarette stench clinging to him. No liquor stinging my nose.

Just him, raw and unfiltered.

His eyes soften as he looks me over.

I can't look away.

He studies my face like he wants to memorize it. Like he's making sure I'm real.

And I realize... he's trembling.

Barely. But he is.

"Are you okay?" I whisper, and he nods on instinct.

My mind screams at me to stay calm, to remember the plan, to watch him, to catch the inconsistencies.

But the way he's looking at me makes my pulse stutter.

It's not lust or anger or money-hungry madness.

It's something heavier.

"I thought we said no more secrets?" I murmur, my voice small and filled with worry. I don't even mean for it to be. But the plan vacates my thoughts the second that I see his hands shaking.

His eyes flicker with something like surprise, and he slowly nods his head this time. "Yeah," he says quietly. "No more secrets."

For a moment, the only sound is the clock ticking on the wall in the foyer.

"Are you in pain?" I ask before I can stop myself.

He hesitates.

And that hesitation ruins me more than a lie ever could.

"Yeah," he finally admits, voice just barely above a whisper.

"You should lie down," I exhale shakily and he opens his mouth slowly.

I think he might protest, but then he gives me a resigned nod. "Okay."

He leads me down the hallway like he's been here before.

Like he already knows the way.

He shouldn't know where the bedroom is, but he does.

He moves slowly, favoring his left side, the muscles in his jaw ticking every time he takes a step. He tries to hide it from me, tries to make his movements smooth and casual, but the pain keeps breaking through, tightening his face when he thinks I can't see it.

When we reach the room, I can't help but reach around him for the blankets. "Let me fix them," I mumble more to myself than him.

He doesn't argue.

He just stands there watching me, eyes unreadable but so open as I smooth out the bedding and pull back the blankets and sheets.

I can feel him behind me, close and warm, the scent of him wrapping around me like a thread pulling me in.

And when I finally turn, he's right there, still standing with one hand pressed to his side, his breathing uneven.

And yet I don't think it's the injury making his lungs strain.

He takes a small step forward, and my breath catches in my throat.

I have to tip my head back to look at him, and I can't remember if Adrian was ever this tall, but I know his eyes were never this dark. His lips were never this full. Skin never this clear.

And he was never this warm.

I know he wasn't.

The heat radiating off of this man is enough to scorch.

It licks up my spine in a way that leaves me dizzy, and it's all I can take not to move when he subtly tilts his head to the side, and his eyes sweep up my body.

"Thank you, baby," he murmurs, and it's so soft pouring from his lips. So sweet I can almost taste it.

"You're welcome," I breathlessly whisper back. I clear my throat and move to his side. "Come on," I murmur much softer than I intend. "Lie down."

He sits on the edge of the bed, exhaling like it costs him something.

And when he lies back, it's with a quiet wince, the motion stiff and strained.

I can see the tension in his throat, the tightness in his arm where the veins jump under his skin. He rolls his head to the side to look up at me, and I feel like I can't breathe when our eyes meet. "Better?" I ask softly.

His lashes lift as he looks at me, long and pretty like a man's lashes have no right to be. "Almost."

The silence hums thick and electric between us, something near tangible, like a string tethering us together. If I plucked it, it would echo off these four walls in the sweetest sound.

"Will you lie with me?" He asks it so softly, barely a whisper.

And I freeze.

Every instinct tells me no.

Every heartbeat tells me yes.

He watches me without pushing or demanding, like he'll take whatever answer I give and live with it.

And that gentleness, whether it's real or rehearsed, is what undoes me.

So I nod.

I slip into the bed beside him, careful and slow so I don't hurt him any further. I lie on my side, leaving inches of air between us, but the warmth from his body still finds me.

His hand hesitates before moving, fingers barely brushing up my spine.

My breath catches, choking out of me before I can relax myself.

He traces a slow, trembling path up my back. Not possessive. Not controlling. Just there, like it would pain him not to touch me this tenderly, like the shape of me belongs underneath the pads of his fingers.

When I finally let myself relax, I rest my head against his chest.

Even though he feigns calm, his heartbeat pitter-patters beneath my ear, sharp and uneven.

He smells so good, like something a little wild and tempting, and my heart races just the same.

He's warm. So warm. Warmer than Adrian ever was.

His arm curls around me, careful of wandering too far, like he's afraid to break me.

For the first time in months, I stop shaking.

He presses his lips into my hair, just barely a touch. More a breath than a kiss, but I swear I feel him trembling again.

When I shift closer, I feel his chest rise beneath me. Then the exhale, long and smooth. The softest sound leaves him, a sigh that sounds like the first relief he's felt in ages.

"I missed you so much," he whispers, the words sinking into my hair, my skin, my bones.

My heart twists painfully.

I shouldn't.

God knows that I shouldn't.

But I whisper back, "I missed you, too."

His heartbeat flies away underneath my palm.

26

ELLISON

Sage is still asleep when I open my eyes.

Her body is pressed against mine, soft and warm, safe, like she should be. Her breath fans across my chest and warms straight through to my heart. Her fingers grasp tight at the fabric of my shirt, like she's afraid I'll disappear if she lets me go.

She needs this.

She needs this just as badly as I do.

She needs someone to see her, to hold her. Someone to take care of her.

No one is more willing to do that than I am.

No one is more prepared and determined.

I lie there for a long moment, staring at the way her hair fans her forehead and cascades down her shoulder.

There is no one more beautiful. No one more stunning.

Even closed, her eyes are hypnotizing. Her dark lashes brush her cheeks, and even in sleep, her eyes seem to flutter behind her eyelids. I want so badly to touch every part of her, to memorize every inch of her body that she'll allow me.

Nobody knows the lengths I'd fall to just to trace patterns into her skin.

I'd like to say that I'm deserving of her, but I know that I'm not.

I've tried to be a good person in my life. I've tried to learn and to teach and to forgive those that have wronged me. I've even tried turning to God when I was at my lowest, but no one understands me.

No one understands how badly I crave. For nothing in particular, I simply crave.

I thought it was for companionship, then for acceptance, and finally, I thought it was for blood.

But there is no craving that could compare to how I hunger to have her all to myself.

If I could keep her in this very room, plastered to my chest, safe from harm, I would.

I'd lock the doors and swallow the key, and I'd keep her here until she found a way to love me.

Ellison Gray is dead, and I'm what remains.

Whatever lingering feelings she had for her husband, they belong to *me* now.

And I plan to wash them all away until nothing remains but love.

That's all I ask of her: learn to love me.

Please.

My fingers trail over the bridge of her nose and she murmurs something indecipherable when she scrunches her face together and exhales against me.

I adore her. Whatever creature she may be, whether it's an angel, a demon, or something more tantalizing, I want her all to myself. I'll convince her to want me back.

My body aches, bone-deep and burning, but I push myself upright anyway, slow enough that she doesn't stir. Her hand falls away, and I regret the loss of warmth immediately.

The floor is cold under my feet when I stand up. The pain hits like a delayed explosion. Shoulder, stomach, everything in between, it all burns, but I grit my teeth and head downstairs.

The kitchen feels more like a memory than somewhere I belong. I move through it on instinct, like I've done this a hundred times.

I remember how she moves here. How she tucks her hair behind her ear when she cooks. How she leans against this same cabinet every morning while she waits for the coffee to brew, impatient as ever.

The fridge hums when I open it, and I almost outright scoff at the contents.

It's nearly empty.

There's some half-drunk waters, a couple of Tupperware containers still half-full but clearly untouched in the past two or three days. My smile widens just a fraction when I see the jar of pickle juice in the door, minus the pickles of course, because Sage devoured those in the first three days she bought them. I've seen her drinking what's left of that shit like it was her morning coffee instead of sour ass dill pickle juice.

Disgusting, if you ask me.

But Sage is my wife, so I can overlook this one flaw.

I frown as I pull open the drawers and find them bare, too.

She always kept this stocked before, so what's she been living on?

Not much, by the looks of it.

I pull out what's left of the eggs, some peppers, half an onion, and some shredded cheese.

Then I find the bread and pull out the grape jelly from the fridge door. I know she likes that, at least.

I'm tugging down a cutting board from the cabinet over the stove when the sound of footsteps pulls my attention back.

Dallas leans in the doorway like he's here to fucking haunt me. His coffee cup is still steaming in his hand, expression somewhere between suspicion and amusement.

He definitely knows.

But I expected that.

I've been watching this man like a hawk.

He doesn't know that, of course.

I had to change my monitoring methods once I realized he had caught on to me hacking into Adrian's feed.

Plus, there was that gnawing feeling in my chest that told me that Dallas was trying to swoop in and take Sage for himself.

I nearly hired someone to put him down out back and throw him in Sage's burn barrel until I overheard his conversations with that other guard. What was his name, again? Anderson?

But Dallas saved himself, at least for now.

He's kept my Sage safe and sound, away from Adrian's father and all of his scheming. For that, I'll play nice unless he gives me a reason not to.

I know that Sage trusts this man, so I have no choice but to keep him around.

"Well, I'll be damned," Dallas finally speaks. "Didn't know you knew how to turn the stove on."

"Morning to you, too, Dallas. How nice of you to join us so bright and early," I say without looking up. My knife clacks against the cutting board each time I slice through a pepper, and I can feel Dallas staring at me like he's willing laser beams to shoot out and obliterate me.

He moves further into the room, slow and predatory. His eyes track my every movement, every decision, like he's taking inventory. "Welcome home," he adds after a moment, and I give him that smug smirk that Adrian always gave me.

He takes a seat at the counter and watches as I throw my peppers into the pan to sauté them. The scent fills the air and the oil sizzles in a way that's comforting. I wonder if it'll rouse Sage from her sleep.

"Should you be moving around that much?" Dallas asks, peering at me over the coffee edge in a casual way.

"I heal fast," I beam at him, and he mutters back something smart like *of course, you do.*

The silence settles heavy between us, just two men pretending not to know the truth.

When Sage finally comes downstairs, her steps are fast and anxious, like she's about to catch me doing something scandalous.

She freezes at the sight of us. Dallas is calm at the counter, sipping his coffee and flipping through the morning paper. And I'm standing by the stove, buttering bread that just popped out of the toaster.

"Good morning," I say, and her eyes dart between us before they finally settle on me. "Oh! Hang on," I wince a little as I rush over to the cabinet. I pull down her favorite coffee cup, a Sage green one with dark blue dripping down the edges.

Her eyes stay glued to me as I pour coffee into her cup and add hazelnut creamer to it. She looks like she might stop me until she sees me adding a fuck-ton of sugar behind it.

How anyone could consume this much sugar in one glass is absurd and probably unhealthy, but she deserves it.

I hold it out to her, and her hands shake a little as she reaches out to take it from me.

But she takes a slow sip and her eyes meet mine when she licks the residue from her lips. "Thank you," she rasps, still quiet from sleep.

"Did I do it right this time?" I ask, and her brows furrow just a tad. I know that Adrian used to screw up the way she takes her coffee. He knew he did it wrong, and the little prick had the audacity to say she was lucky he made her anything at all.

I would never do that to her.

"Yes, it's perfect," her cheeks warm, just a faint pink spreading across her face. I pretend not to notice even though I want to climb the nearest tower and scream to the Heavens that Sage likes my coffee.

"What are you doing?" She asks in a quieter tone.

"I figured I'd make you breakfast since I got up early," I explain.

"I don't really... eat breakfast."

"That's not true," I snort, leaning against the counter to sip my own coffee. "You used to love breakfast."

"I-" She simply blinks at me for a few minutes, her eyes wide and confused like she's trying to work through how I could possibly know these things. "I do, I just... haven't really felt like it recently."

"You should eat more, Sage," I say in a gentle but chastising tone. "Breakfast is the most important meal of the day." I smile at her and see Dallas roll his eyes over the lip of his coffee cup.

Her blush only deepens, and we both pretend not to notice.

She sits down, and she does eat, chewing methodically like she isn't sure if I'm trying to poison her or not.

"Do you mind if we go buy groceries today?" I ask her, and she's slow to nod at me.

"Aren't you still injured?" She questions and I pull a look of offense that she tilts her head at.

"I was stabbed, Sage," I deadpan, and her eyes widen. "I'm not a cripple."

Dallas snorts and Sage simply stares at me.

I probably shouldn't have told her I got stabbed, 'cause now she looks a little freaked out, but that's alright. We'll just smooth it over.

"Anyways," I clap, and she startles, her fork clattering against the plate. "Groceries today. You down?"

"I'm down," she practically whispers.

It doesn't take long to get ready.

The drive is quiet, almost easy to exist amongst one another.

Anderson and Dallas follow close behind us, and I don't mention Sage constantly glancing in her side mirror to check that they're still there.

Inside the store, it almost feels normal.

Sage walks beside me, hand brushing mine every so often until I finally gut up and just reach for hers. When I interlace our fingers, she doesn't pull away even though she stares at me for a moment.

We move through the aisles like a couple that's been doing this for years.

She reads labels while I toss extras into the cart until it's slam full.

Her small laugh when I toss four boxes of coffee in nearly breaks me.

I pay when we check out, and she stares at me then, too.

She murmurs a curious acceptance when I ask if we can stop somewhere on the way home, but I can tell she isn't expecting me to pull into a jewelry store.

Her breath catches when we walk through the doors and I lead her straight to the sales rep walking the floor.

"Hi," I reach out to shake the man's hand and he asks what brings us in today.

"My wife," I gesture towards Sage with a blinding smile. Her eyes are wide and searching, studying me like there's a catch. But there isn't one. "I wanted to get a new wedding ring. The band is just fine, I think. But I wanted her to pick one out that she likes more."

Sage seems breathless the entire time he leads her around the store. Her hand stays in mine unless she needs to try something on, and I want to scream at how pretty some of them look on her finger, but I keep my mouth shut.

"Do you like this one?" She hesitates as she shows me her hand. I take it in my palm, and her chest stops moving altogether.

"It's pretty, but it doesn't feel like you I don't think," I murmur, and she bites her bottom lip before she turns back and shakes her head at the store clerk.

I turn my head to see Dallas watching us through the shop windows, eyes sharp and wild. I can tell he wants to strangle me, so I shoot him a broad smile and turn my attention back to Sage.

She hovers over each case until she pauses. Her eyes land on a ring in the corner. It's much different than what I assumed she'd pick. This one is smaller, a little simple, a thin gold band with a clear diamond that catches the light when she moves. It's not obnoxious and gaudy like her current one.

"Can we see that one?" I ask, pointing to the one she's looking at.

"No, it's okay!" She rushes to stop him, shaking her head.

"You can try it on, baby. It's gorgeous," I tell her. My palm comes up to rest on the small of her back and she clamps her mouth shut as the man reaches for it.

They say God gives his toughest battles to his strongest soldiers, and I fucking believe it, because nothing is more captivating than Sage's expression when that ring slides seamlessly onto her finger.

It's a perfect fit, sliding on and settling there like it's always belonged.

"It's beautiful," the shopkeeper tells her, and Sage goes still for a heartbeat.

"It's my wife that makes it beautiful," I cut in, and her head snaps to me, eyes wide and shocked at my declaration. "What do you think? Do you like it?" I ask her, and she looks down at it once more, her thumb curling down to brush against the gold band before she holds her hand out to look at it further from her face. "How's it feel?"

"I love it," she finally whispers, eyes cutting from the ring to me, and my lips tremble with my resistance at smiling too wide.

"It looks perfect on you," I tell her, and she nods her head.

She tries to hide it, but I see her lips forcing down a smile, too, and I know I've done good this time.

"Is that the one you want, or did you want to try on some others?"

"I want this one," she tells the shopkeeper, and I hand over my debit card.

It's plucked from my fingers, just like Sage was plucked from Heaven.

My hand feels searing on the small of her back.

On the drive home, I take her hand again, and she lets me.

My thumb skims over her new ring, the light catching on it as we drive.

Now it feels right.

It feels real.

Sage protests when I tell her I'll cook dinner for us tonight.

She watches me unpack the groceries and put everything exactly where it belongs, and I know she probably wants to slam her head into the marble counters to figure out how I move in this space like I've been here before.

We settle on cooking dinner together, an idea that I'm quick to accept.

We move around the kitchen like we're meant to orbit each other.

I keep brushing her arm, her back, her wrist. Soft, innocent touches that still make her breath catch every single time.

Dinner is delicious. Everything about Sage is delicious, but her cooking really shines. We eat side by side, and again, it feels so real and right.

After dinner, she goes to shower while I clean up the kitchen and check the alarms.

When it's my turn to shower, I leave the door cracked, and a soft knock comes shortly after I peel my shirt off.

"Can I come in?" Her voice carries, and I nod my head, seeing her already stepping through the doorway.

Her eyes are wide as she takes me in. They linger on the wound, on the bruises still blooming dark across my ribs.

Her hand lifts before she can stop herself.

My stomach tightens when her fingers brush against my belly, light and trembling and warm.

I shudder at the touch.

"What happened?" She whispers.

"Mission went bad," I murmur.

"How?"

"We aren't supposed to talk about it with-"

"But I'm your wife," Sage whispers, fingers still dancing along my skin.

I can't even breathe with the way she looks at me, soft and wide-eyed and worried, like seeing me hurt is hurting her, too.

Maybe it is.

Maybe she hates the thought of me injured and bleeding.

Maybe she feels like this, too.

"That's right," I whisper back, and my hand reaches slowly, like I don't have any control over it. I place my palm against her cheek, fingers splaying wide as my thumb brushes over her skin. She's so warm and gorgeous, and alive. So alive under my hands. So real. "You are."

"What happened next?" She whispers again, and I don't think she understands how she's ruining me.

I don't think she gets how my heart shreds into pieces when she tilts her head to rest it in my palm. She wants to bring me to my knees, and I'll go down willingly. I'd give anything she asked of me if it meant I get to touch her just like this.

"The mission was fucked from start to finish," I answer this time, but even all of my lying can't mask the tremor in my voice, so I don't bother trying. Instead, I tell the truth. "We were tracking a terrorist organization through a village. Another team had been running surveillance for months, but we didn't stand a chance," I murmur as I brush my thumb under her eyelash.

"We were ambushed before we even made it through the city, and our Humvees were targeted. Not many of us made it out. Just me and three other guys, so I heard."

"And your injury," Sage murmurs as she looks down at her wandering fingers. "What happened here?"

"I pulled another guy from one of the Humvees, but we were taking fire," My hands start to shake a little as I explain, and Sage leans more heavily into my hand, like me holding her is enough to ground us both. "I had to call for backup to come get us out since he was injured, but we were ambushed again. A guy got me with a blade before I could stop him."

Sage exhales shakily, but she looks up at me like she's truly worried. "The worst part was not knowing if I'd make it back to you," I whisper.

The way she swallows is audible. "But you're okay, right?"

"I am now that I'm home with you," I can't help but tell her. It's the truth. Wholeheartedly, I would accept any pain in the world if it meant I got to stand right here in her presence.

Her gaze softens and she hesitates before she whispers something that nearly makes my knees give out. "Do you need help showering?"

"I wouldn't turn it down," I manage to lightly tease, even though my pulse is behind my fucking eyelids.

I've imaged Sage down on her knees probably a dozen times before, but never under this context.

Never to be sweet to me.

But she kneels beside the tub, sleeves pushed up, and a determined set to her brow.

When her hands finally touch me, I feel at home for the first time in my life.

She shakes through it the entire time, trying to keep her eyes off of the rest of my body, but I can't help but close mine, relishing in the peace she brings me.

Her fingers comb through my hair, careful and tender, like I hope she'll always be with me.

"Thank you, Sage," I murmur as she brushes my hair from my eyes.

Later, when we crawl into bed, she shifts closer without me asking this time, hesitating only a second before her head finds my chest.

She tucks her face into the junction where my neck meets my shoulder, and her breath against my throat makes me shudder.

My hand slides up her spine, slow and torturous, and she relaxes into my hold.

I can't help it.

I press my lips into her temple and breathe her in.

This.

This right here is what I needed. It's what I wanted.

It's what it was always meant to be.

And I don't care how much of me has to die to keep it this way.

27

SAGE

I wake to warmth.

It's the first thing that reaches me, the heavy, steady kind that seeps into my bones and makes everything feel like a fever dream.

Adrian... *fake* Adrian's arm is slung over my waist, his hand spread wide on my stomach like he's trying to leash me in my sleep. His other arm is wedged under my pillow, cradling my head protectively.

His chest rises and falls against my back, slow and deep, and the sound of his breathing behind my ear pulls something aching from inside me.

He holds me like he can't get close enough.

Like letting go would cost him air.

I'll be honest.

At least to myself.

My Adrian is gone.

My Adrian is gone, and there's an imposter in my home... but it doesn't feel like he's a stranger.

Don't be mindless, Blue.

It's what my father always told me.

And I've tried.

God knows I've tried to keep my head on straight.

I've tried to rationalize and keep a distance. I've tried to keep from falling right into temptation, but there's something about this man... whoever he is.

Every time he speaks, every time he looks at me, touches me... it feels less like we're playing a dangerous game and more like we're catching fire.

I close my eyes and hear his voice in my head. Even when I don't want to, it lingers, whispering for me to let go and give in.

And I want to.

Damn it all, I *want* to.

But I can't.

Not yet.

I have to let him keep up the act. I have to let him keep the illusion running long enough for me to figure out his intentions, whether he's here for the money, to do Andrew's bidding, or if he's truly here for me.

I thought Dallas was wrong.

I thought it was all a far-fetched idea that this man was going this far all for me.

But I can't ignore the way he looks at me. I can't ignore the way he seems like he's holding back from reaching for me. That he doesn't want me out of his sight.

He's a man with secrets. A man who stole my husband's life. A man who treats me better than my husband ever did.

But what does he *want?*

What does he want from *me?*

I stare at the hand against my stomach, tracing the long lines of his fingers. They're not as short and thick as Adrian's were. They're a little rougher, but warmer. His palm flexes faintly, the barest movement against my waist, but it's enough to send a tremor through me.

He needs this, I can't help but think.

Maybe I do too.

Someone to tether us both to the world.

When I turn carefully in his arms, his lashes cast shadows across his cheeks. His face looks different like this, gentler, less guarded.

His hair is a dark mess against the pillow, curling softly over his brow. It's just as black as mine like he was built to match me. The bruises near his temple have softened into a dull gold, fading into skin that still looks a bit too pale.

I study his face, and it sinks into my mind, slow like syrup flooding thick, that this man could have never come home.

He could have died. Stuck somewhere in a foreign country, with no one but me to mourn him. I can't help but wonder if that's what happened to my Adrian. If maybe... somehow, this man replaced him and left him for dead.

I can't help but wonder.

That's how the vicious cycle starts.

It sinks in slow that I'm not sure what the answer would be if someone asked me if it were better or worse that my Adrian didn't come home.

One day soon, I'll call this man on his bluff.

One day soon, I'll ask all the right questions.

Is my Adrian dead?

When did this start, and how long has it been you?

Why are you doing this?

And perhaps the most important one... who are you?

One day I'll find out everything, and I wonder if I'll hate him for it.

I'm still staring when his eyes open.

Like a rain-soaked sky, storm gray eyes land on me, sleep-hazed and exhausted.

I open my mouth to say something, but before I can mutter a single word, he leans forward slowly and presses his lips to mine.

It's unthinking.

An instinctive "Good morning" slipping out as he pulls away before his reason can filter in. His lips are warm and slow, familiar in a way that terrifies me, because they shouldn't be.

Adrian never kissed me like this.

Adrian never kissed me at all.

It's only seconds after he pulls away does he blink fully awake and freeze, realizing what he just did. But neither of us pulls away from each other.

Neither one of us mention it.

When his eyes meet mine, a little hazy still, a little nervous, I whisper back, "Good morning."

Dallas is in the kitchen when I come downstairs, his coffee already steaming and black like his soul.

"He up?"

"Any minute now," I whisper, though I'm not sure which one of us I'm trying to convince.

Dallas stares at me for a long moment before he shakes his head. "That's not Adrian," he finally says, and he may as well slit my throat, because that's what the words do to me.

"I know," I whisper back.

"I don't know who the hell he is," Dallas continues, taking a deep breath. "But I think he's in love with you."

I almost laugh, bitter and in disbelief. "He can't love me, Dallas. He doesn't even know me," I whisper-yell in exasperation.

"I think he knows you a lot better than you know yourself, Sage," he throws back in my face, giving me a look that tells me plain as day that he knows I'm falling for it already.

Before I can answer, the sound of footsteps comes from upstairs and we both go still.

Moments later, *Adrian* walks downstairs, moving carefully, favoring his left side but still trying to hide it. His shirt hangs loose, hair mussed from sleep, and when his eyes find me, they soften instantly.

Dallas mutters something about talking to Anderson and slips out back, leaving me alone to face *Adrian* after our morning kiss.

"What are you doing today?" My new Adrian asks me after a few moments. He leans against the counter, and his hair falls forward a little. So badly do I want to reach out and tuck it out of his face.

"I was thinking about going to work since I didn't go yesterday, but I didn't want to leave you alone," I admit. "I think I'll take the rest of this week off."

"Work?" He tilts his head slightly like he's curious.

Oh, that's right.

You're not the only one lying, husband.

"Yeah," I fidget with the hem of my shirt sleeve. "I, um, I started a security company while you were gone. Just... HOA contracts and private security and stuff like that," I keep it brief.

"You started a company?" A faint smile builds on his lips, genuine pride flickering into his eyes. "Sage, that's amazing."

I don't know if he means it. I don't know if he even realizes what hearing it means to me, but he softly tells me, "I'm so proud of you. That must have been such hard work."

I can't lie to myself about how heavily it settles into my heart.

The day drifts by in a strange, quiet orbit.

We don't do much of anything, and yet everything feels like it's more intense than when my actual husband was here.

Fake Adrian follows me around a lot, talking to me about anything and everything he can think of. The conversation never ceases, and somehow, it's not as annoying as I thought it would be.

He doesn't bother me when I slip off to answer some work emails, or when I go to shower.

I hate to admit that I just need some time to check in with Dallas to see how things at work are going.

But I also check the cameras to see what the man downstairs is doing.

Each time, I hold my breath, thinking that I'll find him doing something devious, and each time, I'm both relieved and disappointed when he isn't.

In the afternoon, I change his bandages for him, and I have to fight the urge to baby him.

It's not like my Adrian, where he bats away my hands and acts like me patching him up is a nuisance.

This man is calm and appreciative of me.

He sits on the edge of the bed, shirt off and skin golden in the sunlight going down on the other side of the windowpanes.

The wound looks better than it did before, but still angry and red around the edges. But he stays patient while I doctor him.

"Hold still," I order, trying to keep my voice steady. But it's hard when his gaze never leaves my face. The intensity makes my fingers fumble with the tape.

When I smooth down the new dressing, my knuckles brush the skin at his hip and his breath hitches, quiet and uncontrolled, and the sound makes my heart hammer against my ribcage.

"All done," I whisper.

"Thank you, Sage," he says back in a low, but unsteady voice. There's a crack in it that makes me dizzy and I have to force myself to walk away from him.

That night, we cook dinner together again.

The room fills with the smell of garlic and roasted tomatoes. My Adrian was allergic to tomatoes, but I don't bother calling him on it.

The radio hums low from the corner, and every time I reach for something, he's already there, hand ready to pass it to me.

With every movement, he brushes against me. Our hands touch so often it stops feeling like it's accidental.

And when I turn around and find him directly behind me, I bump right into him.

His hand catches my waist automatically to keep me from stumbling back, and I look up to meet his eyes.

"Sorry," I whisper.

"Don't be," he murmurs back, and his voice slides down my spine like fresh brewing coffee.

We stand there, suspended in time, breath mingling in the space between us, and then finally, his eyes drop to my lips.

Mine can't help but follow, and it feels like a loaded question when he tilts his head slightly, silently daring me to take what I want.

I don't even realize I'm moving until his breath hits my lips.

The first kiss is slow, testing, wandering.

But then it deepens, unfolding into something that makes the ground beneath my feet feel like it's caving in.

His lips move against mine with a tenderness that burns. My hands slide up to find his chest, and his heart is racing underneath my palm.

I've never been kissed like this. Never in my entire life.

He kisses me like he's starving, hungry and consuming, all at once. When I sigh into him, he makes a sound low in his throat that almost sounds pained.

His hands slip down my waist until he reaches my thighs, and he lifts me like I weigh nothing and sets me on the marble countertop, pressing in between my knees. The world tilts on its axis, heat blooming everywhere that he touches.

My fingers find his hair and bury themselves until I lightly tug, and he groans quietly into my mouth when I pull him closer.

His mouth trails down the corner of my jaw, and I tip my head back on instinct, letting them roam, letting them taste, and I can't fucking breathe with the way his hands tighten against my thighs, like he needs more. More of anything that I'm willing to give him.

When his lips trail my pulse point, the sound I make is mortifying, but I don't have it in me to be embarrassed when his lips return to mine, slower this time, deeper, like he's savoring the taste of me.

When he finally breaks away, it feels like he's forcing himself.

Both of us are breathless, panting against each other until he leans forward and brushes his forehead against mine. His thumb smooths a path upwards and rubs the side of throat before settling where his lips just met, like he wants to feel that my heart is racing just as fast.

"Sorry," I whisper again, just barely a breath.

"I'm not," he whispers back, raw and breathy against my lips. He trembles when he leans forward to press one more firm kiss against my lips, and that one is somehow more intimate than the first. "I've been dreaming about doing that. It's all I've wanted ever since I got home."

"That's all?" I whisper, trembling underneath the weight of his words.

"No, Sage," he shakes his head. "That's not all. But I'm not here to take from you. I'll accept whatever you want to give me."

My heart has never beaten so fiercely, and I fear I won't ever recover from this.

"And what if I want to give you me?"

He closes the inch between us again, and his words are just a whisper against my lips.

"You should know, Sage," his breath catches as he tilts my head back and steps closer, pressing his hips into mine. I suck in a breath sharper than a blade. "You've belonged to me since the moment I first saw you."

I don't know when the first time he saw me was.

I don't know how or why.

I don't even know his name.

But I don't doubt a single word he breathes against my lips.

"If you're lying to me," I whisper, remember the words I once told him over the phone. "Then I'm going to fucking kill you."

His chuckle is low and wrecked against my jaw. "I'll bring you the gun myself, baby."

No.

I don't doubt him at all.

28

SAGE

The warmth around me when I wake is oddly reminiscent of the lips that pressed against mine in the night.

His hands are everywhere. Splayed across my back, palm flattened over the small of my waist, as if he's trying to anchor himself to me in every way possible.

The sheets are in a tangle, one oversized shirt clinging to me and his sweatpants pooled low around my hips. My legs are loosely slotted between his own, foot tucked behind his calf like I too needed him closer some time in the night.

The very smell of him, cedar and vanilla and something dangerously sweet, makes my ribs feel like they're cracking open to make room for him in my heart.

He's asleep or at least pretending to be. His breath is ragged as if he's running from his lies even when he's dreaming, quick and uneven, like his body is still fighting even though he should be at peace.

I could lie here forever, letting the rhythm of him steady the conflicting emotions within me.

For a long minute, I do.

My fingers find the hem of his shirt and brush against the edges, feeling the soft skin of his stomach brush against my pinky finger. Just to feel the heat of him, the steadiness of his warmth against the pad of my fingers.

There's no calculation here. No small, clever strategy for him to hold me this softly. Just a low, aching relief that he's here and real, and for a small sliver of morning, I don't have to be on guard.

He shifts and I feel it, the tiny wince, the muscles shaking from his injury pulling tight, and worry blooms like winter each year, slow and creeping.

He's pretending to be fine for me. Of course he is.

I don't know why, and I don't know if it's to keep me from seeing his weakness, or because he thinks I don't care.

But I do.

I didn't mean to.

I certainly didn't want to.

But there's something about this man... something magnetic that makes me crave him.

This isn't the cold, spoiled Adrian that I had before. This man is intense in every way possible. He's overwhelmingly intimate with the way he touches me. Every time our eyes meet, I see the longing and desire there. He doesn't even try to bury or hide it. It simmers right under the surface, almost like he wants me to see it.

Dallas' words constantly filter through my head.

Does he mean it?

Is he capable of loving me, or is this all just a lie?

And if it is a lie, how long will I let myself live it before the cracks start to splinter?

I lie there for what feels like ages, lost in my thoughts, running my fingertips softly across his shoulder blades until the motion even begins to soothe me.

I barely remember my eyes starting to feel heavy again.

Sleep greets me like an old friend.

When my husband finally starts to stir, rising with the strained cautiousness of a man who knows the cost of sudden motion, he brushes a palm over my face.

It's an absent, possessive thing, exactly the kind of touch that would be meaningless from nearly everyone else. But from this man, it lands like a benediction.

His voice breaks through the haze of sleep, quiet and soft against my ear. "Good morning, baby," he murmurs, half asleep and raspy.

"Morning," I mumble back, the word small and useless, heavy under the fog of sleep.

I can't find it in me to get out of bed just yet, still warm and exhausted despite the extra sleep. Maybe that's my brain trying to tell me something.

He slips out of bed as careful as he can, and my fingers curl into the warmth of the bedsheets he just occupied. It smells just like him and I bury my nose into the fabric, soaking up as much as I can.

When I surface again, the mattress beside me is cooling, and the room feels bigger than it should. My ears strain to pick up any noise downstairs, but there's nothing.

I slip out of bed, cautious and wandering, and make my way down the staircase, but the silence is deafening.

I lift my phone before thinking and then the ringing is breaking through the room.

"Hey," he answers on the first ring. The word is just a breath in my ear, as if he stepped away from someone to keep his voice calm. "You okay?"

"Where are you?" I ask, and it sounds somewhere between worry and anger. I know he can tell.

"I had a doctor's appointment, baby. I'm sorry I didn't tell you. I almost forgot and then you were sleeping so peacefully, I didn't want to wake you."

"You should have woken me!" I respond in frustration. "I would have gone with you! You can't just come home injured after going to literal war, and then just disappear one morning without telling me where you're going!"

It sounds insane.

I know it does.

I half expect him to laugh it off, to brush it aside and tell me to calm down.

I expect the sweetness that I've had all week to evaporate, and anger to replace it.

"I'm sorry, Sage," his voice is soft and airy. "I didn't realize how you might feel waking up with me gone," he takes a deep breath, and it sounds frustrated, but almost like he's angry with himself. "Look, it's at St. Martin Clinic, over by the bay. Just two or three minutes away. They just called me back but I'm sure it'll be a while still. Do you want to ride over? We can grab lunch after."

"Yes," I rasp, and thankfully he doesn't make me feel crazy for it.

The part of me that refuses not to care is being stubborn, but I don't have it in me to feel ashamed as I ask Dallas to drive me there.

I quietly explain that my husband is at a doctor's appointment, and maybe I can find some answers about who he is. Dallas' look in the rearview mirror tells me he knows I'm full of shit just like I'm full of actual concern.

The clinic is incredibly sterile, all polished edges and stern looking workers.

But when I ask for Adrian, they lead me right back to his room.

His eyes lift fast when the door opens, and the relief that crosses his face is so unguarded that I feel tears sting the back of my eyes. Maybe he did want me here. Maybe he truly wasn't trying to keep me away.

In the exam room, the doctor recites Adrian's life as if she's reading it right off his bones. He confirms every little detail, his name, date of birth, prior injuries, service history. Even the lie the higher-up military officials created to get Adrian into the military without sending him off to basic training.

He answers every question with a smooth confidence of a man who truly believes it's his own history.

He slides over Adrian's ID and insurance, his signature matching so precisely now that I feel the ground tilt.

She cleans up his wound and says his stitches held well, but he'll definitely have a scar, but he doesn't seem to care.

Somehow, we're now one of those married couples who schedule follow-ups and after visit summaries together, like we've been doing it for ten years.

He keeps my hand tight in his as he drives us over to a deli that I love. I didn't even have to tell him about this place and somehow he knows.

It makes me start to wonder if maybe I'm the crazy one. If maybe I made it all up in my head and he really is Adrian, but now, some twisted part of me doesn't even want him to be.

A part of me, and I'm not sure how deep that part goes, wants him to be someone else. To be clean of all Hart blood and just exist as whoever he is.

Part of me wishes the pretense would drop and he'd just tell me who he is so I could love *that* version, that man that seems to care for me like he can't help it. Like he doesn't want to help it.

We get our food to go and eat side by side at the kitchen counter.

He pauses between bites just to smooth a palm over the small of my back as he stands. Or to bracket my hip with his fingers as he leans past me to reach for a napkin. The touches aren't demanding but feel like he does them to get some occasional proof that I haven't dissolved in front of his eyes.

When he asks me to go swimming, the yes falls from my lips so fast that it's embarrassing.

He dives in first.

The water parts easily around him, and I swear even that looks natural, like he belongs to this place, this life, this body.

I settle onto a float, pretending not to stare but licking my lips every time he rises out of the water. The way that his swim trunks dip low on his hips should be fucking illegal.

But I try to leave him alone while he swims laps back and forth like he's Michael Phelps on a mission.

That is, until he swims closer, eyes glinting with mischief. "You just gonna float there while I do all the work?"

"I'm supervising," I say, tugging my sunglasses down as I look him over.

"I dunno," he says in a disbelieving voice. He looks up and down the length of my float. "You look like you need to cool down."

"You wouldn't dare." I deadpan, but God, does that smirk look absolutely threatening on his face. He looks like a cat that's found something to knock off of the counter. He tilts his head dangerously and I start shaking my head. "Wouldn't I?"

"You wouldn't do that to me, would you, *Adrian?*" The name hits him just like I wanted it to. For a heartbeat, something dark flickers behind his eyes. And then he smiles, low and wicked. "Hold your breath, baby."

"Don't!" He flips the float and the world goes blue. Cold rushes in, shocking and frigid, and the laughter bubbles up before I break the surface, hair slick and dripping. He's already there, catching me by the waist, both of us gasping and laughing like idiots.

"I will kill you," I choke out, hitting his shoulder. But he laughs harder, and it spills out of him, unguarded and wild, nothing like any of the practiced ones he's given me before.

But the laughter fades as quickly as it came. I'm still in his arms. My legs still locked around his waist. His hands splayed across my back.

And everything feels hot all of a sudden.

His touch, his warmth, the length I feel pressing against me beneath the surface.

My arms slip around his neck to pull me a little closer to him, but it's him that leans down to kiss me.

His hand slides upwards to find my jaw, and I feel the flush building in my skin as he pulls me closer against him.

God, this man knew how to kiss.

It was nothing like the dead pressure that Adrian gave me in his poor attempts.

This man kisses like he's hungry. He kisses like he craves to taste me. And maybe he does.

His fingertips run across my jaw before finding a sensitive place behind my ear that makes me shiver. His tongue slips into my mouth in a way that feels claiming this time, like he needs more and more and more.

I can't help but let out an embarrassing sound when he nips at my lower lip before his tongue finds mine again. I just know he's trying to break me. He's trying to make me go insane. My hands reach up to tangle in his hair and I shift so I can straddle him better.

And then I let out a nervous huff when he suddenly lifts me.

The water rushes down as he moves through the water, closer and closer to the stairs until he's climbing out and leading me back inside.

Water drips all over the marble flooring, and for once, I don't give a damn about the mess he's making on my carefully crafted masterpiece.

I let him lead me upstairs, and my hair soaks the sheets when he drops me onto our bed.

I never wanted Adrian before. Not once.

But this man standing above me, letting his eyes run up the length of my body... I've never wanted anything more.

My legs part to the side on instinct when his eyes trail downwards, and he licks his lips as he reaches out.

His fingers brush against my inner thigh, and I can't fucking breathe all of the sudden.

I want him to let go. To break through all of those walls he's crafted to maintain the illusion that he's Adrian Hart. I wanted to see all of the things he restrains from me.

To have him unleash it all on me. To know how he really feels. How bad he really wants me.

I deserve it.

The whole world feels like it catches fire when he places his knee on the bed between my legs and starts crawling over me.

He groans when his fingers find my stomach, sliding up my ribcage until they catch on my swimsuit top. And then there's hesitation. He pauses there, like he's not sure if he's allowed, and I don't have the self-control to tell him no.

"Please," I beg, and he doesn't need to be told twice. His fingertips slide under the fabric, cupping my breasts before his head is dipping down, and stars explode into my vision.

There is no fucking reason this should be so good. No reason his tongue lapping at me should make me dizzy and breathless, but damn it, it does.

His tongue rolls over my nipple before his lips settle there and suck, and I'm certain it's painful how tightly I'm gripping his hair. I'm not sure if I'm trying to slow him down or bring him close, but I lose all will to figure it out when I feel his fingers sliding down my skin towards my thighs.

I glance down, and nearly send myself into cardiac arrest, because this man is looking up at me. Tongue swirling around my nipple, head cocked back to see my expressions as he dipped his hands lower. His eyes are dark, so, so dark, full of hunger and want and something I've never seen on a man's face before. There's no way to describe the desire that I see in his eyes. No way to explain it.

Dallas was right.

This man wants me.

"I want you to feel good, baby." Oh, God, even his fucking voice. My muscles pull tight when his fingers tug on my swimsuit bottoms, and I'm going to die at the hand of a man who I barely know. A man with a name that's unknown to me.

He tugs at the strings of my bottoms and then he's tugging them off.

Like this, I'm stuck open and exposed. There's nowhere to go when he's got me underneath him.

And it should be frightening. It should be nerve-wracking. But it's not. It's not at all.

Even though I'm vulnerable in a way that makes my heart ache, I don't doubt that he wants to please me.

All I can think is what I want to say right here underneath him, safe, and soft, and his.

"Look how fucking pretty you are," he whispers, and I nearly choke on my tongue. When I lift my head, his eyes are glued between my legs. Is he-is he calling my vagina *pretty?* There's no way this man is real. What the actual fuck.

His voice sounds absolutely wrecked, eyes heavy-lidded as he brings his palm down to cup me, and I shudder violently at how big his hands are.

"All of you is just so pretty, baby. Pretty, and sweet, and mine," he rasps.

My breath stutters when his fingers slide down, thumb carefully pressing between my legs, moving in slow circles over my clit in a way that's torturously slow. Heat builds from my stomach and slips into every single limb.

I buck my hips up, wanting his hands closer, faster. I just want more, and I know he's capable of giving it to me.

"There you go, sweetheart. Good?" He asks. He knows the answer, this sick fuck. Of course, it's good. The little whimpers slipping out of my mouth cement that, but he asks me anyway, and all I can do is rapidly nod my head, breathless and shaky.

"Can I give you more, Sage? Do you want more?"

"Please," I beg, and his own breath catches at how desperate I sound.

But his hands double their efforts. He leans down and kisses me, his tongue tangling with mine, wet and messy and deliciously sinful as his fingers curl inside of me, and I squeeze my thighs together, trying to get him deeper. His hips keep me from going anywhere, and my efforts are useless, but his fingers move a little faster, and he eats up the moan that spills from my lips into his mouth.

"Trying to work your hips?" He tsks and pulls away to look down at where I'm squirming against his fingers. "Just relax, baby. Let me do the work for you."

"Please," I rasp again, because apparently that's the only word I know.

"I'm gonna fuck you until all you remember is my name, baby," he rasps and steals another kiss from my lips.

I want to scream at him that I don't even know his name. All I know is the name he stole, and that feels wrong to call him.

I want to know who he is.

I want to know his name. Who the man that pleasures me this well is.

But he can't even tell me.

"Such a pretty fucking pussy," he groans, licking a line up my throat, and I shudder underneath him, already seconds from coming apart just from the touch of his hands.

"More," I rasp frantically. "More, more, I-"

"You what, Sage?" His fingers circle my clit again, and I cry out, letting little broken sounds pour out as he gives me a little more pressure. "You want my cock, don't you? Just don't know how to be patient. My sweet wife, always wants things to be her way."

My head falls back against the pillows, breath catching on another desperate noise, and my hands squeeze the bedsheets, needing something to ground me so I don't float away to Heaven.

"Making a fucking mess, aren't you, baby?" He doesn't stop rubbing my clit until I'm crying out, soaking through the sheets and making a mess of his hands, just like he said. He soothes me through it, slow and careful, hands slowing slightly as he wraps the other one around my hip and slows me down a little.

"There you go, sweetheart. Take it nice and slow, hm?"

I'm nodding before he even finishes speaking, not even really hearing what he's saying to me.

All I know is that I need him, and I need him now.

He gives me mercy, and he presses his fingers back into me. One, then two, then three, and I'm melting into the sheets again, my chest finally relaxing, pliant and perfect as I know I'm about to be handed exactly what I want.

And fuck, I love him like this. I love his touch and the sounds he makes and the feral look in his eyes.

He doesn't even know how he's unraveling me, how he's opening me up like I'm a gift, but only for him.

Adrian never touched me like this. He never brought me any care or pleasure. He only took.

He only took from me, and never gave anything in return.

And now I know that if I were to have to choose between this imposter and my husband, I would choose this man.

I would choose this man, this liar, this imposter, over my own husband.

What does that say about me?

"I can't wait to take you, Sage," he rasps, leaning down to kiss my shoulder. "You open up for me so well. Just take everything I have to give you. I love it," he tells me in a low, strained voice.

I love it, too.

I can't even tell him that I love it. My voice is caught in my throat and all that comes out is low whimpers as I grasp at his wrist between my legs.

He's so good for me, too. So, so good. I never even knew I could trust him like this. I never knew I wanted this or even needed this, until he started giving it to me so easily. Until I trusted him to.

And I do.

I do trust him to.

"For you," I rasp and he chuckles so sweetly under his breath.

"That's right, sweetheart. Head's all fogged over, and you still know that you belong to *me*, don't you? That *I'm* your husband, and *I'm* the one who takes care of you, who wants you to feel good, that *I'm* the one that loves you like this."

Love.

Love.

Did he say love?

He withdraws his fingers and leans forward, shuffling a little further between my legs until he's right there, and I can't help but lift my hips, trying to get closer to him, and I hear that vicious, breathy laugh all over again.

"Patience, baby," he whispers, and I shake my head no.

I can't even breathe as he settles himself over me, lips finding mine again. My hands curl around his waist and settle against his lower back, pulling him closer and closer, and he groans into my lips.

His cock brushes between my legs and I moan into his mouth, whispering please over and over again until he has some mercy on me.

"Give it to me, please," I plead, and he licks the words right out of my mouth. His length keeps brushing against me as he moves almost like he can't even help it, like he just needs the friction too, but he's too focused on kissing me, relaxing me further into the sheets, making me go lax and pliant all over again.

Every inch of me is trembling, but he still takes his time.

Until he reaches for my calves and pushes my legs up, folding my knees closer to my chest.

I barely have time to look down before his cock is pushing into me slowly.

My breathing goes unsteady again, and his eyes are closed like he's never felt anything better, and maybe he hasn't.

Maybe I'm exactly what he needs.

I squeeze around him and he groans low in his throat and squeezes my hip to stop me. "Baby, you have to relax or this is going to be over quick."

"Just give it to me," I petulantly whine, and I can see a little bit of his resolve crumble behind his eyes.

He pushes into me hard and unforgiving all at once, and I cry out at the fullness. My nails dig into his lower back, legs slipping again and tightening around his waist.

"Oh, fuck, this is so close to Heaven," he rasps against my throat, burying his face into my neck.

"C-close?" I whisper. "Not Heaven?" I don't even know how I got the words out with how overwhelmed I am.

"It feels like Heaven," he chuckles darkly, trying to breathe through it just like I am. "But what I'm about to do to you is going to land me a first-class ticket into hell, Sage," he rasps. I'm going to hell with him. I swear it. I'll hold his hand on the trip there.

His hands tug at mine, making my nails scratch his back as he brings them back to the bedsheets. He pins my wrists to the bed and hovers over me, something devilish and seductive and dark in his eyes.

And then his hips are moving.

It's all I can do to lie there and take it. Stretched out underneath him, pinned down and breathless, I've got no choice but to take what he gives me.

And God, does he give.

He thrusts so deeply that I can feel every delicious inch, every ridge and curve of his cock, the heat of it pulsing inside of me in a way that made me shake from the intensity.

"Sage," he breathlessly finds my lips again, and my name sounds like a curse and a cure all at once. "Fuck, you belong to me, don't you? Were made just for me? To be mine? My wife?"

"Y-you belong to me!" I moan, high-pitched and desperate. "You belong to me, too. M-mine too."

"That's right," he rasps and catches my lips again, hands sliding up to hold my face so tenderly. "That's right, Sage. You don't even-" he cuts off with a low groan. "Fuck, you don't even know what I'd do for you. How I'd-how I'd kill to keep you."

My head screams alarm bells, and red flags wave like a banner across my eyes, but they dull into nothing when I hear how wrecked he sounds. The red-tape looks like baby soft pink when he kisses me.

"I'm never going to hurt you again, Sage. I promise. I'll give you e-everything you've ever wanted. I'll take such good care of you. You'll never, oh-fuck, you'll never want for nothing," he buries his face back into my neck, hands turning painfully tight on my hips, and I feel it. That slow slip on his control and restraint. The way his thrusts turn deeper and his breath shudders as he tenses up.

And when he shatters, spilling into me, I go down together with him.

Everything burns white, and I swear I can see the lightning in his storm-grey eyes as he looks at me like he's never seen me before.

Everything feels so heavy as I try to catch my breath, limbs loosening and satiated, head clouded over with blissful awareness.

Soft kisses meet my lips, my nose, my cheek, the space between my eyebrows.

Everywhere they can reach, I feel them until my head starts to drift away.

When I close my eyes, all I see is red.

I don't know if it's the glaring caution tape or my blood rushing from my heart from the endorphins that I feel.

But I know I'll never let it go.

I'll never give it up now that I've had it.

I let my mind go and let my husband's lips trail my skin.

I think I sleep.

I'm not sure, but when my eyes open again, I'm in my husband's long-sleeve oversized shirt and his sweatpants. They're too big, loose on my hips and hanging, but they're warm and smell like him. He must have dressed me after cleaning me up.

The bedsheets have been stripped, and I wonder how good I had to be fucked in order not to wake to any of this.

By the time I drift downstairs, the house smells like cracked pepper and garlic and butter, the marinade still clinging to the room even though it sounds like my husband's outside getting the grill ready to cook.

"Adrian?" I call, and I cringe at the name. It doesn't fit him at all. But I don't know what else to call him.

I start a pot of coffee in the kitchen and pull out some potatoes to peel, and some broccoli from the freezer.

I rinse off my cutting board and set it on the counter.

Then I start hunting my house shoes, not liking the way my bare feet are freezing against the marble floor.

But as soon as I go to pass through the foyer, the front door cracks against the wall hard enough to make the frame rattle, and men are flooding into my foyer like a dark tide, with Andrew Hart in the front, his mouth shaped into a sneer that strips the oxygen from my lungs.

"Where is he?" He snaps, scanning the room like it owes him answers, and when his gaze lands on me, it sharpens into the smile of someone who likes to remind a body exactly how small it can feel. "Why the hell wasn't I informed my son is home?"

"I-he-" tumbles out of me on instinct, that old stammer I learned at nineteen rushing up out of the basement where I keep the broken things.

"Shut up, bitch," he says, almost idly, and all the heat drains out of my limbs at once.

This is bad.

This is really fucking bad.

The click of a hammer pulled back freezes even the second hand on the clock.

Everything stops moving.

"Adrian," I whisper, not because I think the name will save me but because the fear is climbing out of me so quickly that I can't control it.

He doesn't look at me. He doesn't have to. I can feel him in the doorway, a stillness so contained it might be mistaken for calm if you didn't know what it cost.

ELLISON

My gun finds Andrew's temple like it was meant to live there, the metal cool under my hand while the men in suits take a collective half-step towards me in both shock and fear.

There are seven of them that I can see and probably two I can't.

Enough that I know this would end badly for anybody who isn't me.

"Did I not tell you there'd be changes," I say, not raising my voice because men like Andrew mistake volume for power, and I like to take away their favorite toys.

"Have you lost your goddamn mind?" He asks through his teeth, the words careful so they don't bump the barrel.

I lean just enough that he registers the weight of my words. "You used up my patience on the phone," I tell him, which is the polite version of the sentence that wants to claw its way out of me.

"Get that thing off me."

"Apologize," I say, and it's amazing how quiet a room can get when the request is simple, and the price is not. "For insulting my wife," I add when he glances at Sage like he wants to see her bleeding out on the stairwell, "in her own fucking home."

He laughs, and I feel the trigger settle under my finger in that familiar way my body recognizes as permission; I don't give it, but I let him see the possibility and he gets the message, jaw flexing on whatever passes for dignity in him.

"My mistake," he grinds out, and then, like he can't help himself, he looks at Sage and says her name as if it's poison he'd like to spit out.

"Adrian." It's whispered so quietly, and my chest aches at the sound.

"It's okay, sweetheart," I say without taking my eyes off him, because I can feel the tremor in her even from here, and I need her to take that breath. She's still damp from the pool and in my shirt and sweats with bare ankles and wet hair, and I have never hated a man the way I hate this one for making that beauty share space with fear.

"You need to learn not to break into people's houses," I tell him, almost gently, because the truth spoken softly is the most dangerous weapon I own. "Next time I might just pull the fucking trigger and ask questions later."

"You are out of your mind," he says as if the thought pleases him, smoothing his lapel like he's standing in a mirror, then, with that petty little spark that keeps weak men alive, "Don't worry. I'll help you find it very soon."

"Get out," I say, not because I need him to listen but because I want him to remember I told him to.

He steps in closer, testing, measuring, *gambling* that the son he made is still the boy who feared him, and it's almost a shame that I'm the wrong man for that test. "You think you're a hotshot because you learned to hold a gun?"

His hand goes for his breast pocket; Sage breathes my name like a wire pulled tight and I lift a palm to still her without looking, because the most important thing about love is that it stands between you and the bullet. And that's exactly what I plan to do if he tries to harm a single hair on her head.

The envelope he produces is black and sleek, and he watches my face with the greedy interest of a child waiting for a flinch that doesn't come. "Invitation," he says, too pleased with himself. "Your coming-home celebration to show off your honorable discharge."

"We don't want it," I tell him, and it's almost funny how his eyes light with the opportunity to say the next line.

"You'll be there if you know what's good for both of you. Your guests have already been notified, and there are appearances to keep, son. Even your wife's family will be there."

He turns, his men folding around him like trained dogs. One sets a large box on the entry table and says, "Mr. Hart expects Mrs. Hart to wear this," with a look that would be the last expression his face ever made if the wrong person were in this doorway. Then the door closes on the back of their arrogance and the house exhales all at once.

I deadbolt the door immediately and arm the alarm with a new code he will never guess, and knock the lid off the box with the muzzle of my gun because I'm not wasting clean fingers on anything he touched.

The yellow that grins up at us is the exact color of something I'd throw in Sage's burn barrel outside.

"You're not wearing that," I say, already reaching, and Sage moves as if she forgot her body knew how, crossing the space and folding around me like she's trying to fit herself inside my ribs.

She's shaking so hard the metal wobbles in my hand. I set the gun down and give her my arms instead, one hand to the back of her head, mouth at her temple, breathing with her until the rhythm matches mine and the tremor eases. "I'm sorry if I scared you," I tell her as I tuck the hair behind her ear so I can see her eyes, and then, because truth is the only thing I want to say to her, "I meant what I said, baby. I'll take care of you."

"He-he scared me," her voice shakes as she looks up at me, and I hate it so much. I want Andrew Hart's actual heart in the palm of my hand so I can fucking crush it between my fingers.

"Come on," I murmur softly, reaching for her hand. "Let's grill these steaks. You need to eat something."

Outside, the light is soft, and the grill is hot. The dress goes up fast, the flame catching the ruffles until it drowns inside the barrel next to the patio. She wraps her arms around my middle from behind, face pressed between my shoulder blades, and I cover her forearms with my hands and rub slow circles on the smooth skin until her breath loosens.

"I won't let him dictate our lives," I say to the yard and to the trees and to whatever else listens. "If he bothers you, you tell me, Sage. I'll kill him if I have to."

"Okay," she says into my shirt.

We eat inside at the island, the two of us turned toward each other in that unconscious way that says orbit more than intention. And while she sips one glass of wine and teases me for watching her mouth, I'm thinking that the hunger I feel isn't hunger at all, but something else entirely.

Love.

Because Sage belongs to me, and I do love her. In whatever way that I'm capable.

When the plates are in the sink and she touches my wrist with a small, shaking hand and says, "Come to bed," I do because I would follow that voice anywhere.

Upstairs I don't pretend to be anything other than what I am: a man who learned late and intends to spend everything he has left learning well.

I take my time and let the pace be set by the curve of her breath, and if I kiss devotion into the place where she breaks, that's between me and the God I don't believe in.

When I sink into her, I'm not Adrian Hart.

I'm Ellison again, and I love her more every time she sighs into my mouth.

She falls asleep with my shirt on her skin and my stolen name caught soft behind her teeth, and I lie awake in the long quiet after, counting the shadows as they move and promising them, the walls, the bed, and my own body that if it takes my hands to end a bloodline so she can live in a house that only knows warmth, then I will gladly wear the sin and the sentence.

Downstairs the coals are dying and the night still smells like pepper and smoke. I get up to reset the alarms, recheck the doors, and stand for a long moment at the threshold to the hall where she sleeps, letting the thought of her safe settle the way the last blade settled into my abdomen.

I finally go back to bed and sink into her warmth.

All I feel is her pulse beneath my palm and her fingers digging into my shirt like she never wants to let me go.

29

ELLISON

I never thought I'd see her looking any more gorgeous than the first time I laid eyes on her.

But holy fuck, was I wrong.

Sage in all black is sickening.

She's nothing short of elegant and dangerous. Black is undoubtedly her color. It's the kind of color that eats the light around her and turns her into the most magnetic thing in the room.

The dress fits like sin, long and sleek, hugging every curve of her body, and I almost say fuck it and just take her back to bed for the rest of the night. There's nothing loud about it, no fancy sequins, no cutouts that show slips of skin. Just that perfect simplicity that makes the whole world shut up and stare.

And they can stare all they want to, but Sage belongs to me and me *only*.

She's standing in front of the mirror when I walk in, pinning one side of her hair back so it shows off the diamonds in her ears. They glitter faintly when she tilts her head, catching the lamplight, and I wonder how she can make everything look more beautiful just by putting it on.

For a moment, I forget to breathe.

She is so gorgeous, so perfect, and my hands itch just to have her back in my grasp.

"You're beautiful," I say, and it comes out too low and much too honest.

She looks at me through the reflection, and her smile builds just like the pink flush against her skin. "You think?"

"I don't think," I murmur, stepping closer until I can see the flutter of her pulse at the base of her neck. "I know."

When she turns, her eyes catch mine, and she tilts her head back to lean forward to kiss me. How we became this comfortable in the past few days, I'll never understand, but I'm not trading it for anything. This is how it should always be between us. Her breath catches when I pull the small velvet box from my pocket. "Before we go."

Her brows knit, soft with confusion, until I open it. The diamond catches the light instantly, a single, perfect stone suspended on a fine silver chain.

Her breath hitches. "Adrian," she whispers as she takes it in. "Is that... is that your mother's stone? From my first ring?"

I nod once. "I had it reset. Figured it'd be better here than collecting dust in a drawer."

Her hand trembles when she touches it, thumb grazing the edge of the gem. "You shouldn't have-"

"I wanted to," I cut her off quietly. "I thought it would look good on you. I know the ring wasn't either of our choice, but the diamond was still beautiful. You make everything look timeless either way, but I figured you'd appreciate it."

Her eyes soften, a flicker of warmth breaking through the nerves. She turns around, gathering her hair to the side, and tilts her head so I can see what I'm doing. "Put it on me?"

"Of course, baby." The moment the clasp clicks, her skin smells like the lingering coconut body wash from the shower, and the faint sweetness of vanilla. My fingers brush the back of her neck, just barely, and she shivers. I'm realizing that the longer we're here, the worse my self-control gets. We aren't ever going to leave if I keep touching her.

When she turns back around, the diamond rests right above her heart, catching light like a matchstick every time she moves.

"Perfect," I whisper. "You're perfect."

Her eyes drop to my chest, and she smiles faintly when she notices the suit. "You match me."

"All black for my better half," I say.

She blushes, the pink rising fast across her cheeks, and I have to look away for a second just to get my control back.

The party is exactly what I expected.

A mausoleum dressed in gold.

Andrew's estate looks like money with a hangover, gaudy chandeliers, marble floors that echo too loudly, people who smile too wide for cameras. It's nothing like the beauty that Sage tried to turn our house into. I can tell that Adrian had tried and failed to mimic his father's style.

We arrive together, hand in hand, the car doors closing like a bad fucking omen. Flashbulbs go off from the reporters waiting at the gate, and I just know this entire night is going to be a spectacle.

Andrew greets us at the entrance like a man hosting his own coronation. His smile is tight, his suit sharp, his eyes colder than I remember even just last night.

"Son," he says, clapping my shoulder hard enough to bruise. "And my beautiful daughter-in-law. You clean up well."

I'm not going to let her out of my fucking sight tonight. Not for one second.

I don't trust Andrew anywhere near her, and I won't give him an opportunity to hurt her.

"Thank you, sir," I manage, my jaw so tight it aches.

He's already motioning for us to step further inside, his hand lingering too long on Sage's back. I hate that. The possessive touch. The silent control.

All night, he works the room like a vulture, boasting about his son's bravery, his miraculous recovery, his spotless record.

Like a Hart could have any hand in what I did to get my men to safety.

Every few minutes, he finds a reason to separate us. To pull me into another conversation, another toast, another round of forced smiles.

Sage never strays far. Every time I look for her, she's there at the edge of the crowd, eyes scanning until she finds mine.

Dallas is somewhere lingering, and so are the others. I carefully instructed them to keep tabs on her all night.

She doesn't know that I can't stand being more than five feet away from her.

I hold my drink, untouched, pretending to listen while the old men talk about contracts and war and investments that don't exist. My patience wears thin with every fake laugh.

Then Andrew's hand lands heavy on my shoulder again. "Son, a word."

It's not a request.

He leads me out of the ballroom, through one of the long halls lined with portraits and silver-framed mirrors. The music fades behind us. The laughter disappears. The air feels colder here, heavier.

The door shuts, and I turn to face him.

"What's this about?"

Andrew exhales, slow and suffocating, and all I can think is how I'd love it if he never took another breath. "You tell me. You're acting strange. You've been avoiding me since you got back. You won't return calls, won't show up at the office, and now-" he waves a hand toward the door "-you're parading her around like she's some kind of trophy."

My jaw flexes. "Sage is my wife."

He laughs, short and humorless. "Don't insult my intelligence, Adrian." I almost scoff in his face. How intelligent can you be if you can't even realize that I'm not your son?

"Then stop insulting mine," I snap back.

He narrows his eyes. "I don't know what's gotten into you, but it ends tonight. I won't have you embarrassing this family."

"I'm not the one who does that," I say, voice low and venomous.

The silence between us stretches until it burns.

But then Andrew steps closer, close enough that I can smell the whiskey on his breath. "You're going to listen to me, son."

I meet his eyes, unflinching. "I'm not your son."

That stops him cold.

For a second, his expression slips, just enough to show something like confusion, something ugly, something afraid.

Then he laughs again, softer this time. "You've really lost it, haven't you?"

He circles me slowly, like a predator sizing up prey. "You think wearing a suit and putting a new ring on her finger makes you a man? Makes you anything other than what *I* made you?"

I turn my head just enough to track him. "You didn't make me into anything. All you did was set up our marriage. I did all the rest."

"You're weak, Adrian," he spits the words at me.

"No," I respond in a low tone. "No, I'm not."

He stops beside me, voice dropping to a growl. "Then prove it. Put her down like the bitch she is. Tonight."

My heart stutters once, sharp and clean. He truly has a fucking screw loose if he thinks I'm going to harm Sage in any way.

If anything, tonight will be the night that I start plotting his death down to the very last detail.

He takes a step closer, close enough that his words scrape against my skin. "You humiliate me in front of those people, or I end her life myself tomorrow. You understand?"

The world narrows to a pinpoint. My blood goes still.

I can hear the music faintly through the walls, the muted laughter of people who have no idea that murder is being promised in the next room.

My hand tightens at my side, the ring on my finger biting into my palm.

When I speak, my voice is calm. Too calm. "If you ever touch her-"

He smiles, cruel and cold. "You'll what? Pretend like you're going to shoot me again?"

The air feels thin. I take a slow step forward until we're eye to eye. "No," I say softly. "I'll bury you this time."

Andrew's smile fades. His eyes flicker with something I can't quite name, fear, maybe, or recognition finally that he's not the only predator in this room.

Then he straightens his jacket, tone suddenly smooth again. "Careful, son. You're starting to sound like me."

He walks out without looking back.

I stay standing there, fists clenched, pulse hammering in my throat, the image of Sage in her black dress burning behind my eyes.

He wants me to destroy her. To undo *everything* I've built just because he wants to.

But what he doesn't understand is that I'd rather burn the entire world down before I ever let him lay a hand on her.

30

SAGE

It's not the kind of night you come back from.

The car hums beneath us, carrying a silence that tastes metallic. He hasn't spoken since we left the party, not one word. Just that muscle ticking in his jaw and his reflection in the glass, hollow-eyed and far away.

I shouldn't know what I know.

But I do.

Now I wonder if this will be our undoing.

Put her down like the bitch she is, or I'll end her myself.

Adrian's father's voice through the door, steady, venomous, and final.

He has never wanted me here. I knew that. But accepting it stings.

I don't belong with the Harts, nor do I belong with the Ledgers. And now I'm not sure I belong anywhere.

Now I'm not sure if tonight will be the night when my father's plan will come to light.

The night I might have to kill my husband once and for all.

I remember Andrew's words and how hateful they sounded as he instructed my husband to kill me.

And the pause that followed.

The pause that ruined everything.

That pause is the reason I may lose my life tonight.

Now the steering wheel groans beneath his grip, and I swear I can feel the storm inside him trying to break free.

When we get home, he moves through the kitchen like someone performing a role they've practiced too long. Jacket off. Tie loosened. Sleeves rolled high enough to show the veins along his forearms. He talks about steak again, about feeding me something other than some tasteless, expensive party food that may have honestly been poisoned.

But his calm isn't calm. It's containment.

"Is everything okay?" I finally ask when we get home. "You've been quiet."

He only hums in response, and this is the first time he's ever made me feel dismissed. The first time I've ever felt unsafe in his presence.

He doesn't even look up when he hums, just keeps setting out the knife and cutting board on the counter.

I watch him for a moment as he stares at the knife, and a thousand different scenarios rush through my head.

My blood might be coating that blade soon.

"Adrian?" I say softly.

He doesn't look up. "Hmm?"

My throat tightens. "You're scaring me."

That makes him pause. His hand hovers over the knife handle like he's thinking too hard about my words, but then I see his shoulders soften like he's forcing the tension in his body to ease. He laughs once, a brittle, disbelieving thing. "Don't be scared, sweetheart. It's just been a long night."

The fridge light spills across his face when he opens the door. My husband's face, but wrong around the edges.

The face I thought I could love soon.

He picks up the knife and starts chopping.

Thud. Thud. Thud.

Each strike cuts closer to the truth and my hands start to violently shake each time the blade hits the cutting board.

"I'm gonna grab my slippers," I whisper.

He hums again without turning. "Okay, baby."

Upstairs, my hands shake so badly I can barely get the safe open. The gun's weight drags at my wrist, heavy as a heartbeat.

Dallas told me I might need this one day, and I remember thinking how insane that sounded. I remember wondering if it would ever become my truth.

I always thought guns were the easy way out, but nothing is easy about this night.

When I go back downstairs, he's still at the counter, slicing red against wood, tomato juice bleeding out into the surface.

I stare at the back of his head for a moment, my heart in my throat, wondering if I can even do this. If I can kill a man I thought I'd fall in love with. If I can bring myself to pull the trigger.

I wanted him so badly. I wanted this to work so badly. I was even willing to overlook that our entire life is a lie. That he is a stranger that I've been trying to trust.

I was trying so hard.

The tears sting the back of my eyelids and when I swallow, my throat feels so tight, I fear I might choke before I even do what needs to be done.

"Adrian," I say again, quieter this time.

He doesn't answer. The knife keeps moving, the blade making a steady, obscene clock of thuds.

My hands are slick with sweat. The gun is heavier than I remember, heavier than the idea of it should be, and when I slip it out, the world narrows to the cold of the barrel and the shape of his back.

He's still cutting when I step through the doorway.

The kitchen light pools around him, throwing his shoulders into sharp relief. For a second I think maybe I can do it. Maybe I can be the final thing that becomes his end and someone else's beginning. The thought is horrible and cold, and I hate it.

I never wanted to be this way.

I never wanted to turn into a monster.

Dallas' reminder to keep my hands clean echoes through my skull and I can barely breathe.

"Adrian." I whisper and every desperate syllable burns my throat.

He turns so fast my breath leaves me. His hands are like a blur, a reach, a grab, the gun sliding across the tile. The metal clatters and my heart drops with it.

We lunge at the same time.

He's stronger than I expect. He's faster than I'd allowed myself to believe. I go for the gun, and he goes for my wrists.

Our bodies collide with a sharp, painful slap against the floor. The tile is colder than I thought possible. The gun skids away again and we both scramble.

Adrenaline explodes through me.

My hands claw for anything, for the weight, for the safety of the action, and all I feel is panic, hot, animal panic that screams *this is how it ends.*

I kick and thrash, fingers scrabbling at his forearm, at his shirt, at the edge of the rug. He pins my elbow to the tile with an ease that makes my bones ache. His other hand clamps over my wrist so tightly I think it will bruise, and I start crying. I can't even help the way the sobs pour out of me.

"Stop!" He huffs. It's not a calm word. It's ragged and raw and bleeding with emotion. "Sage, stop!"

"Get off me!" I shriek. My voice is brittle as glass. The sound of it ricochets off the cabinets, into the dark of the house, and for a second, I imagine Andrew Hart's voice answering me from the rafters, telling someone to shut me up.

He presses harder. His weight settles across my sternum, hot and terrifying, and the air whooshes from my lungs.

My face hits the tile and then the world is a blur of light and his cologne, sweet and suffocating along with the pounding in my ears. He pins both of my wrists with fingers that are not cruel but are iron tight. I try to twist, to wrench free, and his forearm digs into my wrist with a firmness that tells me he won't let go.

Tears sting my eyes. I taste metal from where I've bitten down on my tongue. My whole body shakes with the effort to get to that gun. The urge to pull the trigger isn't abstract anymore; it's a tool, a promise, an end.

"Don't," he says again, and this time his voice is shredded. "Please don't do this." He flinches, body shaking on top of me. "You think I'd hurt you?"

I don't believe him. I have no reason to. I have a camera-memory of Andrew's voice ordering death, and the pause that followed like a held breath.

I think about the way Adrian's face could flatten into something that looked like nothing human at all. I think about the coldness in the way his father spoke. I think about the evening's laughter and masks and how thin a person becomes when they want to create their own illusion.

I wrench my body away again, trying to break free. He shifts, and we roll. My elbow slams into the edge of the counter and pain blossoms, bright and white, up my arm. My knee pins under him; his weight crashes along my ribs. The gun is a fraction of an inch from my fingertips. I see the barrel catch the light and I panic.

I lunge.

He moves like lightning, a motion taught by years of practice and war. His body is suddenly between me and the gun, and his hand knocks mine aside.

The impact drives the breath from me, and the tile slides cool beneath my cheek. He puts both palms on either side of my shoulders and pins me there, his chest a hard, vibrating thing over mine.

He's on top of me, knees pressed to the floor, and I am an animal trapped beneath him, heart thudding as if it could break free.

"Stop," he says, softer now, voice breaking. "Sage, look at me."

I can only see the whites of my own tears. The panic claws louder. "You're going to kill me," I sob. "You're going to-"

His face flinches as if my words struck him. He leans in so close his breath fans across mine. "You think that I," he breathes. "You think I would do that to you? After *everything?*"

"Then why-" My words shred into a hiccup. "Why would you let him say it? Why did you listen? Why didn't you stop him if you're not him?"

His jaw hardens. There's a tremor in the muscles there, like cords pulled tight. For a long, ragged moment he says nothing, like he's making sure the words he's about to give me are believable.

"I didn't listen because I thought it would pass," he finally answers, voice hoarse. "Because I thought Andrew giving commands was-" He swallows, and the sound is like gravel. "Because I didn't want him to know how much I cared, Sage."

I flinch under the confession. "You *cared?* You *cared* enough to-" I let out a loud, involuntary sob. "I don't even know who you are."

His face is close enough I can see the tiny, uncontrollable twitch at the corner of his mouth. He looks almost afraid of himself. "I cared enough to want to protect you. I cared enough to study the man I thought I'd have to be."

The kitchen tilts. My fingers curl into his sleeve like a lifeline even as my other hand strains against his grip.

Is he about to...?

"I served with your husband," he says. The words are small, but they carry like explosions. "Adrian and I, we were in the same unit. Everybody swore we looked just alike. That we were brothers in any other life." He breathes in, slow and painful, like even admitting any of this is breaking his ribs open. "I saw you on a screen once. You were talking to him; you were arguing. I had never seen something like that... how someone could have a wife that cares and then turn around and brag about what he did to other women. He... he'd make jokes about his affairs like they were trophies. He talked about you like you were a thing he owned. It made me sick, Sage; it made me fucking sick," the admission bursts out of his chest and I'm trembling in shock and confusion.

I knew it.

I fucking knew it all along.

He presses his forehead to mine, the action so sudden that my vision crosses with his. Up close, his eyes are storm-gray and raw. The intimacy of it knocks my panic into a new register, confusion layered on fear layered on sharp, weird pity.

"That's when it started," he whispers. "Not in a clean way. It was ugly at first. Wanting to be him. Wanting what he had. But it turned... into this ache to fix what he'd break. To have you, Sage. I had no choice but to study him so I could-"

"You studied him?" I say, incredulous through the fog of adrenaline.

"I *learned* him," he corrects. "I learned his walk, his laugh, his cadence. I sat in his seat and learned the coffee he bought at nine-thirty. I listened to the men who called him friend recount things he'd done. They joked that we were nearly the same. So it was easy to step into him." His laugh there is hollow. "It was the stupidest, most monstrous idea. But I thought if I could be him- if I could go home as him, I could be close to you. I thought I could protect you from *him.*"

"Protect me?" I choke on the word. "By... by pretending to be my husband? By *lying* for months?"

He closes his eyes and the movement is almost childlike. "I know how that sounds. It sounds evil. It sounds cruel and manipulative. But I never meant to cause you any harm or pain, Sage. I always wanted to take you from a life I thought would hurt you. I kept thinking I could fix it all before you ever knew. That if I tried hard enough, I could make you happy and you could-you could learn to love me."

My fingers are slick with sweat and tears. The gun lies a few feet away and I almost forget its very existence. My elbow throbs where it hit the counter, splintering through me, but it seems like I'm not the only one in pain.

He swallows. "When the Humvee flipped-" His voice breaks, the past colliding with the present. "He didn't make it out. He was dead when I could finally crawl free. I didn't kill him. I *swear to God* I didn't. I took his tags, Sage, because if I didn't come back here-if I didn't go home-Andrew would have sent someone worse than he'd been, or he'd tear this family apart in a way I couldn't put back together. I thought if I could be him, I could keep you safe. It was stupid. Cowardly. All of it." He laughs then, a sound that's no humor. "But every night since, I've been terrified that you'd see through it. That you'd see the man I'm not."

Heat and cold war in my chest. My mind tries to ration disbelief, anger, grief, and an odd, corrosive undercurrent of longing that makes me hate myself. He is on top of me, his face only inches away, his breath hot and carrying that same scent that I've come to love, and he looks like a man who has been clawing his way back from an abyss.

"If you'd wanted to meet me as yourself," I say, because I need him to know I'm thinking, because the thought of lying in his bed and waking up to this is unbearable, "you could have. You could have come forward. You could have just told me. Why did you lie?"

"Because Andrew Hart wouldn't let me anywhere near you," he says simply. It's not an excuse; it's a fact. "He'd have stopped me before I had the chance. I thought-God, I thought I was doing the only thing that mattered: getting you away from him. From the life he would've made for you or taken from you. I thought I could do better. I thought I could learn to be a man worthy of you, Sage."

My lungs burn. I can barely remember how to breathe without his body anchoring me to the floor. He loosens his grip an infinitesimal degree and I feel dizzy with the freedom of it, like oxygen rushing back in.

"If you think I'm capable of what his father suggested," he says, voice pitched low and raw, "then I'll give you the gun back and you can end me. Do it. I will never stop you. I'd rather you kill me than live with the knowledge you thought I'd hurt you."

"Don't say that," I whisper, but my hands are trembling so badly that the words are a ragged thing.

He meets my eyes, looks until there's nowhere left to hide and nothing left to dress up the truth. "I love you," he says, voice raw and aching and terrifyingly truthful.

"I have loved you in ways I couldn't understand. I am not proud of how I came to you. I *am* ashamed of the lies. But the feeling isn't a lie. I already love you, Sage. I will wait. I will learn how to be honest. I will be patient while you learn me too. I'll go slow. I'll do it right. I promise you. I will do right by you, every damn day."

He backs off of me slowly, and I hesitate, moving as slowly as possible, waiting to see if he'll stop me, but he doesn't.

He lets me sit up and scramble away until my back hits the wall.

He reaches slowly, carefully, and picks the gun up with two hands. He doesn't point it. He sets it gently into my lap, palms open, surrendered. The gesture is absurdly tender.

"If you don't believe me, take it," he says. "If you think this is the end, end it now. I won't stop you."

My thumb runs the cool metal. My pulse is a drum in my throat. Every rational piece of me screams to pull the trigger and rid the world of the deceit, of the man who held me down and claims to love me.

But my hand trembles for different reasons now: the weight of choice, the tilt of pity and the ache of something that might be love but I'm not sure.

He kneels in front of me then, voice shaking so hard it's barely sound.

"I never meant to hurt you, Sage," he whispers, and now I can finally see the tears in his eyes. "I'll do whatever you want. If you want me gone, I'll leave tonight. If you want me dead, I won't fight. But if you'll let me, just let me, I'll spend the rest of my life making this right. I'll take care of you, love you, worship you the way I should have from the start. I'll go slow. You can learn me piece by piece, until you know every truth I tried to bury."

He looks up, eyes glistening, throat working like the words are knives.

"My feelings are real, Sage. I swear it. You can take everything from me, my name, my past, the breath in my lungs, but you can't take that. I already love you. I'll wait for you to love me too. I'll wait forever if I have to."

The room hums with the sound of his heartbeat. Mine. The world holding its breath.

"I don't even know who you are," I whisper, and it burns my throat in ways I can't explain. My tears build to match his. My breath catches in my throat. The gun feels like a gravestone in my hands, and I want nothing more than to throw it back down. To be done with this all and let go of the weight of this. "I don't even know your real name."

"My name..." he whispers, and I stop breathing while I wait. His eyes are still conflicted, and my hands are trembling. "Is Ellison Gray."

I can't move. The gun trembles in my hands, and I can't fucking move.

He leans closer, voice barely a whisper as he looks at me with eyes full of unshed tears. "I'm not him, Sage. I'm not Adrian. But I could love you better than he ever did. I promise I could. It would be so easy for me. So easy, just like it has been. We could be that, all the time. I could love you like that all the time," he pleads, and I don't want to believe it. I don't want to trust it. I don't want to.

But something breaks in my chest.

I lower the weapon until it clatters to the ground.

He exhales loudly, the breath sounding wrecked. "Please, Sage. Please let me at least try." He leans forward, slow like he's approaching a wounded animal, and my entire body is shaking from fear and adrenaline and a longing so fierce that I might break apart into tiny pieces.

His hand hesitantly closes around mine, and they're just as damp with sweat, just as shaky.

The air between us is thick enough to choke on.

He's still on his knees, eyes locked on mine, his hand folded around mine like he's afraid I'll vanish if he lets go. Neither of us moves. The gun sits between us, cold and silent, a witness to what's unfolding here.

For a long, awful moment, all I can hear is the ticking of the kitchen clock and our uneven breaths.

The fight's gone from my body, leaving behind only the shiver of adrenaline ebbing through my veins. My wrists ache where he held me down. His shirt is wrinkled and damp with sweat; a streak of red from the tomato stains the cuff near his wrist. The knife still lies abandoned on the counter.

He exhales shakily. The sound breaks something in me all over again.

"I'll make it right," he says again, quieter this time, as if he's not talking to me at all. "I swear, I'll make it right, Sage, please."

I want to tell him there's no fixing this. That there's no coming back from deceit this deep. But my mouth won't open. My throat feels raw, scraped clean by screaming.

He reaches for me tentatively, fingertips brushing the edge of my jaw. The touch makes me flinch and he pulls back immediately, devastated by his own reflex. "I'm sorry," he whispers. "I won't touch you again unless you ask me to."

The words shouldn't sound honest, but they do.

Goddamn it all, they do.

I push myself upright slowly. My knees sting against the tile. My hair is stuck to my cheeks with sweat and tears. He rises with me, uncertain, every movement cautious, as though I'm made of glass and his hands are heavy enough to break me.

The kitchen feels too bright, too open. The refrigerator hums quietly.

The entire world is still moving and we're having a standoff on the kitchen floor.

"Why?" I whisper finally. "Why wouldn't you just tell me?"

He looks at me like the question guts him. "Because I couldn't stop loving you," he says, and it's so soft, so genuine. "Even when I shouldn't have. Even when I didn't have the right. I was scared that you'd turn me away, Sage. I'm still scared that you'll turn me away."

My chest caves in around the ache of it. My body wants to recoil but my heart doesn't move.

He steps closer, one hesitant inch, then another, until the space between us is a trembling breath.

I can feel the heat coming off him, that impossible warmth that once made me feel safe.

Now it's a fire I don't know if I want to run from or into.

He lifts his hand again, slower this time. When I don't pull away, his palm finds my cheek. His thumb trembles against my skin.

"I know that I'm fucked up, and I know what I've done is wrong, okay? I know that it's wrong. I've scared you, and I've lied and hurt you in the process. That's exactly what I never wanted to happen, and it's my fault that it is. I'm just asking you to try. To try to trust, to try to love. Not Adrian. I won't-I won't pretend anymore, Sage. If you could just try to love me, then we could do this together. We could do this together, whatever it is. Even if you don't want to live this life. I don't need anything but you. We could run tonight if that's what you wanted. I'd go anywhere, as long as I get to have you. Please, I'm asking you just to try to love me," he pleads, the words turning wet towards the end.

My breath stutters. His eyes shine wet in the low light, all that control stripped bare.

A man, not a mask. A liar, not a killer.

"Ellison," I whisper. The name tastes foreign, but it rolls off of my tongue so sweet.

He nods once, almost imperceptibly. "Yes."

And something inside me dissolves.

It's not forgiveness, not trust, but the thin, terrible thread of fury I've been using to hold myself together. What's left beneath it is exhaustion.

He holds out a trembling hand between us, and I stare at it.

For a moment, I try to imagine.

I try to think of what it could be. Of what I could have.

The memories of our conversations and touches play through my head over and over again and I try to remember any time I didn't want him.

I try to remember any time I wanted to push him away.

But all I can remember is how softly he touched me.

All I can remember is how he whispered my name.

All I can remember is how he looks at me like he can't live without me.

Slowly, like it might burn me if I move too fast, I lift my own hand.

His breath catches, wet and ragged as he watches me, and his fingers twitch like he wants so badly to reach out and take my hand, but he restrains himself.

When our palms meet, it feels like I'm signing my death sentence.

But I've never felt a greater relief.

I step into him because standing hurts.

Because shaking alone in the middle of a kitchen made up of lies hurts worse.

His arms come around me like instinct, hesitant at first, then firm and crushing. His chin dips into my hair. His whole body shakes with a sound dangerously close to a sob.

"I'm sorry," he says again. It's all he can say. "I'm so sorry, Sage, I'm so sorry."

I should push him away. I should scream until the neighbors call someone.

Instead, I just stand there, trembling, his heartbeat thudding against my ear, my fingers clutching the fabric at his back. I don't even know if I'm holding him up or if he's holding me.

The clock still ticks. The refrigerator still hums. The world still spins on.

Eventually, he draws back enough to look at me. His forehead presses to mine, and his voice drops to a broken whisper.

"I promise you that I won't hurt you again. I promise you, Sage. I know you might not believe me right now, but I love you. I truly do love you, and I promise you that I won't ever take you for granted. I won't lie again, and I'll tell you everything. I'll answer any question that you have. Whatever you need from me, I'll hand it over."

I close my eyes and lean against his chest.

My heart feels splintered. My body is tired. Morning feels a lifetime away.

But finally, I nod.

He exhales against me like he's been drowning for years.

He bends down, picks up the gun, empties the magazine with steady hands, and sets it on the counter beside the knife.

No more words. Just the soft click of metal. Then he turns back to me with tired, hollow eyes.

"I'll sleep on the couch," he says, voice barely above a whisper. "You can keep the bedroom door locked. If you wake up and want me gone, I'll be gone before sunrise."

He turns to walk away from me, and I hate the way it feels like the edges of my heart are going to cut my lungs open.

"Wait," I choke out, and when he slows and quietly turns towards me, the tears well up and pour over my lash line so fast that I can't stop them.

"Sage," he whispers my name again as he steps back towards me, and I fall into his hold again, choking on my breath until I feel like I might drown in my own tears.

My legs feel too weak to hold me and I start to slide to the floor, but his hands catch me.

He picks me up just like he did so many other times, holding me close to his chest, soothing his palms over my skin, and he quietly makes his way upstairs.

I can't let him go.

Not even when he sits me down in the bed and tries to move away to pull the blankets over me.

I can't let him go.

I won't.

He climbs into bed with me and holds me while I cry.

I don't know how long I sit there before the adrenaline drains and the shaking stops and dulls into something fragile.

The weight of our lies settles heavy in the walls.

This is not the kind of night you come back from.

I try to think of when this all began, and I can't pinpoint when it started.

The deceit and anger simmer underneath my exhaustion.

The hands caressing my skin are the softest I've ever felt.

They held me like iron bands earlier and now they feel like silk, soothing and devoted to ease me.

I want to be angry.

I want to say I want to kill him. To end the lies once and for all.

But all I can think of is the fact that I've been complicit.

I knew he wasn't my husband.

I knew it all along.

He may be a liar, but I've got lies of my own, and when they shake loose, this fragile house of cards is going to collapse.

"Ellison," I whisper into his collarbone, the words a quiet rasp pouring from my lips.

He hums again, just like he did in the kitchen, just like he did right before I thought he was going to kill me.

I shouldn't.

God knows I shouldn't.

I say it anyways.

"I love you, too."

The hands on my skin tighten and his breath shudders against my hair.

"I know you do, baby. It was me you were in love with from the very start."

I want to say he's wrong.

But he's not.

And maybe that's the cruelest truth of all.